MAGIC FORGED

Hall of Blood and Mercy Book 1

K. M. SHEA

MAGIC FORGED
Copyright © 2020 by K. M. Shea

Cover Art by Natasha Snow Designs
Edited by Deborah Grace White

All rights reserved. No part of this book may be used or reproduced in any number whatsoever without written permission of the author, except in the case of quotations embodied in articles and reviews.

This is a work of fiction. Names, characters, places, and incidents are either the product of the author's imagination, or are used fictitiously. Any resemblance to actual persons, living or dead, or historic events is entirely coincidental.

ISBN: 978-1-950635-07-8

www.kmshea.com

*For my Champions.
Thanks for giving vampires a try.*

CHAPTER ONE

Hazel

I crouched behind a rusty, blue mail drop box and held my breath.

It wasn't the most auspicious of hiding places, but it was closer to the smelly, dank alleyway I intended to hide in than any of my other cover options.

I made a face at the rusty grit it smeared on my hand, but carefully peered around the side of the box.

Gideon of House Tellier—or as I called him, the Idiot—was still poking in the bushes where I had originally hidden outside the bank across the street.

It was now or never.

I scuttled into the alleyway that cut between a popular café, Dream Bean, and what used to be the building of a now defunct newspaper. I had to pick my way around the bags of trash that bubbled over from the café's dumpster, but I didn't mind. The trash smelled strongly of coffee grounds and almost covered up the scent of rotting food.

It wasn't too bad a place to hide. I'd been in a lot worse.

I circled around to the back of the café—which was supposed to be a neutral zone. Actually, all of downtown was neutral, but tell that to the clowns of House Tellier or any of the other wizards who thought they could push me around.

At twenty-two, you'd think I'd be past the age of bullying, but the supernatural community reflects the wild, I guess. The strongest thrive while the rest are all dinner. With my tiny sliver of magic, I was lower than dinner. I wasn't even a snack.

My cellphone erupted in a cheerful and *loud* song. I bit back a curse as I yanked it out of my jacket pocket and fumbled to silence it.

When I caught a glance of the caller ID, I swiped to answer. I doubled my pace so I power-walked across Dream Bean's tiny parking lot and hopped on the boardwalk that stretched around the perimeter of the lake that squatted in the middle of town. "Hey, Mom."

"Hello, my sunshine! How are you?"

I glanced back over my shoulder, but I didn't see Gideon the Idiot, so it was safe to follow the boardwalk away from downtown. "A bit busy," I said vaguely. Whenever possible, I tried not to let my parents know about my...*run-ins* with some of the wizards from other Houses. It only made my mom anxious and my dad angry, but it wasn't like they could do more than they already had. It wasn't *their* fault I had such sucky magic. "Did you need something? I'm on my way back to the House."

"Yes. Your father and I need to talk to you."

"Okay. I'll find you when I get back."

"No, we'll meet you at the Curia Cloisters," she said, naming the one public magical building in town. It served as a meeting hall, court, and safe house for anyone in the magical community, so it was pretty weird for us to meet there as opposed to House Medeis, which was way more private.

I peered back over my shoulder—still no Gideon. "Is everything okay?"

"Of course!" my mother said in a cheerful voice that sounded totally fake. "It's just...we've realized we need to make some changes."

"Change can be good," I said carefully.

"Yes, it will be for the good of the House," she said. "Though I don't know that anyone is going to like the scale of it. But we'll need your help."

"Uh-huh," I doubtfully said.

"You're the Heir, Hazel," my mother said—as if she needed to remind me. It's not like I wasn't painfully aware I was the weakest Medeis Heir in our centuries-old history or anything. "You can do so much. You'll see how House Medeis will rely on you, and your father and I have a lot we need to talk to you about."

"Okay," I said, still not believing her.

She and Dad always told me I needed to accept myself and embrace my weaknesses and strengths. Because having to crouch behind rusty mailboxes and frequently make escapes down smelly alleyways was something to celebrate, apparently.

The boardwalk creaked as I marched on. "I still have to run back to the House so I can get my car. The Curia Cloisters are too far away for me to walk."

"There's no rush," Mom said. "Your father and I are driving there now—we'll reserve a meeting room while we wait for you."

"Gotcha. I'll call when I'm closer."

"Okay, drive safe."

"Love you, sunshine!" Dad shouted, barely audible from Mom's end of the phone.

"Love you both! Bye."

I hung up and slipped my phone back into my pocket. I stepped off the boardwalk—I had left the hum of downtown traffic behind and had entered the quieter suburbs. House Medeis was still a good fifteen-minute walk away, but it would be faster to zigzag through the quaint streets filled with old Victorian houses, brick mansions, and colonial style homes.

I stopped dead in my tracks, however, when I felt the tangy prickle of wizard magic.

Without hesitating I burst into a run—I almost always wore running shoes for this very reason—before I risked a glance over my shoulder.

Nothing.

I frowned and ran smack dab into Gideon—who is massive enough to rival a defensive lineman—bouncing off him with the force of my own momentum.

He caught me by the arm and wrenched me back to him. "Going somewhere, *Medeis*?"

"Let go of me!"

"So you can run again? Nah." He held his free hand out and gathered magic that flickered like fire in his palm. His wizard mark—which was distinctly spiky and more brown than black—appeared, slicing down his cheekbone and making a break toward his jawline.

Ho boy. This did not look good.

I kept my expression placid and didn't fight him as I fidgeted, readjusting my stance so I faced him. "Isn't this a little pathetic? It's not like beating me up is going to give you any kind of bragging rights."

Gideon held his palm so close to my face the hum of magic crackled in my ears. "It's not about strength, it's about asserting what should be obvious," he said. "You shouldn't be the Medeis Heir. You're too weak. Your House will never be able to depend on you."

"That's House Medeis's business, not yours." I rested my weight on the leg closest to Gideon and drew the other back, lining my shot up.

He didn't seem to notice. But I tried to cover my plan by sucking air in and snapping my fingers, pulling the tiny bit of magic I could channel from the air and pushing it through my blood and down to my fingers where I turned it into a tiny flame that I flicked at him.

Gideon scoffed as the flame hit his t-shirt and fizzled, easily put out with a firm snap of his shirt. "No," he scoffed. "It's *all* wizards' business. Allowing one of the oldest wizarding Houses in the Midwest to be run by a wizard with *your* level of power makes us a laughingstock, and we're already considered the weakest in our society." He pointed to the tiny patch of blackened fabric for evidence of my weak powers—which was a birthday candle next to the glowing ball he held in his open palm.

The heat of my wizard mark—which I knew from staring in the mirror was a stark black and made of one lonely, pathetic loop under my right eye—slowly faded from my face as I let go of my magic. "Ahhh," I said. "I understand now."

Gideon squinted down at me and cocked his head in his confusion.

"It's because you're compensating," I seriously added.

"Why you—" Gideon moved to mash his magic into my face—which would have at least given me third degree burns, if not worse. But I was ready. I smashed my foot into his kneecap, kicking as hard as I could.

Gideon's leg buckled, and he tipped forward, off balance enough that I was able to rip my arm from his grasp and scramble backwards.

He took a swipe at me with his magic, but only touched a bit of my hair, singeing it.

I fled, the horrible smell of burnt hair trailing behind me as Gideon roared.

"You're going to pay for that, Medeis!"

I didn't even bother to see if he was following—his thundering footfalls chased after me as I darted across a grassy park.

Three ladies and their kids stood in the woodchips surrounding the park playground equipment, their mouths hanging open as they gazed at Gideon with wonder.

They had to be regular humans—no one else would look so awed.

A few of the kids shrieked and clapped in joy. "Wizards!"

I glanced back at Gideon—whose entire fist was now encased with magic.

He mustered a smile. "Training, it's necessary," he lied.

I snorted and jumped a park bench.

Even though supernaturals were "public," and had been for almost two decades, we still weren't supposed to flash our magic around. The last thing we wanted to do was frighten the humans, who greatly outnumbered *all* magical species and could potentially exterminate us if they felt threatened.

Apparently, our community's leaders were overly concerned, though, given that none of the mothers or their kids seemed to feel "threatened" while watching a gorilla of a guy with a fistful of fire chase me in broad daylight.

When I reached the sidewalk on the opposite end of the park, Gideon chucked the fireball.

I tried to dodge it, but I wasn't fast enough, and it hit me on the left shoulder. It sizzled, burning a hole in my clothes, and it was so hot it baked my skin. I bit down on a yelp—that would have made the sicko *happy*—and inhaled air in a sharp hiss between clenched teeth.

My shoulder throbbed, but if he caught me, it would only mean more pain. I limped across the street, picking up speed as I shook it off.

Unfortunately, my distraction with the pain—however short-lived—had given Gideon time to catch up with me.

He was almost on me as I sprinted up the block. I came to a four-way intersection and glanced up the road.

A motorcade of shiny black cars bore down the street, barreling closer. A fancy emblem was emblazoned on the sides of the front car—a limo—but the rest were all unmarked SUVs.

I saw the black dragon roaring at the center of the drawn emblem, and my heart stuttered.

The roaring dragon was something *everyone* in the Midwest feared—at least anyone with any sense of self-preservation.

But Gideon was less than half a block behind me. If I waited for the motorcade, he'd catch me, and if I ran around the block again he'd be on me pretty quick.

My shoulder ached, but although fear made my heart pound in my throat with enough force to strangle me, I darted across the street, narrowly missing being hit by the lead car.

Gideon skidded to a stop at the crosswalk as the lead car rumbled by, but when the SUV just behind it slowed to a crawl, he swore, turned on his heels, and ran back toward the park.

I didn't stop running either. Gideon wasn't going to be able to catch me now, but I needed to get away from the motorcade.

Only one magical group used a dragon as their emblem in this city: the Drake Family. The most powerful vampire Family in the Midwest. And they wouldn't hesitate to maim us just for irritating them.

Thankfully, the cars barreled on, and I made it home without any more "fun".

Well, I was almost hit by a blood delivery car—vampires had to be fed *somehow*—about four blocks up from the House. But neither Gideon nor a member of the infamous Drake Family stalked me home, so I'd count it as a win.

I breathed a sigh of relief as I considered jumping the knee-high wrought-iron fence that surrounded House Medeis. But considering I was the Heir I thought it best to pay my respects, so I trotted up the front sidewalk.

Even with my small abilities, I could feel the magic of the House bloom around me.

"Hey there," I said with affection, greeting the House as I might a pet.

Thankfully, the House didn't seem to mind my wussy powers.

Its magic greeted me with a content purr as a butterfly danced among the flowers that lined the front porch.

The magical building was three stories tall and was cobbled out of stretches of blue siding with white trim and blocks of gray, ivy covered rock. Three turrets poked out of the House—two smaller ones in the front with the tallest in the back more closely resembling a bell tower. But instead of a bell it housed the House Beacon—a glowing orb that usually glowed blue with veins of gold.

The lawn was big—House Medeis had a giant lot—and there was a huge flower garden that started in front and stretched around to the back. A large koi pond and a cheerfully trickling fountain that was ornamented with diapered baby angel statues was also settled in the backyard.

A bit eclectic in both looks and architecture, the best way to describe it would be to say if a Victorian house and a French chateau had a building baby, House Medeis would be the offspring.

There were a bunch of cars in the long gravel driveway—which wasn't unusual. Although House Medeis belonged to my immediate family, we still had a fairly large wizard House.

Let me explain. Vampires have Families, werewolves have Packs, fae have Courts, and wizards have Houses.

Though the term "wizard House" refers to the physical building—like House Medeis—it can also refer to the wizards who live there together as a sort of large magical family, not bound by blood, but by similar passions and desires...and a big magic House.

My parents ran House Medeis because the House itself was theirs, but there were roughly twenty adult wizards who belonged to House Medeis who we counted as family and who lived here with us.

I playfully slapped my hand on the fancy white porch railing, wincing when it made my shoulder twinge.

"I better disinfect that before I head out," I muttered. "Great Aunt Marraine ought to be home, and she's the least likely to blab to Dad and Mom. Maybe I should ask her."

I heaved the front door open and popped inside, immediately kicking off my shoes. (House Medeis got crabby if you walked its floors with your shoes on. It only takes so many times of getting your sneakers chucked at your head before you learn this, even as a child.)

"I'm home," I called out to any other members of House Medeis who might be around. "But not for long. I'm just stopping by to grab my car, then—"

"Hazel?" Great Aunt Marraine appeared in the hallway—the bright blue streak she dyed into her curly white hair made her impossible to mistake.

"Yep." I shook my arm out, trying to get the sting out of my shoulder wound, and padded closer, pausing when I saw how puffy and red her eyes were. "What's wrong?"

Great Aunt Marraine pressed her hands to her ample bosom, but at my words her face crumpled, and she pulled me into a hug. "It's your parents. There's been an accident."

The world seemed to slow as she pressed my face into her shoulder. "What?" I asked with numb lips.

"There was a car crash and...and..."

I heard ringing in my ears.

Great Aunt Marraine sobbed. "Hazel...they're dead."

CHAPTER TWO

Hazel

The funeral and wake were crowded with everyone from House Medeis and well-wishers from the magical community—representatives from werewolf Packs, fae Courts, vampire Families, and the other wizarding Houses we were allied with.

I tried to smile and forced myself to accept handshakes and embraces, but all I wanted to do was scream.

What went wrong?

I was supposed to meet my parents for a talk, and now I stood in front of their *coffins*.

The police officers who had responded told me it was an accident. A drunk driver—in the middle of the day.

She hit their car at an intersection, killing my parents—two of the most powerful wizards in the city—on impact.

It was so wrong. But the nightmare had gone on long enough for me to know it was real.

I tried to swallow and almost choked. My mouth was too dry.

I glanced over my shoulders at the unforgiving, black coffins and shuddered. I quickly gazed forward again, meeting the stony expressions of the leaders of the local supernaturals.

Sam, the Alpha of Pack Whitefrost, scratched his beard, the wrinkles on his forehead deepening as he spoke with Lady Vif, the representative of the fae Summer Court.

My parents had been good friends with both of them, but they wouldn't meet my gaze.

Breathe, I had to remind myself. *Breathe!* I wanted to scream and demand to know how this could have happened, but I had to stay calm.

I—weak magic and all—was all House Medeis had.

Though my eyes stung with unshed tears and I wanted to crumple, I couldn't.

I had been the Heir.

Now I was the House Medeis Adept. The leader.

And not only did I have an old, magical home depending on me, but everyone who had been sworn into our family as well.

For them, I wouldn't break. At least, not on the outside. I couldn't do anything to stop the pain from tearing my heart from end to end.

That was why I looked out at the werewolf Alphas, the fae nobles, the visiting vampires, and all the other powers that be that had come for the funeral, and I knew the truth.

They were predators, circling me. They were trying to gauge me and see what I'd mean for House Medeis, and how that would impact the supernatural community

Based on their expressions—the vampires' curled upper lips, the wolfish grins of the werewolves, the smug smiles of the other wizards—it did not look good.

I didn't blame them for their low opinion of me.

As the last Medeis I *had* to inherit the House. If I died, House Medeis would change names—and lose some of its respect, power, and members in the process. It would disband and be reborn or, in reality, be re-branded in a new image. If you didn't entirely separate from the old family line, the House would eventually rebel. Yeah, it sounds like a bunch of elitist crap—and for the most part I still think it is—but a magical House throwing a temper tantrum is never good. So even though I was the weakest wizard in the House, I was now the Adept.

"Do you need a break, Adept?" Great Aunt Marraine asked.

My stomach churned at the title I knew shouldn't have come to me for decades. "It's fine."

Great Aunt Marraine studied me through bottlecap glasses that made her eyes large and owlish. "The House allowed the caterers in—though it was a near thing. All will be ready for the luncheon."

"Thanks, Great Aunt Marraine."

"Of course, dear." She looked past me. Judging by the weight in her gaze, she was studying my parents' coffins. "They were taken from us too early."

My throat squeezed, and I could only manage to stare out at the mourners.

"But," Great Aunt Marraine continued, "you'll be a fine Adept."

I couldn't help the frown that made my forehead wrinkle as I shifted my stare to her. Had she finally cracked? Great Aunt Marraine was old when I was born, but she'd always been spry—and sassy enough to know that an Adept who could barely start a campfire wasn't much of an Adept at all.

She reached out and smoothed my blond hair away from my face. "The blood of the Medeis wizards flows in your veins, Hazel. You'll thrive. And when we get back to the House you need to eat. The caterer made your father's favorite triple chocolate brownies. You ought to have one or a dozen, get some more meat on these bird bones of yours."

I tried to smile at her, but the thought that my dad and I would never split another brownie was enough to make a pins and needles sensation prickle in my lungs. "I will," I lied.

"Good." Aunt Marraine nodded, then waddled away—her unusual gingham dress a spot of bright blue in the sea of black.

I watched her until I noticed Mason drift away from the House Tellier representatives and walk in my direction.

Mason was one of the best wizards in House Medeis, and was an extremely distant relative. I think his great, great, great grandmother had been a Medeis, but it was so far back I couldn't remember the specifics, and the connection was so diluted the House didn't consider his blood to be part of my family line. He was in his mid-thirties, about ten years older than me, so I hadn't hung out with him when we were kids. But I'd always admired his talent for magic.

He offered me a practiced smile and hugged me—which I was not expecting, and was more than a little awkward. His arms were stiff, and I mostly just felt super hot due to his proximity. "You do our House credit, Hazel," he said.

"Thanks." I started to grip the fabric of my black skirt when a quick glance down confirmed the material was already crushed and wrinkled. "I'm starting to think this day will never end."

"It was a terrible accident," Mason said. "And a great loss for the wizarding community." He smiled and nodded to a female wizard from House Rothchild dressed in periwinkle blue. Rothchild was one of our allies, but I doubt the House relationship was what had the other wizard smiling.

I was clinically aware Mason was classically good-looking, with a fine smile, broad shoulders, and clean-cut appearance. But given who my friends were, I was immune to it, and instead pondered how someone could *smile* at a time like this.

The stifling air in the room had me sweating. I had to get away and do something, or I was going to suffocate. "Maybe I should start packing up the pictures," I muttered as I stared at the easels and tables that displayed printed photos of my parents.

I didn't mean for Mason to hear, but he did anyway. He shook his head and folded his arms across his chest. "You can't."

I blinked. "*What?*"

"You shouldn't," he smoothly corrected. "You're our Adept now. How would it look to everyone else?"

"Like I'm grieving the loss of my parents?" I had to peer up at him, but that didn't mean much. I'm pretty short, so I have to peer up at practically everyone.

"You're our Adept," he repeated. "You need to be more aware of what that means, and what it means to House Medeis."

This was probably why Mason and I didn't talk much. He was a super big fan of having a pecking order in the House and observing tradition—neither of which I loved, though I probably should have because it was most likely the only thing that made him support me as Adept.

"You're over thinking it," I said, doing my best to sound pleasant rather than sour. "My parents loaded the dishwasher and took trash out just like everyone else in House Medeis. No one is going to judge us if I help take some of the pictures down so I can get away from these *coffins*." The last word seemed to hit my gag reflex on the way out of my mouth.

Mason pressed his lips together, but before he could dig in and really complain, my salvation arrived.

"Dear Adept," Felix said with a voice as balmy as a beach sunset. "You've been standing for hours. Why don't you sit for a bit?"

"Yeah." Momoko appeared just behind his shoulder and eyed me doubtfully. "You look like you might throw up."

Together, Felix and Momoko made a striking image.

For starters, Felix personified beauty. No, he wasn't handsome, but *awesomely* beautiful. He outshone a lot of vampires and fae lords and ladies with his bright gold hair, unfathomably blue eyes, slender body, and angelic smile that worked almost as well as a fae persuasion spell.

The toddler that sat on his hip and drooled on his crisp black dress shirt didn't dampen his general aura of beauty, but instead seemed to amplify it.

Momoko, though also gorgeous, was his exact opposite. She had midnight black hair, eyes so dark they appeared black, and generally looked like she enjoyed lurking around graveyards with the amount of black and gray she wore.

Despite her appearance, Momoko was more of an optimist than Felix, and Felix had the personality of a warthog, and spent hours weightlifting every week in a failed attempt to bulk up. But both of them used their appearances to put people off balance, and they wielded their looks with the same finesse they handled their magic.

It worked, even on people who knew them, like Mason.

"Ahh, Felix and Momoko. I wondered where you two had run off." Mason nodded at the duo, but shifted ever-so-slightly away from them.

Felix smiled, setting the volume of his sparkling looks on full blast. "We were occupying Ivy and some of the other children." He patted the dozing toddler on the back with the ease of practice.

"Until we saw how terrible Hazel looked," Momoko bluntly said. "Come on, Adept. You can leave your post for a bit."

Mason rocked back on his heels. "Perhaps that is a good idea," he delicately said. "Surely I and the other senior members of House Medeis can be stand ins for the moment."

"Thanks, Mason."

"It is my honor, Adept."

Momoko didn't wait for any more chit-chat. She circled an arm around my shoulders and towed me away, managing to make it look more like a helpful embrace than bodily corralling me. Even though Momoko was a shade under average height, she was still taller than me. That hadn't been frustrating as a kid. Nope, definitely not.

"Sorry, Hazel," Momoko said in a voice much softer than the

jaded one she had spoken to Mason with. "We should have come sooner."

"No, I am Adept now." I sighed big enough to make my bangs flutter. "I needed to be there to receive everyone. And I'll have to go back eventually." I offered the pair a shaky smile. "Though I'm hoping House Medeis will hide me for a few minutes when we move there for the luncheon." We slipped into the foyer of the funeral parlor and made our escape outside without anyone noticing.

Out in the cool spring air the sweaty heat that clouded around me finally dissipated, and some of the tightness in my chest eased.

Felix peered over his shoulder at the closed doors. "What a bunch of vultures."

Momoko hugged me tightly then joined our childhood friend in scowling at the parlor doors. "I hope House Medeis eats their shoes if they dare to come over."

"If it doesn't, we could throw their shoes in the trash and blame it on the House." The wind ruffled Felix's blond hair. "It's not like anyone could prove the House didn't do it."

"I thought we tried that excuse as kids when some of the brattier wizard kids from House Rothchild visited," I said. "I don't think it ended well for us."

"Now you're the Adept," Felix pointed out. "Through a horrific circumstance, yes. But that doesn't mean we can't use it to our advantage."

I grinned. "If we didn't, I'd be disappointed with all three of us." My smile dropped from my lips as I joined them in looking at the funeral parlor. "Thanks, guys. I didn't think it was possible for me to laugh today."

Felix and Momoko leaned in until their shoulders touched mine.

We stayed like that, standing under the stormy gray sky with the wind snapping our hair and clothes, until the doors to the funeral parlor opened.

"There you three are." Mr. Clark—one of the senior wizards in House Medeis and Felix's dad, as testified by his soulful blue eyes Felix had inherited—shoved his hands in the pockets of his black trousers and joined us outside. He paused just short of us and bowed his head. "Adept."

The pins were back in my throat. "Please don't, Mr. Clark."

He shook his head. "It's Ed, now."

I almost shuddered at the thought. "You've been Mr. Clark my whole life."

"And now you're the Adept," he said. "You'll be calling all of us in House Medeis by our first names."

I scrubbed my face with my palms. "I don't think I can do this."

"You can," Mr. Clark said firmly. "House Medeis believes in you." He held out his arms to take Ivy—his granddaughter and the daughter of Felix's older brother, Franco, who was also a member of House Medeis. "But you don't have to do it all at once. This came as a shock and a tragedy to everyone. We can take it slow with you as you adjust, Hazel."

His voice was so understanding I couldn't look at him. Instead I stared at Ivy, who blearily stirred as she realized she'd been handed off. When she saw me, she smiled and tugged at her necklace—which I suspect was self-made as it mostly consisted of macaroni and colored yarn. "Hazel!" she said in her cute voice.

I cracked a smile. "Hello, Ivy. Did you have a nice nap?"

Ivy yanked on her necklace, making the metal loop someone—her mother, I suspected—had threaded through the necklace to weigh it down, smack her face. "This is for you!"

I made the necessary oohing noises. "It's very pretty."

"Mommy said you're sad."

I felt my smile splinter. "Just a bit."

Mr. Clark stabilized her when she squirmed in his arms, trying to get the necklace off, but the little girl stopped trying when another wizard left the funeral parlor.

"Mr. Bear!" Ivy called out in delight.

The wizard—a large man who was hulking enough to rival a werewolf—smiled. "Hello there, Ivy-girl!"

"Hello, Mr. Baree," Felix said in his very rare but true tone of respect—probably because the man had all the muscle and bulk Felix wanted.

Mr. Baree grinned at Felix, but like Mr. Clark, he bowed his head to me. "Adept." He folded his meaty arms across his chest and squinted down at me.

"I can go back inside." I didn't bother to attempt a smile, but I inhaled deeply and rolled my shoulders back—which probably did more to convince them anyway.

"We can wait," Mr. Baree said.

"It's expected."

Mr. Baree snorted. "What's expected can take a swan dive off a steep cliff. This isn't a sprint, Adept, it's a lifestyle. You can take your time and settle in. No one is expecting you to be perfect the week your parents pass away."

Mr. Clark rested his hand on my shoulder. "Roy is right. You're the last in the Medeis line. House Medeis needs you, which means it's important that you survive and don't burn yourself out."

Mr. Baree nodded. "The House comes first," he said, repeating the ancient adage I'd heard probably the day I was born. "Which means you're now our top priority. If some folks are displeased or House Medeis loses a bit of its austerity, it doesn't matter. You are far more important."

He meant to be encouraging.

Or supportive.

Or...*something*.

But those words made my stomach heave.

It felt so *wrong*! How could you prioritize like that? Sure, it was how wizarding Houses were supposed to operate, but I'd never seen it so brutally displayed for me.

Everyone in House Medeis would prioritize my wellbeing over *everything.*

"Right, well, I'm fine. So, in we go!" I trundled into motion—if I stood there and listened any more there was a very good chance I was going to throw up. "Are there any more representatives from our close allies I should greet?" I chattered to fill the silence.

"Not any that matter," Felix sniffed.

"Well said," Mr. Baree growled.

I slipped back inside the funeral parlor before the others could join me.

My eyes automatically slid to the viewing room where my parents' coffins were, but I jerked my gaze away and peered around the foyer.

Mason was standing with someone at the viewing room door.

Perfect, I could ask him if I had missed anything.

I slipped through the straggling mourners—with my height I got mistaken as a high school student pretty often, so no one paid any attention as I padded around them, bits and pieces of their conversation reaching me.

"Drake struck down a law that would have allotted space for another wolf Pack in northern Minnesota."

"You're surprised?"

"No, just disgusted he can control our Regional Committee of Magic."

"Vampires rule the Midwest, my friend..."

The rest of the exchange fell out of my hearing range as I edged around the two tall women—werewolves, judging by the gold gleams in their eyes.

Ugh. Politics.

Politics I'd soon have to worry about as the House Medeis Adept.

I briefly shut my eyes. My life had become a waking nightmare. Losing my parents had torn a hole in my heart, and being responsible for House Medeis was a different level of horror. But the politics, the leading...how was I going to manage it? Especially once everyone in my House started going back to work.

Adept was considered a full-time position, so I'd spend my days waffling through my new workload. But besides Great Aunt Marraine, everyone else had jobs—or school. (The only reason I still didn't have college was because I had luckily finished my business degree a semester early, in the winter.)

A part of me felt angry with my parents that they hadn't better prepared me, but it wasn't their fault. Heirs receive the first part of their training when they turn twenty, and then receive more responsibilities and training after they reach twenty-five.

I hadn't ever questioned that policy before...until now.

Another breath and a correction to my posture, and I made myself cross the remaining distance to Mason. I was surprised to find he was talking to a wizard from House Tellier. Medeis and Tellier weren't enemies, but we weren't friendly either given Gideon's tendency to bother me and Momoko's methods of revenge—which usually involved lightning.

The two spoke in lowered tones, though Mason smiled when he saw me. "Ahh, Adept, we were just talking about you."

"Yes." The House Tellier wizard smiled, but it seemed flat and insincere. "When do you think we might observe the grand occasion of your Ascension?"

Ascension was the old and showy ceremony that basically was the handoff of the House to the Heir-turned-Adept. There were a few speeches to give, and I'd get officially sworn in as Adept, but the most important part was that I would make my vows to the House and bind it to me.

The House would then physically change in accordance with my magic and the kind of person I was. It would still keep that Victorian-house-crossed-with-a-chateau feel to it, but it might grow bigger (unlikely) or smaller (most probable), grow some new gardens, or—as had been my dearest childhood dream—sprout a pool.

"I don't imagine for a couple weeks," I said. "There's still a lot to...settle." My gaze again strayed to the viewing room before I yanked it back.

Mason's smile turned overpoweringly sympathetic, like too much sugar in your coffee. "Of course, Adept. You need time to mourn your parents."

"And to notify the Wizard Council, gather the records, and find the House Medeis signet ring," the House Tellier wizard added. "Unless you already have it?"

"No." I clasped my hands behind my back so I wouldn't be tempted to make any rude gestures I would later regret. "Given the tragedy, having my parents' will read hasn't been a priority."

The two wizards exchanged an indiscernible look.

"Of course, Adept," Mason said smoothly. "If I can be of any service in the meantime, just ask."

I had been eyeing the Tellier wizard, but when Mason spoke I shifted my attention to him. *He said that already. Is he just putting on a show for House Tellier?* It seemed my future in politics was grimmer than I thought. "Thanks."

Mason bowed slightly. "It is my honor—the House comes first, after all."

———

THREE WEEKS PASSED, and the unbearable pain left by my parents' death settled into a dull ache.

Laughing came more easily, but sleeping was rough. I spent hours every night walking House Medeis.

The magical House was both comforting and a stark reminder that I was less than an Adept should have been—less trained *and* less skilled.

I'm going to have to come up with a method to supplement my magical power, I reluctantly concluded. *Or House Medeis will crumble even though I'm the rightful Heir. I mean, kicking kneecaps and being as squirmy as an eel works for facing off with people like Gideon, but that's not going to help with politics. But what would work? Stronger allies would be ideal, but who would* want *to befriend us that didn't want to when my parents were alive?*

I scratched under the elastic waistband of my owl fleece pajama pants. Though it was late spring, nights were still cool, and House Medeis was always a bit drafty—a good thing given wizards tended to run hot most of the time.

The House grumbled under my feet as it turned on a dusty chandelier for me while I ambled down one of the long hallways.

Maybe I should give the senior Medeis wizards more power. It would be unusual, but not entirely unheard of—or unexpected.

I popped into the bathroom and pulled on the knob for cold water, filling my ceramic mug. I turned off the tap before I took a sip, making a face at the steaming hot water.

It seems that the ice-cold shower I had earlier was not because Felix used too much water on the gardens, but because the House is upset. How...wonderful.

I set the mug down on the counter and leaned against a wall covered in blue damask wallpaper. "I'm sorry," I told the creaking building. "I know you're growing weaker because I haven't had my Ascension yet. I'll get it sorted out soon."

The water pipes groaned ominously, and the black and white tile under my feet rumbled.

"I'll call my parents' lawyer in the morning," I hastily added. "We still haven't had their will read or the deed transferred, and the signet is stored with all of that. I think."

My answer must have satisfied the House, because it finally shut up. I considered trying for cold water again, but decided not to push it.

If I had Ascended and become the proper Adept, I could command the House to give me whatever kind of water I wanted.

Supposedly I'd be able to sort of communicate with it rather than just guess at the source of its foul moods. But until then, it seemed like I'd be getting hot drinking water and cold showers.

I exited the bathroom and shuffled back up the hallway. I was trying to decide between heading to the library to find a book to read or going to the kitchen for a snack when a door creaked.

Curious, I swung around and jumped when I found Mason standing right behind me. "Geez, Mason, you scared me." I took a few steps backwards, but Mason grabbed me by the shoulders, stopping me.

His face was shadowed in the flickering hallway light. "We need to talk."

"Sure," I agreed as I adjusted my fleece pajama pants again. "Sometime tomorrow or...?" I frowned when I studied Mason and saw he wasn't dressed in sleepwear like me, but a crisp, pristine suit with the House Medeis coat of arms—which had a rampant leopard and a white unicorn rearing over a shield—over its breastpocket.

"Now," Mason said.

The wind shrieked as it whistled through the trees just outside, and I thought I felt House Medeis quiver.

"Fine," I said. "What about?" I tried to ease out of his grasp, but he dug his fingers into my shoulders.

"You're aware we are related?" Mason said.

"Distantly, yeah. Aren't you, like, my third cousin three times removed—or something?"

Mason relaxed, slightly. "Yes, I have Medeis blood in my veins—though it's so little, wizard law won't count it. But what I lack in pedigree I make up for in power."

Why is there something unnerving about the way he's talking? I tried to lean so he would have to step more into the light—I might be able to read something in his expression—but he pulled me back.

I licked my lips. "You're obviously known for being strong in magic. It's why you're the youngest senior wizard in House

Medeis." He was weirding me out enough that I tried to nonchalantly feel the pocket in my pajama pants for my cellphone, but I must have left it in my room.

"Precisely—whereas you have the blue blood of the Medeis, but are practically a dud," Mason said.

I sighed and fluffed my hair with a hand. "Is this about me not having much magic? Because I already know we'll have to come up with another alternative to keep our power consolidated. But that's something I should be discussing with *all* the senior wizards—"

"I've already come up with the alternative we will take."

I narrowed my eyes at him. "*Will we?*"

"We should get married."

My forehead puckered, and my mouth dropped open. "What did you say?"

"It's the most logical move," Mason said. "You can't run House Medeis alone."

"Mason." My voice was hot with frustration. "I'll admit to being a weak Adept. But it is an *insane* jump to get from there to 'we should get married'!"

"You're unable to protect yourself or House Medeis," Mason said.

"Yeah," I agreed. "I have no delusions about my power. But there are about a *thousand* different plans we can enact that don't involve the two of us getting hitched. You don't even like me!"

"The House comes before all."

"That's nice, but I draw the line at an arranged marriage!" My voice was growing louder with my disbelief.

"Adept? Is everything okay?" Felix poked his head out of his bedroom, his gold hair shining in the dull light as he peered suspiciously at Mason.

I gritted my teeth but forcibly smiled. "Yes. I was just having a *discussion* with Mason." I yanked myself from Mason's grasp, and he let his arms drop.

Mason offered me a smile. "Won't you even consider it?"

Was this why he'd been so friendly the past few weeks? Not because of my parents' death, but because he was hoping to sway me?

"No," I said, "I won't consider it because it's *not necessary*."

Felix frowned and fully emerged from his room, pausing to roughly kick a few other bedroom doors.

"It's the fastest way," Mason said. "And speed is vital in this case."

I sourly pressed my lips together to keep from shrieking. "Not important enough to make you propose in the middle of the night!"

Felix made a choking noise as Momoko, Great Aunt Marraine, and Franco—Felix's older brother—emerged from their quarters.

Momoko yawned and stretched her arms above her head. "What's going on?"

"Mason has apparently lost it," Felix said.

"Maybe if he was sleeping right now this wouldn't be a problem." Great Aunt Marraine struggled to put on her thick, blue framed glasses. Her hair was in curlers, and she looked fierce as she tied her purple bathrobe.

Mason glanced back at our family, and I sighed—it wasn't my intention to publicly embarrass him. Who knows, maybe that was why he approached me at night?

"I'm twenty-two, Mason," I reminded him. "I've been the Adept for three weeks. Figuring out the new power balance doesn't have to be an instant thing."

Mason stared up at the ceiling. "It would have been easier this way."

I furrowed my eyebrows. "What are you talking about?"

An explosion rocked the House, making the lights shake and the walls groan.

CHAPTER THREE

Hazel

"House Medeis?" I slapped a shaking hand on the wall, trying to judge the House's state, but it was no use: I hadn't Ascended yet, and I had too little magic to get a good feel for it.

"That came from the front hall," Great Aunt Marraine shouted.

"Let's go!" Felix and Franco sprinted down the hallway and darted into the corridor that held the main staircase.

I moved to follow them, but Mason grabbed me by the wrist. "Not yet, Adept," he said.

"Let her go, Mason." Momoko stalked closer, her wizard mark surfacing as she funneled magic.

Mason glanced at her, and something felt *off*. When his wizard mark—which stretched all the way to his jaw—surfaced, I stiffened. He made a flicking motion, blasting Momoko with blue magic. She crashed into the wall with a groan.

I lashed out, kicking Mason in the gut. "What are you *doing*?"

He coughed, but yanked me closer. His mistake—years of being bullied made me anticipate his reaction. As soon as I smacked into his chest, I stood on my tiptoes and summoned what little magic I could channel to my fingers, which I then jabbed into his eyes. I might not have a lot, but apply it to just the right spot on a person and it will still work!

The magic crackled, and Mason swore as he released me, clawing at his face.

I scurried around him, sprinting to Momoko's side. "Everyone, wake up!" I tried to keep an eye on Mason as I inspected Momoko, trying to judge how badly she was hurt. Thankfully, more House Medeis wizards emerged from their rooms.

"I'm fine." Momoko leaped to her feet and shook out her hands. Her wizard mark was darker than ever as she made a pulling gesture, producing more magic before she advanced on Mason with a snarl.

A few of the senior wizards popped out of their rooms, half dressed.

I spotted Mr. Baree among them, quickly calling magic to his hands when he noticed the way Momoko placed herself between Mason and me. "Mr. Baree, wake the others in the other wing. Something's going on!"

I had to shout to be heard above the rattling, but the House wasn't reacting much besides creaking floorboards, so I couldn't tell what was happening.

What had Mason done?

Yells echoed from downstairs, but Mason stood between the stairway and the rest of us. When I cautiously started to approach, Great Aunt Marraine and two other wizards stepped in front of me.

"We have to see what's downstairs." I watched Momoko and Mrs. Clark—Felix's mom—stalk closer to Mason.

"We can't risk you, Adept," Great Aunt Marraine grimly said.

"But—"

"We're under attack!" Felix bounded up the stairs, turning around to cast whirling balls of magic behind him. "House Tellier busted through the front gate! They're swarming—" A bolt of orange magic struck Felix, and he fell with an ominous thud.

House Tellier wizards—led by Gideon the Idiot—stormed the stairway. They weren't hiding their House—they all wore black sweaters or blazers with the orange and yellow House Tellier crest on the front.

My brain struggled to understand. There hadn't been serious physical fighting between wizard Houses since World War II. That Tellier would *attack* us was unthinkable—and why would they even do it? What could they possibly gain from this?

"I asked you nicely, Hazel." Mason briefly looked back and exchanged nods with Gideon as the House Tellier wizards trotted down the hallway. "Now I'm ordering you: marry me."

I had been trying to count the House Tellier wizards—it looked like they outnumbered those of us in this hallway, though who knew if they'd already subdued the rest of the family in the other wing? I felt my empty pocket again and cursed my nonchalance in leaving my cellphone in my bedroom, but Mason's words yanked me out of my thoughts.

"Do you seriously not know what year it is?" I snapped. "Because this *isn't* the medieval ages. You can't buy me for a cow because you want my House!"

He didn't even blink at the accusation that he was after House Medeis.

Instead, he smiled politely. "This isn't an economical exchange but a political move. I deserve to be Adept and lead House Medeis. You—made out of the same overly optimistic and pacifist stock as your parents but lacking their admirable power—do not."

His words made my knees shake.

This wasn't just an attack; it was a coup. Mason wanted to lead, but without my blood to legitimize him the House would rebel and chaos would rule. His attempt to belittle me and use my low powers was just a shield to cover how power hungry he was.

He had to be, no one would have called my parents pacifists. Being part of House Medeis meant you took a vow to honor life!

I tried to swallow, but almost choked as Mr. Baree and the other House Medeis wizards crowded around me in a protective huddle.

"But it seems you've misunderstood," Mason continued. "If you *don't* marry me, I'll start killing off the House Medeis wizards one by one and take it by force instead. We'll begin with...your friend."

He glanced back over his shoulder, and two House Tellier wizards dragged Felix, still unconscious, up to him.

"Felix!" I lunged, but Mr. Baree caught me and held me back.

"You can't, Adept." Mr. Baree had to tip his head back to avoid my fists as I tried to thrash free. "If he gets you, it's over."

"He's attacked the House—do you really think he'll let Felix go?" I snapped.

"It doesn't matter," Mr. Baree firmly said. "The House comes before everything."

The House!

I whipped my gaze back to Mason. He was holding a ball of magic that crackled like electricity as he curiously watched me, his hand hovering just over Felix's heart.

"House Medeis," I shouted. "Can't you do something?"

The building rattled and groaned, but nothing happened.

"It can't, in fact." Mason still wore his usual smile, looking as kind and calm as he had at my parents' funeral. "I waited *just* until you stretched its power to its weakest. You never Ascended and bonded with it, so there is very little it can do to protect you."

I could hear my heartbeat in my eardrums.

How. How could this happen? It was *unfathomable*.

"Roy, did you get a hold of the others?" Mrs. Clark asked.

Mr. Baree shook his head.

"Felix!" Momoko shouted.

"Decide, Adept," Mason said pleasantly. "Marry me, or Felix dies."

I tried to wriggle in Mr. Baree's grasp, but being part hulk and part bear he didn't flinch, even when I elbowed him in the stomach.

Great Aunt Marraine leaned closer on the pretense of soothing me, but she spoke in a lowered voice. "What are the chances after he makes Hazel marry him he'll force her to Ascend, and then have her killed?"

"If I agree it will buy us time," I snapped. "He can't make me Ascend tomorrow—we don't have all my parents' papers or the House signet ring!"

Mr. Baree barely moved his lips as he spoke, his eyes hooked on Mason. "You're the last in your line, Adept. Your life isn't something we can gamble with."

"Adept, I'm waiting," Mason warned, his voice losing its pleasant edge.

Momoko had turned around to watch us, but she exchanged a look with Mrs. Clark, lifted her chin, and moved to stand in front of the small huddle of House Medeis wizards. "You won't get away with this, Mason."

Mason raised an eyebrow. "What a cliché thing to say."

"When the Regional Committee of Magic hears about this, they'll arrest you!"

"No, actually, they won't." Mason flexed his fingers, but didn't move them any closer to Felix's chest. "The law states clearly that House inheritance must be handled within the House—the Regional Committee of Magic and our local Wizard Council aren't allowed to interfere."

Momoko scowled. "And the House Tellier rats aren't 'interfering'?"

"Hey!" Gideon scowled.

While Momoko continued to challenge Mason, the senior wizards kept up the whispered conversation.

"We have to get the Adept out," Mrs. Clark said.

"Indeed," Great Aunt Marraine agreed.

"We'll cover your retreat, Hazel, while you run," Mrs. Clark whispered. "Go to the Rothchilds. My car is parked at the end of the driveway. Here." She discreetly pressed her car keys into my hands.

"I can't leave you all like this," I hissed.

"You have to," Mr. Baree said. "Neither you nor the House has the ability to protect us, and the House *must* survive."

I winced, but he was right. I hadn't Ascended, so I couldn't lean on the House for power, yet. I was in no condition to fight Mason. But I couldn't *abandon* them. "How many will he kill?" I asked.

Great Aunt Marraine chuckled humorlessly. "With you gone and not around to threaten he won't kill anyone. Harm, perhaps, but he is not so stupid to shed the blood of House Medeis wizards *in* House Medeis itself without the payout he wants. We can outlast him."

I shook my head, but before I could stubbornly voice my discontent, Mr. Baree interrupted me. "You *must* leave us, Hazel. For the House."

For the House.

In that moment, I *hated* House Medeis. It came before the people who were my family—which hurt something in my chest.

But as I looked from Great Aunt Marraine to Mr. Baree, I could see the determination in their eyes. They would sacrifice themselves for me. So that House Medeis would survive.

And just as I was powerless to protect them, I was equally powerless to stop them.

I gripped Mrs. Clark's keys so hard they bit into my palm.

"Now!" Mrs. Clark barked.

Momoko burst forward, firing off her magic in shimmering clouds. One hit Gideon, who dropped to his knees with a mewl of pain.

Mr. Baree dragged me to the end of the hallway, plopping me down on a massive window seat. He unlocked one of the windows in the honey-comb shaped window seat and kicked out the screen.

"Stop him!" Mason shouted.

"House Medeis, don't let them through!" Mrs. Clark cried.

The air crackled with magic, and with a numbing horror I realized I didn't hear Momoko's shouts among the others.

"Wait—" I objected as Mr. Baree set me on the edge of the window.

He ignored me. "Don't stop until you reach House Rothchild."

"Okay," I agreed. I craned my neck as I looked back, trying to see Momoko through the storm of magic behind us. "But this is the third story—" My throat closed with terror when Mr. Baree shoved me out of the House, dumping me into thin air.

I slammed into the decorative eaves that jutted over a fancy second story window just below me. My momentum made me roll off it and skid over the side before I could even try to grab at a shingle.

I hit railing that corralled a tiny second-floor balcony. That took the air out of me, but it also slowed me down so when I fell over the side and landed in a lilac bush in the gardens below, I fell without much harm, miraculously still clutching the car keys.

I struggled to breathe for a moment, simultaneously terrified and confused. Had there always been a lilac bush on this side of the House? I didn't think so...

"Thanks," I squeaked when I got enough air.

The House was silent, though I could still hear shouts and the explosive boom of magic coming from within its walls.

"After her! She made it to the ground floor!"

Run. I had to run. Momoko, Felix, and the others had paid for my escape. I wasn't going to let it be in vain.

I fought my way out of the bush, scratching my bare feet on some branches. Once on my feet, I stayed in the shadows of the few trees planted on the front lawn and stopped only when I saw the gate that normally blocked House Medeis's driveway at night. It was ripped off its hinges and tossed to the side, another example of House Tellier's brutality.

I couldn't let myself cry, this was *not* the time for it, but I did hiccup as I threw myself at Mrs. Clark's car—a blue Toyota.

It took me a few fumbling moments before I figured out her car was a press-button starter, but I managed to throw the car into reverse. Tires squealing, I backed the short distance out of the driveway—thank goodness Mrs. Clark had parked just inside the now busted gates—then threw the car into drive when I careened into the street.

Cursing that I still lacked a cellphone, I floored it, shooting down the darkened street as a few wizards emerged from House Medeis.

My heart pounded in my throat and I clutched the steering wheel with shaking hands, still barely able to believe what had happened.

House Medeis had been invaded, and I was running for my life, and for my family.

HOUSE ROTHCHILD WAS ONLY a ten-minute drive away, but it felt like hours of my life passed on that trip.

I slammed on the brakes at the curb just outside House Rothchild and threw the car into park before it fully stopped.

I almost fell out of the car when I kicked the door open, scrambling to the front gate and scraping my bare feet on the chiseled sidewalk. There was a buzzer on one of the gateposts, which I frantically pressed.

The gate didn't open, and though there were three lit windows on the main floor, no other lights turned on.

"Come on," I whispered as I tapped the buzzer so many times

I lost track. "Wake up!" I strained my ears, listening for any sign of Mason and House Tellier driving after me.

Only crickets chirped.

Nothing on the street—or in the House—stirred.

House Rothchild was more of a colonial architecture style—rectangular, white, and with an endless front porch. Between the sole streetlight and the dim lights that flickered in House Rothchild's front windows, I could see three people sitting on the front porch.

I jumped up and down and waved my hand. "I'm Hazel Medeis!" I shouted.

They didn't move.

"House Medeis has been attacked! Please let me in!" I gripped the spokes of the gate and glanced back over my shoulder—still no sign of other cars. When I peered at House Rothchild's front porch I saw someone stand, and I let my shoulders drop.

Finally, I'd be safe with House Rothchild. I'd have to explain to their Adept what had happened, but we had a sworn alliance between our Houses. They would help.

As I watched, the three figures all stood, walked across the porch, and went inside.

Shortly after, the lights turned out, and no matter how much I pushed the front buzzer, no one stirred.

House Rothchild wouldn't help me.

A sob filled my throat, but I forcibly pushed it down as I hurried back to my car. "It's okay," I whispered to myself as I threw the car in drive. "We have lots of wizard allies. Someone will help."

Except, they didn't.

CHAPTER FOUR

Hazel

I went to the four other wizard Houses we were allied with. No one came to the door. No one would even see me.

Desperate, I drove to the Curia Cloisters.

I screeched into the cloister parking lot, and the car jumped the curb before I could stop it.

I abandoned it and ran for the doors—which were well lit and open.

It was still dark outside—I think it was only three in the morning—but the cloisters were open all night given the nocturnal tendencies of some magical species.

I sprinted up the sidewalk and into the cloisters, almost running down the brownie janitor who was mopping up what looked like a puddle of slime.

"I'm sorry, can you tell me who's here tonight?" I said between gasps for air.

"The vampires are holding a meeting in the assembly hall to discuss the recent vampire murders," the short statured brownie said.

"Anyone *besides* the vampires?" I asked desperately.

Vampires were among the strongest supernaturals. As a result, they tended to look down on the rest of us, and they barely adhered to society laws. Seeking refuge with the vampires was my *last* choice.

"Anyone from the Regional Committee of Magic? Any Pack Alphas or fae nobility?" I continued.

The janitor adjusted his hat. "A few Alphas are discussing hunting rights in the red meeting room."

"Thank you!" I almost skidded out on the wet floor as I ran down the hallway, familiar enough with the cloisters to know my way to the red meeting room.

Hopefully I knew at least one of the Alphas present for the meeting.

Usually the various magical species kept to their own, but my parents had been among the strongest in their generation in the Midwest, so some werewolf Alphas and fae nobles knew them. If I was lucky, an Alpha would take me in out of pity.

With the rejection from the other wizard Houses, I was running out of options. I couldn't easily drive out to some of the more obscure wizard Houses in neighboring states. I had so little magic it would be dangerous, and with House Tellier helping Mason, it would be easy for him to find me.

The Alphas must have finished their discussion. When I reached the red meeting room the doors were open, and the Alphas were all lingering around the large horse-shoe shaped table placed at the center of the room.

Three of the Alphas were male, the remaining one was female. It was she who was curiously watching the door when I skidded around the corner and almost smacked into the doorframe.

"Please," I panted. "I need help."

One of the werewolves was Sam, the Alpha of Pack Whitefrost. He had attended my parents' funeral, and while the other werewolves warily studied me, he stood up taller. "You're Hazel, Rand and Rose's daughter," he said.

"And the new Adept of House Medeis," another one of the werewolves added.

I nodded and swallowed the bitter taste of my panic. "House Medeis was attacked."

"*What?*" the Alphas snapped.

"Mason—one of my senior wizards. He staged a takeover." I sagged against the doorframe, my gaze darting between the werewolves, looking for any hints of compassion. "He got House Tellier to attack us."

"He's after your position?" Sam asked.

I nodded. "I escaped, but the rest of my House was captured. Can you help me?"

Sam rubbed the back of his neck and was silent.

I gazed from him to the other Alphas. "Please? What he's doing breaks committee law."

"Have you sought refuge with other wizard Houses?" the female Alpha suggested.

"They're refusing to help me," I bitterly said. "They won't even talk to me."

Sam sighed. "I'm sorry, Hazel, but…we don't interfere with other species' business. It leads to infighting and war. The supernatural community is already weak. We can't risk it."

I shut my eyes, forcing back the tears that threatened to escape.

"Why don't you officially hand over your Adept position to Mason and forgo your right to leadership?" the third male Alpha suggested.

"She can't," the female werewolf wryly said. "To wizards, the House is their top priority. If she does that, she'll bring ruin on House Medeis."

The second male werewolf scowled. "Pack should be first," he grumbled.

Painfully, I opened my eyes. "You really won't help me?"

Sam looked away—signaling just how uncomfortable the situation made him as usually it was considered a sign of weakness to his kind. "I'm sorry, Adept."

I wanted to crumple into a heap on the ground. The cloisters had been my last resort. Where could I go now?

The other male Alphas also looked away. The female Alpha alone was studying me.

Should I risk traveling to one of the other out-of-state wizard Houses? It might be my only chance.

I heard shouts echoing up the hallway. I poked my head out of the room and saw a group of wizards stalking closer. Mason was leading them.

I glanced back at the Alphas. Judging by their flickering gazes they heard the other wizards.

They really weren't going to help.

What could I do now? My family had sacrificed themselves for me, and I was about to get caught! Wasn't there another way?

My thoughts focused sharply on my final option and the only other beings in the cloisters: the vampires.

I zipped out of the red meeting room and darted down a different hallway from the one Mason and his goons were in, my bare feet thudding painfully on the unforgiving marble floor.

"There she is!"

"Get her!"

I felt the tangy sensation of wizard magic, but sprinted around a corner before they could throw anything at me. Even so, I wasn't entirely sure if I was running to safety, or throwing myself into an even greater danger.

There was no way the vampires would take me in as a political refugee. I wasn't important enough, and frankly it wasn't their way. But vampires and fae were known to take on humans as servants and—in the vampires' case—blood donors.

I couldn't be a blood donor because I was a wizard, but *maybe* one of the vampires would take me as a servant. I would have preferred to serve a fae Court, but I was out of time.

The vampires were my last hope.

I took a few twisting corridor loops that would keep me out of sight. It took me a little longer to get to the assembly hall, but it also made it harder for Mason to figure out where I was.

The assembly hall was the second largest room in the Curia Cloisters—it was actually multiple floors high for viewing purposes. But I didn't fancy jumping down on the vampires, or using a side door—they might maim me just to make a point—so I scrambled to the main entrance.

It had two doors—both of them were large, wood paneled monstrosities—and they were luckily the tiniest bit ajar.

I had to use both hands to muscle the door open enough for me to slip in, and it creaked loudly enough to wake a sleeping werewolf.

Mason's shouts were starting to grow closer, which meant there was a good chance he'd heard the door creak, so I yanked the door shut behind me, my shoulders heaving with the exertion.

I wanted to rest my forehead on the cool door, but already the hair on the back of my neck was prickling. I slowly turned around, keeping my hands at my side.

I paled when I realized my vampire audience was much larger than I had expected. I thought it was informal—like the werewolves' meeting—but slightly larger.

Turns out, I was totally wrong.

In fact, based on the filled chairs that spiraled the circumference of the room, about half of the vampire Families in the Midwest had a representative present. And all of them were staring at me with glittering red eyes.

Vampires are considered some of the oldest supernaturals, so the style and range of clothes in the room varied by centuries.

A female vampire sitting on the left side of the room wore a Victorian era gown with thick, poofy skirts held out by a crinoline, and a bonnet-like headdress that tied in a large bow at her chin. The most modern looking vampire I saw was a male with his hair slicked back wearing a plaid suitcoat and loose trousers in colors that made him look like he had stepped out of a 1950's advertisement.

With all the different costumes, it might sound like a masquerade, but the unnatural stillness of vampires matched with their utter lack of emotion, the unnatural paleness of their skin, and the overwhelming predator sense they inspired made me aware that they weren't dressed up for the fun of it, but rather because *they were that old.*

My heart beat faster from an entirely different type of danger, and I swallowed loudly as I grabbed fistfuls of my stupid fleece pajama pants.

"I apologize for interrupting your important meeting." I bent over in a deep bow. "My name is Hazel Medeis, and..."

I heard shouting in the hallway, and something banged against the door.

I jumped, making the pads of my feet ache.

"Hazel Medeis, the new Adept of House Medeis?" The question came from a female vampire lounging on her chair in a beaded, loose-fitting dress that looked like something from the 1920s.

"Yes," I said in a dry, scratchy voice.

"Why do you interrupt this private and sacred meeting of vampires with your garish presence, Adept Hazel of House Medeis?" a male vampire sneered, his upper lip curling back. He had a pointed beard and wide mustache and wore a sort of red jerkin-doublet-thing that made him look like he was a musketeer.

I tried and failed to lick my lips as someone knocked on the door behind me. "It is not my intention to offend. Rather, I am here to request refuge. A member of my House has staged a coup."

The musketeer scoffed and leaned back in his chair. "No self-respecting Family would take on a refugee of your diminutive and unimportant status. We don't bother ourselves with the politics of ants."

"I am aware of this, which is why I would like to request a servant's position." I had to spit the words out of my mouth, they were so unwillingly lodged in my throat. Every piece of self-preservation screamed at me to run from the room, but as dangerous as the vampires were, I had a better chance of surviving with them than with Mason.

They wouldn't be interested in trying to manipulate House Medeis, as wizards posed no threat to them, but because I was a wizard, neither could they drink my blood. If I was a servant, they *might* leave me alone, which would give me a chance to recoup.

The musketeer looked down his long, aquiline nose at me. "What use would a *rat-blood* be to us?" he scoffed.

The female in the beaded dress thoughtfully played with her jeweled necklaces while the male in the plaid suitcoat set an unlit cigarette in his mouth as he studied me.

"You don't look like you could do anything useful." The flapper-era female said doubtfully. "I don't suppose you are trained in lawn management, hand scrubbing laundry, or pastry making?"

"No." I glanced over my shoulder—Mason and his goons hadn't stopped knocking, but since they hadn't burst in after me they must have figured out who I was speaking to. "But I am a quick learner and have a background with technology."

Plaid Suitcoat waved his hand. "What use is technology?" The way he narrowed his eyes made me think it was a rhetorical question. "Your parents were quite powerful wizards. Did you inherit their abilities?"

If I had been anywhere else, I would have shut my eyes. I'd come to accept my lack of magic while in college, but it was the source of all my problems tonight, which was a bitter pill to swallow. "No," I said. "I'm not powerful at all."

"Ah. In that case, run along." Plaid Suitcoat leaned back in his chair. "You really are useless. Off with you."

The pounding had stopped, and instead Mason called through the door. "I beg your pardon, but I believe a dangerous renegade has impeded upon you. Please allow my men and me to peacefully retrieve her."

I peered down the side of the room—perhaps I could run out a side door? But would the vampires let me, or would they kill me in their indifference?

I took a step sideways. Flapper-Dress peeled her lips back, revealing slightly elongated, sharpened fang teeth. "You were told to leave, rat-blood."

What do I do? Death by fang, or traitor?

"The Drake Family will accept your pledge of servitude." The deep, rich voice made me freeze in my tracks, and fear quivered in my stomach.

The Drake Family?

CHAPTER FIVE

Hazel

I, along with all the other vampires in the room, stared at the very back of the room. Lounging on a leather office chair placed behind an imposing desk on top of a raised platform was Killian Drake.

His dark hair looked black in the dim assembly hall lighting, though it was stylishly mussed on the top and cut short on the sides. His strong jawline, full lips, and high cheekbones made him a top predator—not because vampires valued appearances, although they did—but because he could swindle humans to do whatever he wanted with a wicked grin. His skin was pale like all vampires, but he didn't have the gaunt pallor some of his fellows did. Instead he reminded me of pure, unblemished snow.

But what terrified me most was how *modern* he looked. His hair, obviously, but unlike the other vampires, he was dressed in a designer suit that was not only outrageously expensive, but also showed just how informed he was on current trends.

An informed vampire was the most dangerous sort—even more so than a hungry and mad one.

Killian pushed up a dark eyebrow as he stared imperiously down at me. "A pet wizard sounds amusing—even one so weak as you, Adept Medeis."

A cold sweat dripped down the side of my forehead. I had made a grave miscalculation.

I hadn't *dreamed* Killian Drake—the vampire Eminent of the Midwest—would be present. He usually only emerged to frighten the Midwest Regional Committee of Magic, or to beat his opponents into submission.

Why was he here? What had the janitor said the meeting was for again?

No one—not even the other vampires—moved a muscle, which was a really, really bad sign because it meant *they* were also scared.

But what else could I do?

Survive. Live to fight another day, because being a servant to the Drake Family means I could still survive—hopefully long enough to kick Mason out—even if it means serving a figurative demon.

I inhaled, but started to lower myself to one knee.

"Come closer, Adept Medeis," Killian ordered in his smokey voice that had the faintest trace of a British accent. "You should see the eyes of your new master as you swear fealty."

Barefoot, I shuffled down the velvet carpet runner, stopping at the base of the platform.

This close to Killian I could see his eyes were such a dark red they were almost black—the same black as oblivion. He yawned, revealing his vampire fangs, and I managed not to openly shudder.

I knelt on the cold marble and stared up at Killian's black tie—unable to look him in the face.

A woman stood at the base of the stairs that led onto the platform. She had tawny brown skin, dark brown hair that was pulled back into a no-nonsense braid, and wore a pantsuit that was most likely the same expensive designer as Killian. She was tall and leggy, so it only took her about three steps to reach me.

"Do you know the pledge?" she asked in a lowered voice.

It took me three tries before I was able to swallow my spit. "No."

She pulled a leather book on a stand placed off to the side. Each page she turned wheezed out a puff of dust, but it only took her a few moments before she found what she was looking for. "Here." She tapped a paragraph of text and handed the book off to me.

The weight of the book made my arms buckle, and it was hand written in ink so faded it was almost illegible, but I stubbornly clung to it as I stared down at the words that would make me a Drake Family servant.

Faintly, I heard another knock on the door as Mason called out again, "*I beg your pardon…please allow us to retrieve the renegade.*"

This was it. I was signing my life away to a monster to escape a smaller, less powerful one.

But my parents had left me House Medeis, and my family had sacrificed themselves to see that I lived.

I would survive Killian Drake, no matter what.

I licked my lips. "I, Hazel Medeis, swear my loyalty, service, and fealty to Eminent Killian Drake, and the entirety of the Drake Family. I will not betray them under penalty of death, no matter what pain and threats I face."

"Drake Family accepts your pledge, and in return we will see to your physical wellbeing and safety." He said it so casually, but I swear I could feel the words echo in my bones. "And—" he said, adlibbing from the script outlined in the dusty book, "if you forsake your vows, I will personally see to it that you are dealt the most painful of deaths, and will destroy your beloved House brick by brick."

I winced at the unnecessary threat. "I will not betray you, sir."

"Mm." Killian stood, making him even taller than I had imagined, and addressed the other vampires. "This will end today's discussion. You have all wasted enough of my time proving you are unknowledgeable idiots. Find out more information on the murderer, or it will be *your* body I will send back to your Family Elders."

He was off the steps and striding down the carpet runner in the blink of an eye, unnaturally fast with his vampire speed.

The woman in the pantsuit took the book from me and set it back on the stand, then indicated that I should follow Killian.

I hesitated.

"Come along, servant," Killian called.

I darted after him, feeling every bruise forming on the bottom of my feet.

"In my day pledges were made in Latin, but those were more civilized times," a heavily accented voice sniffed as I rushed after Killian.

Killian paused at the main entrance, cocking his head at the doors—which Mason was now timidly knocking on.

The vampire slightly narrowed his eyes, then lashed out, delivering a kick that hit both of the doors and made them crash open.

Mason must have been standing in the doors' way, because he was sprawled on the ground, pressed against the far wall with a stunned look of shock and pain pasted on his face.

He saw me and scrambled to his feet, then froze. Paused halfway in the process of standing, he flicked his eyes in Killian Drake's direction and gulped loudly.

Killian didn't even look at him. He merely adjusted his cufflinks, then started down the hallway.

Remembering how I had struggled with the heavy doors, I glanced at them as I passed through, but was careful to stay close to Killian's shadow, aware Mason was once again staring at me.

The dark-haired female vampire followed behind me, pausing to close the doors. She stared at Mason and his goons for several long moments, then put her right hand in a deep pocket of her suitcoat.

Mason and the House Tellier wizards bowed, but they didn't even dare mumble as they fled down the hallway.

The message had been clear enough—I was off limits. For now.

I DON'T KNOW if it was the exhaustion, relief, or trauma of the night, but when I followed Killian out to the motorcade, I didn't question the female vampire ushering me into a black SUV that she drove.

I fell asleep, and didn't wake up until we were in the underground parking lot of the Drake Family's estate.

The female vampire led me to what looked like a windowless coat closet and told me to wait there, then left.

My eyes felt like heavy weights, and the events of the night threatened to set in as I sat down on a wooden bench positioned by the darkened doorway. I shut my eyes for what felt like just a moment, but when I opened them again, I was lying flat on a cushy couch.

I rocketed upright, gripping the back of the couch as I blinked and tried to get my bearings.

I was in what looked like a fancy sort of...*parlor*? There was a marble fireplace, giant windows covered with half drawn shades that seemed to block *a lot* of light, and there were lots of comfortable, *expensive* couches artfully arranged around the room, along with what looked like an original Claude Monet painting from his Water Lilies series.

The night's events hit me like a car, and I remembered with stark clarity exactly whom I had sworn myself to, and what I was running from.

I held in a groan as I propped my elbows up on my legs and bent slightly so I could rub my eyes. I'd been betrayed...but why?

Mason had been perfectly happy with my parents as the House Medeis Adepts. Was he really that enraged with my lack of magic?

But that was improbable. House Medeis was by far the most peaceful wizarding House in the region—and not just when my parents ran it. Medeis had *always* been considered peaceful—or pacifists by the more violent minded, like House Tellier.

No one joined House Medeis unless they shared the same ideals—under no circumstances were you to take a life, you had to be slow to fight, and on and on. No one who joined House Medeis would *want* to overthrow me. And not just because it would do a lot of damage to the actual House, but because fighting was the exact opposite of what House Medeis stood for!

My eyes were threatening to sting with tears, but I held them back by releasing the groan I'd been holding in for an equally long time.

In less than a month I'd lost my parents and my House. And the only way I could survive was to pledge myself to the vampires.

My life officially sucked.

"Oh, so you're awake?"

I removed my thumbs from my eyelids and peered up at a thin woman with bright red hair and smile lines so deep they gave her a perpetual grin. She was maybe in her mid-40s, and wore a white shirt with a black skirt and apron that made her look a bit like a waiter, but her sleeves were rolled up to her elbows and she had yellow banana earrings hanging from the lobes of her ears.

"I'm Debra." She cheerfully extended her hand.

When I took it she pumped my arm a few times. "Hazel," I said.

"Well, Hazel, seeing how you arrived in the middle of the night and seemed a mite exhausted, we let you sleep a bit." Debra looked me up and down as she put her hands on her hips.

"Thank you," I said. "What time is it?"

"Almost noon. Here." She handed me a snack packet of

seasoned pistachios and motioned for me to follow her. "A snack to hold you over. You'll have lunch with me, but I'm to give you a quick tour first."

She strode out of the room, and I staggered after her, wincing at my bruised feet and scruffy pajama pants.

"Do you think I could change first?" I peered up and down the hallway—it was surprisingly modern with bright white panels and white limestone columns and arches placed by the largest doors.

"Ahh yes, we'll end with your room—where your uniform is waiting and you can take a shower to make you feel like a decent person." Debra kept her pace quick and still managed to talk to me over her shoulder, even as she side-stepped a man toting a large crystal vase with bird-of-paradise flowers jutting from it. "Since you'll just be working in the kitchens until we can find an official role for you, you'll only have to know your way around a small portion of the mansion. Unless you signed up to be a blood donor?"

It seemed the female vampire had dumped me on the other servants without an explanation—not necessarily a bad thing. Hopefully it meant Killian was going to ignore me and just use my presence as a statement. (I wasn't sure what *kind* of statement—hopefully one that would keep me alive.)

"I can't be a donor," I said. "I'm a wizard."

Debra screeched to a stop and swiveled so she could stare at me. "Oh. Well. Then, yes, you'll be in the kitchens for a while."

Her reaction was pretty expected, given the circumstances.

You see, wizards are almost completely helpless against vampires.

Technically vampires are vulnerable to magic, but vampires are also a thousand times faster than us wizards. Wizards are pretty much just regular humans who can use magic, so yeah, the vampires with their unnatural speed would always have the upper hand. Fae, though, can use their brand of magic against vampires because they can keep pace with them.

But wizards? A vampire could take a wizard out with his/her speed before a wizard could even summon a flicker of magic. Add in the fact that vampires are physically tougher, ageless, and way stronger, and you have yourself a genuine predator of wizards.

Except!

Our blood tastes awful.

No joke—vampires can't even swallow it. Supposedly it smells like roadkill and hits their gag reflex so if they even taste a drop of it, they heave. It's why they call us rat-bloods.

This is probably the only thing that preserved us wizards as a race, and a lot of people theorize it's actually a survival adaption our magic creates on our behalf—kind of like poisonous animals—because there's a property to our blood that would normally have vampires' attention and make them hunt us ruthlessly.

If a vampire manages to drink wizard blood, it makes that vampire immune to the wizard's magic.

We wizards pull raw magic through our blood and use it in its purest form. Fae have to use tools—wands, staffs, and stones—to manage it and transform it, but not us wizards.

But the only way a vampire can stomach drinking a wizard's blood is if a wizard trusts the vampire completely, and the vamp returns that trust.

There's no way to fool this test, because it's magic itself that makes the blood unpalatable, so a vampire can't manipulate a wizard into trust and then drink her blood—the magic will know, and it will still taste like roadkill.

Vampires are a super paranoid and suspicious lot—I suppose when you've been alive as long as they have it's natural. So, there aren't many cases of vampires being able to drink wizard blood—at least not too many in the past century. Things used to be different, but there's no use sighing over what supernaturals have become.

The point is, there was no way I could be a blood donor. Even if I lost all sense of self-preservation and was swindled into trusting one of the House Drake vampires, a vampire wouldn't ever fully trust me, so my blood would always smell awful and taste gag-inducing-rancid.

Debra trundled down the hallway, so I hurried to keep up.

"The Drake Family uses the top two floors of Drake Hall as private quarters," Debra said, surprising me. "The main level holds the communal rooms—the dining hall, the kitchens, parlors, meeting rooms, and a very grand ballroom. The basement has the training grounds."

I mentally spooked—did the Drake Family have a dungeon downstairs? Was "training" code for torture? "What sort of training grounds?" I tried to casually ask as we marched past a glass door that looked like it opened up into a plant filled conservatory.

"The shooting range, a track, the weight room, the boxing ring, the dojo—everything the Drake Family needs to train. Well." Debra thoughtfully paused in front of a window, which overlooked gardens almost as magnificent as the ones that circled House Medeis. "The pool is outdoors—just beyond those trees. But they don't use it."

"You don't say?" I asked, my voice faint.

A *pool*? The Drake Family had a *pool*? Why? They were vampires! Given their reputation I could see the need for the weight center, dojo, and the rest of it—even the shooting range was understandable given that some of the Drake vampires might favor crossbows or daggers. But a *swimming pool*?

What, was it for nighttime pool parties? HAH!

Vampires preferred to operate as if the world was centuries younger—although they did make exceptions for things like electricity, indoor plumbing, etc. But I'd never heard of a vampire Family having an HD TV, much less a swimming pool!

"The kitchen and all the servants' quarters are located near the back of Drake Hall," Debra said. "Blood donors have rooms in the same hallway as ours, but they aren't expected to work."

"How many blood donors live here?" I asked.

"Currently? Twelve."

I nodded as we made a sharp turn. "And how many vampires?"

Debra turned an eyebrow up at what she must have imagined was an inappropriate question, but she answered anyway. "Thirty-eight of them—though the Drake Family is much larger. A number of Drake vampires elect to live off the hall grounds or are positioned around the Midwest to serve as the Eminence wishes."

Ah. In other words, Killian Drake scattered his men across the Midwest to better control it. I nodded, because she seemed to expect some sort of response, before her words actually dawned on me. "Wait. Twelve blood donors, for thirty-eight vampires?"

Did they drink the donors dry and toss their bodies out in the pool? Twelve humans couldn't possibly satisfy almost forty vampires!

A bell rang, interrupting us before Debra could explain the uneven mathematical equation. She gave me a business-like nod, then marched to what was clearly a back entrance to the house, given that it was surrounded by coat closets, and flung the door open.

A female vamp stood at the doorway, balancing a cardboard box in either hand. "I've got this week's blood delivery." She smiled and gave Debra a slight nod in greeting.

"You know the way?" Debra asked.

"Yep!" She hopped inside and made a beeline down the hallway. She must have been a newer vamp—her hair was dyed an ombre blond, and though she wore a delivery jacket in her company colors, she had a pair of dark jeans on.

I was a little surprised—vampires don't typically hold down jobs outside of their Family. She probably was an Unclaimed—a vampire that didn't pledge allegiance to or belong to a vampire Family. It's the vampire version of werewolf Lone Wolves.

She darted through an open doorway—the kitchen, judging by

the sound of rattling dishes and the sharp tap of a knife on a cutting board—but returned to the hallway in a flash.

Debra smiled pleasantly as the delivery vampire trotted back outside, but held the door open. "Most Drake Family vampires drink packaged blood."

"Really?" I asked, trying to hide my skepticism.

Lots of vampires drank packaged blood—it was a cheaper and more easily law-abiding alternative to keeping blood donors on retainer, something the average vampire couldn't afford.

But blood donors were a sign of status. Most of the powerful vampire Families kept more blood donors than members so they *never* had to drink from a blood pack.

There was no way Killian freaking Drake's vampire Family dined mostly on blood packs.

"Really," Debra assured me. She stepped back, giving the delivery vampire a clear path when she returned with two more boxes. "In fact, Killian Drake *only* drinks packaged blood."

I had to work hard to keep my jaw from dropping. "The *Eminence*," I squeaked, my voice going high, "only drinks *blood packs?*"

Debra gave me a smile that was half wry half smug. "Indeed."

The delivery vampire made four more trips while we waited in silence.

There had to be a reason for Killian Drake's pre-packaged diet. I didn't believe for a minute that the *Eminence*—the vampire leader of the Midwest—drank packaged blood due to the cost or the reluctance to see humans as dinner.

Once Debra had signed off on the blood delivery, she marched down to the kitchens.

Standing in the doorway, I was overwhelmed by the spotless white of the kitchen. The elaborate wooden cupboards and the fancy molding on the edges and corners were all painted white. White marble topped every counter, the walls were a shining white—the only relief was the stainless-steel appliances and sinks.

And yeah, you got that right—there were multiple sinks, and four fridges that I saw—though I was willing to bet there was a walk-in fridge somewhere for the blood packs.

Scurrying through this intimidating domain was: a pair of chefs, three assistants, a baker who was busy rolling out cookie dough, and a teenage boy who must have been the dedicated dishwasher given that he was elbow deep in soap suds.

It seemed a little overkill given the number of blood donors in the house, but vampires could technically eat regular human food. Not much—and it didn't have any nutritional value for them—but if most of them drank packaged blood it wouldn't be *too* surprising that they prefer to have a human meal occasionally.

Two well-dressed females—both of them looked in their early thirties or so—were perched at one of two kitchen islands with an equally well-dressed man. All three of them were humans—you could tell by their colored eyes.

Vampires always have red eyes. The exact hue and shade of red varied per vamp, but was a dead-giveaway—and one they couldn't easily hide.

This meant all three of them were probably blood donors since they weren't dressed in the white and black kitchen uniforms and they seemed occupied with nibbling on food.

Debra waited a moment or two, but the kitchen staff were too busy working and chatting to notice her, and the blood donors were pretty focused on the baker's progress with the cookie dough.

Eventually she gave in and clapped twice. "Everyone, this is Hazel Medeis. She is a newly sworn servant to the Drake Family, and will be serving here in the kitchens until we find a permanent spot for her. Please help and direct her as needed."

The baker—a plump middle-aged woman—smiled. "Welcome to Drake Hall!"

The chefs—a man and a woman who stood close enough

together I was starting to assume they were an item—eyed me up and down.

"Are you any good at food prep?" the male chef asked.

Debra held a finger in the air. "I'm not handing her over just yet—she needs a tour of the hall. But I'm going to leave her here for a moment while I call housekeeping to confirm her room location. You'll give her something to eat?"

The kitchen staff nodded.

Debra laid a hand on my arm. "Stay here, I won't be but a few minutes." She swept off, her heels clicking on the stone tiled floor.

One of the woman blood donors smiled at me and patted the counter. "Take a seat!"

"Thanks." I padded across the kitchen, tiredly rubbing my eyes.

Some of the staff were staring at me, and it took me a moment to realize it was probably my fleece pajama pants and dirty, scratched up feet. (Or it could have been the hair. My blond hair was probably a rat's nest by now.)

The realization didn't come with the flush of embarrassment you would normally expect. I just didn't care anymore—a product of the traumatic night I'd gone through. But I recognized that I wouldn't gain anything by freaking these people out, and I was going to be stuck playing a long game if I ever hoped to kick out Mason, so I tried to smile.

"Long night?" the friendly blood donor asked.

"Yeah. Really long." I plopped down two chairs from her, and my smile turned a little more genuine when the female chef slapped a plate down in front of me that held a ham sandwich almost as big as my head. "Thank you."

She slightly pursed her lips as she studied me. "Hazel Medeis… of House Medeis?"

I cringed—I hadn't expected humans to recognize my last name. "Yep."

"So, you're a wizard, then?"

I picked up the giant sandwich, trying to figure out what end was best to start with. "A weak one, but yeah."

The chef nodded and folded her arms across her chest, seemingly satisfied. "I expect they hired you because of all the murders?"

CHAPTER SIX

Hazel

I mentally repeated her question twice before I set my sandwich down in my confusion. "I'm sorry...*what?*"

"Playing dumb, hm?" the male blood donor said in a growly voice, though his toothy smile was warm. "Probably not a bad idea—if the sicko responsible doesn't know you're a wizard you can better protect us."

"What's the count up to now?" the dishwasher asked. He almost lost his black framed glasses in the suds when he peered into the depths of his sink.

"Have there been any new murders?" a kitchen assistant asked.

"Not since Nick's death yesterday," the female chef grimly said.

"He was a vampire from the Kotov Family," the baker sighed. "Such a loss."

"In Drake Hall we lost Wanda, Kevin, and a maid!" The other female blood donor, who had been staring at her plate this whole time, hotly declared. Her face was a little red and her eyes glassy with unshed tears. "They may be humans, but they still count!"

The male blood donor patted her hands. "The Drake Family will avenge them."

"I heard Killian Drake himself is getting involved," the male chef said. "That's what last night's meeting was for. And her, probably." He nodded his head in my direction.

I had been puzzling through the conversation and steadily working away at my sandwich—I don't know if it was because I was starving or if it was the magic of crispy bacon layered with ham and slightly melted cheese, but I swear it was the best sandwich ever. Unfortunately, when the talk finally worked back around to me, my mouth was full, and I almost choked on crumbs. "Really," I said when I finally managed to swallow my food. "I have no idea what any of you are talking about. I pledged myself to the Drake Family because of a...situation. I'm not here to help with finding a murderer."

The atmosphere in the kitchen dampened instantly.

"Oh." The woman chef's shoulders drooped.

"Wait a moment—you're Hazel Medeis." The baker paused in the middle of pressing a heart-shaped cookie cutter into the dough. "You're the new House Medeis Adept."

It seemed I hadn't completely cleared my throat of all the crumbs, as it abruptly squeezed shut. "Yeah, that's me."

The baker eyed me. "Did they kick you out because you don't have any power?"

"Martha!" the female chef snapped.

"It's not a secret," the baker argued. "I read about it when I was scanning the minutes of the latest Regional Committee of Magic to see what they said about the murders."

The topic appeared to have safely returned to the murders given the winces around the room—though I got the feeling several of the staff were sending me thinly veiled looks of sympathy.

I wanted to take another bite of my sandwich—a crazed murderer running around was hardly noteworthy to me. Not since Mason had implied he was happy to murder my friends and family to get me to marry him, which pretty much topped the creepy meter for me. But if there *was* a psycho out to get the Drake Family—or vampires in general—given my recent luck it seemed like there was a good chance I'd blunder into him. So, it was probably best if I learned more.

I wiped my mouth off. "How long have these murders been a problem?"

"A month, maybe?" The dishwasher boy scratched his head, leaving a glob of soap bubbles in his hair. "That's when we lost Wanda. She was a blood donor."

"The Drake Family will handle it," the male chef firmly said. "They care for their own, and though one could not accuse them of being fond of humans, they never shirk their duty toward us."

I bet they didn't. The more the staff were under the vampires' thumbs, the easier it would be to subdue or get rid of a problematic servant or blood donor.

Don't get me wrong. Not all vampire Families are power hungry and obsessed with influence—though the majority of them are.

Most newer vampires—like the delivery vamp—are way more chill and calmer once they make the complete transformation.

The problem is that these days it's *really hard* for an old vamp to successfully sire a new vampire. Like, if there were more than ten new vampires in the Midwest per year, I'd be shocked.

This wasn't a problem just for vamps, though. Werewolves were almost at the same level.

You'd think wizards and fae—being born—would escape this, but instead it just seemed like each new generation being born was less powerful than the previous.

Magic was...well...dying. We tried to keep it a secret from humans, but over the past two generations it had become unfailingly obvious that if we didn't do something fast, supernaturals would die out altogether—or leave only the crazy psychos alive like the oldest of vampires and the most deranged fae kings and queens.

That was why we went public when we did. We were hoping by turning humans into our allies, we might be able to find a solution to magic's weakening.

"If the murderer attacked you, Hazel, would you be able to fight it off?" the chattier of the two women blood donors asked.

I scratched my cheek. "Not if they killed a vampire."

"Nick—rest his soul—was a mid-level member of the Kotov Family," the baker said. "The Kotov Family is competent, which probably makes him roughly on par with the weakest vampire in the Drake Family."

"Yeah, but the Drake Family is the most powerful in the Midwest," I pointed out. "And wizards can't take out vampires on our best day. If Nick Kotov was as strong as even the weakest Drake vampire, whoever killed him is super powerful, or really well prepared. And, as was mentioned, I don't have strong magical abilities."

"We'll trust in the Drake Family," the male blood donor decreed. "They'll handle it."

The dishwasher boy and the quiet female blood donor didn't seem nearly so convinced, but they delicately changed the topic to the dinner menu, which was when the vampire strolled in.

His suit was so perfectly pressed and his tie was so snug I swear he couldn't have looked down without breaking his neck. (Was the suit thing a dress code around here? Because matched with his slicked back, bright red hair it made him look like a model for men's cologne.)

"Sir!" the male chef barked. "How can we help you?"

"I have no need of help." Though his pale skin gave him a delicate, almost anemic look, his red eyes flashed with a cruel savagery that revealed his true nature. "I'm here to fetch a blood pack for the Eminence."

One of the assistants scurried across the kitchen, throwing open the door of what I had assumed was a pantry, but was actually a walk-in cooler.

The vampire boredly looked around, leaning against a countertop with the casualness of a satisfied predator as the kitchen staff and blood donors beamed at him.

I shrank back in my seat and did my best not to be noticeable—the less vampire attention I received the better.

Of course, this meant he looked right at me instead of watching the blood donor sitting a seat down from me who was clearly trying to get his attention.

I stared at my plate and didn't dare look up—a good defense mechanism.

Vampires didn't have mind control powers per se. But they could dazzle a person into complacency, which was close enough for me.

The vampire narrowed his eyes and delicately tilted his head back, sniffing the air. "What's a rat-blood doing here?"

I stayed huddled on my chair and kept my eyes on the counter. "I'm a new kitchen servant. I said my vows to Killian Drake last night."

The vampire scoffed and took a step closer, but was fortunately blocked when the over-eager assistant zipped out of the fridge and skidded between us, holding a blood pack on a silver platter.

"Would you like me to deliver it to the Eminence, sir?" the assistant asked.

"No." The vampire grabbed the blood pack and meandered out of the kitchen without looking back.

"That was Rupert," the chatty woman blood donor confided to me. "He's like Killian and drinks packaged blood—which is a real shame."

The male blood donor rolled his eyes, but added, "You don't need to be afraid of him."

I squinted at him. "He's a vampire. It's healthy to be afraid of him—you *should* be afraid of him."

"Nah," the female blood donor said. "Not here in Drake Hall! The vampires care for us."

There was nothing in Rupert's manners that had hinted at that, and knowing how little Killian Drake cared for anyone not a vampire, and that he had a history of eliminating anyone who got in his way, I was not inclined to believe them.

The skepticism must have showed on my face, because the blood donors spent the rest of the time trying to convince me of the vampires' cold but real kindness until Debra came for me.

It gave me the shivers to see just how little the blood donors understood about the creatures drinking their blood.

———

A week passed, and I numbly settled into my new routine—which was a never-ending schedule of working, sleeping, and eating.

I liked it.

I was thankful that I didn't have to think, and I didn't even try to process Mason's betrayal. But sometimes at night I'd wake up in a sweat, remembering with vivid clarity the way Felix sagged as Mason's magic hovered over his heart.

I hadn't wanted something that would distract me from my parents' death, buuut it seems like I got it anyway.

I did odd jobs in the kitchen—putting away clean dishes, fetching ingredients for the chefs, arranging the baked goods on pretty trays—and I did my best to be friendly to my co-workers, so they accepted me readily enough. (Though I think they found my guarded manners toward our vampire bosses a little offensive.

But that mostly just showed how little humans understood about our world.)

My biggest concern was the vampires.

I did everything I could to stay out of their way and escape notice. Thankfully, it wasn't hard since no one could accuse a vampire of harboring excessive amounts of noblesse oblige.

I didn't actually see them too often—I volunteered for early morning shifts and errands where I would be least likely to run into them. But after a week of living with the Drake Family, I actually got a glimpse of some of the elite vampires training.

It was evening. The sun hovered on the horizon, casting a blood red splash of color on the gunmetal gray clouds, and the vampires were holding practices outside.

I was carefully trotting along the outer wall of the massive mansion. I'd been sent to retrieve some fresh mint for one of the dishes that was going to be served with dinner. The mint was part of the herb garden tucked into the fold of the massive backyard garden. And just beyond that garden were the vampires.

It looked like they were practicing swordplay, but they were moving so fast it was hard to see.

It was pretty gutsy of them to practice in the sun—or maybe that was the point? Sunlight can't instantly turn a vamp into dust, but it slows them down mentally and physically, and it's an unpleasant sensation. But, watching the deadly Drake vampires, I suspected that was probably why they were outside—and why they were moving so fast even as the red sky glowed above them.

I paused at a patio door that would lead me into the mansion, and glanced back over my shoulder.

The vampires were streaks of black and white, their swords colliding in movements that I could track only with my ears. I wondered...could I learn to be competent with weapons to make up for my poor magic?

Grit scraped stone, and I jumped as I peered farther up the

walkway, freezing when I saw the tell-tale black and white suit of a vampire.

I had come to find that *all* Drake vampires wore expensive suits, and this vampire was standing in the shadows so I couldn't make out if it was Rupert or any of the other vampires I'd seen glimpses of. It didn't matter though. His presence was enough to make me jerk out a stiff bow and dart into the mansion.

I carried my basket of mint sprigs to the kitchen, doing my best to stay out of the way as the rest of the kitchen staff frantically tore around, rushing to prepare the evening meal.

"I've got the mint," I called.

"Good, out of the way," someone ordered.

I jumped back to the doorway to avoid being bowled over, and caught sight of Debra marching down the hallway.

"Hazel—perfect. Do you have any chores at the moment?" Debra smiled and glanced down at her wristwatch.

"No."

"Would you help two of the maids outside? Rupert informed me that the dragon statues lining the driveway need to be cleaned. The maids are almost finished, but they're running behind. Their shift is about to end, and The Eminence does *not* like to see the cleaning staff out after sundown."

Yeah, and I was sure it was out of concern for his staff. *Right*. The jerk probably just didn't like his view being spoiled, or something equally prissy.

Knowing my thoughts could get me bitten—or worse—I forced a smile to my lips. "Sure thing! Do I need to take any supplies out there?"

"No, no. They'll have it all. Thank you, Hazel."

I gave Debra a thumbs up. "Sure thing! We'll finish fast."

The older woman seemed bemused by my enthusiasm, but she did wave to me before I turned up the hallway and slipped outside through the delivery door.

Since time seemed to be of the essence, I jogged down the

stinking long driveway and quickly realized why the maids were behind schedule. There were dragon statues every fifty feet or so of this paved monstrosity, and whoever designed it seemed to think it was necessary to snake back and forth across the immaculate lawn and around every tree that formed the front perimeter of the property.

I wasn't exactly sure how much land the Drake Family had, but I was betting it was *a lot*. "And who wants to bet there are annoying dragon statues on every acre of it?" I muttered to myself as I jogged.

I was grateful for the cool night air. Spring was warming into a hot summer, and my uniform—a white dress shirt with black slacks that made me feel like a waiter day in and day out—stuck to me as I started to sweat despite the sweet chill in the air.

I found the maids attacking a dragon statue with sudsy rags and grim expressions.

I waved to them as I approached. "Hey—I'm Hazel. Debra sent me to help you."

One of the ladies—an older woman with gray hair—smiled widely. "Aren't you a sight for sore eyes? The name's Bea, that's Ellie." She nodded at the other maid—a doe-eyed, college-aged student.

Ellie gave me a weak smile as she polished the inside of the statue's nostrils. "Hello."

"We just have that statue left—could you be a dear and get started on it?" Bea pointed across the driveway, to the twin of the stone dragon they were vigorously scrubbing.

I swiped a wet brush and one of their buckets, then settled in to wash the stone monstrosity—which was bigger than me.

We were quiet—concentrating on our work—but I enjoyed listening to the birds as they fluttered in the trees above us. The rough stone of the statue felt like sandpaper whenever my grasp on my brush slipped and I banged my knuckles on it. I tried to scrape mold off a front fang, and I contemplated what I had left to do for the day.

While dinner was served, I'd need to go through the walk-in cooler that held the blood packs. We just got a delivery today, so I'd need to re-order the packs and put the older ones in the front, or they'd expire and go bad. (I'd discovered last week that the servants just served the vampires whatever was freshest and tossed the rest. It was a colossal waste of money, but my main incentive was that it made me gleeful that the vampires were getting served older blood.)

"How long have you worked in Drake Hall, Hazel?" Bea called across the driveway.

I shook myself from my slightly vindictive thoughts. "Just a week."

"Gosh, a green one, are you?" Bea smiled as she buffed the statue's front foot. "I've seen you around—I thought for sure you were Connie's replacement."

"Connie?"

Bea's smile dimmed slightly. "Ah, she passed on recently."

I recalled the kitchen gossip that a maid and two blood donors had been killed before the vampire. Connie must have been the maid. I chewed on my lip and wondered how many more questions I could ask. Given all the "fun" I'd gone through the last few weeks I understood it was a tough topic, but as a wizard I hadn't heard about the murders.

"It's kind of rude of me to ask," I started. "But...how did she die?"

"She was a victim of the murders that have been plaguing the vampire community of late," Bea said. "Of course, it's mostly been blood donors and servants of the most honored Families, but there've been a few slayings as well."

"Are all the victims killed in the same method?" I asked.

"No." Bea tossed her rag in her bucket and pressed her lips together. "It seems the vampires have more violent ends—they're found completely drained and often with grievous wounds. The humans are more peacefully killed—if you can call any sort of *murder* peaceful." She shook her head and picked up the bucket, coming to join me. "These are terrible times."

"Yeah," I echoed.

"Didn't you know about the murders before you got here?" Ellie joined us and started in on the statue's tail. "I'm friends with one of the kitchen assistants. She said you're a wizard. Wouldn't that make you part of their society?" She pointed back in the direction of the mansion.

I snorted. "No. Supernaturals don't mix well. We tend to stick to our own—besides, we've got laws to keep us from meddling with each other. And no one wants to bother." My last few words came out more bitter than I meant for them to, but neither Bea nor Ellie seemed to notice.

"That's sad," Ellie quietly said.

I shrugged. "It's been that way for a long time—at least half a century." I trailed off as I cocked my head and listened.

It was quiet.

Our voices were the only noises in a forest that had been alive with bird songs just a few minutes ago. They couldn't have all nested down for the night—the sun was still up. But the last few weeks had, more than anything, only amplified the paranoia installed in me from a lifetime of bullying.

I dropped my brush in the bucket and peered into the shadows of the tree-shaded lane. I heard leaves rustle, and narrowed my eyes.

"Hazel?" Ellie asked.

More leaves rustled.

"I hear something." I lowered my voice to a whisper as I slowly turned in a circle.

My eyes caught a tiny bit of movement, and I froze. Fifty feet away, looming behind a tree, was a nightmare of a creature. It somewhat resembled a giant, wingless wasp with six sapling sized legs and a stinger that was approximately the size of a dagger poking out of its rear. It was bigger than Bea and stood upright on its back legs, its four other legs moving around it like a spider feeling for a web. It had the serrated jaws of a beetle, and its head and back were covered by a grayish brown exoskeleton. It blended in so well with the forest I would have missed it, if not for the silver, scythe-like claws that tipped its four front appendages and glittered in the fading light.

It had to be a creature from the fae dimension. But what was it doing *here*?

More importantly, what did we do? There was no way we could fight the thing! And judging by its size and willowy frame I didn't think we could outrun it. But would help come before it killed us?

I slid my eyes in the direction of Drake Hall, but I couldn't even see the end of the forested section of the stupidly long driveway. I glanced at Bea and Ellie, trying to gauge them.

"What is it?" Ellie whispered.

Ellie was built like a track runner, but Bea was older—old enough that I didn't think she'd be able to manage much more than a jog. If we ran, the creature would go for her first.

Bea squinted at me, then followed my gaze to the creature. "Heaven have mercy," she breathed.

Ellie opened her mouth wide—probably to scream—but Bea grimly slapped a hand over her lips. "Don't, Ellie," she warned in a hoarse whisper, then glanced at me. "We should run for it."

"It will kill at least one of us even if we run, possibly all of us," I said.

"Don't play games, girl. I know I'll be its first target," Bea said. "Least I can do is run in the opposite direction to lead it away."

For a moment, I struggled with her offer. Tradition said I needed to survive for the sake of House Medeis. But I believed in doing what was right. Back at the House, my family had made my decision for me. Here, though, I had a choice.

I knew what I had to do.

"No." I tilted my head back as I mentally rummaged through the battle tactics and strategies I had learned in my tussles with other wizards, and read about in books in House Medeis's incredible library. "I'll face it. Both of you run and get help—start screaming as soon as you leave the trees."

I could last long enough to stop it from chasing them before the vampires could hear them. *Probably*.

It didn't matter how grim my prospects were. I couldn't let Bea sacrifice herself for us. It wasn't right.

"Hazel—" Ellie squeaked when Bea dropped her hand from the college student's mouth.

"Now—run!" I barked.

Ellie ran as swift as a deer, pausing occasionally to glance back at Bea—who jogged behind her.

I also ran.

But instead of running away, I ran toward the creature.

I barreled through the underbrush in my slacks and dress shirt, perhaps the worst prepared I'd ever been for a fight. Intent on keeping the thing occupied, I started shouting.

The creature had turned in Ellie and Bea's direction, but when it perceived my...war-cry...it slowly turned back around.

When I had crossed half the distance to the monster, I abruptly turned, shutting my mouth with a jarring click and peeling off into the forest.

It started after me, first following at an ambling, awkward walk before it settled into a lope that was a lot faster than I liked.

In seconds, it was almost on top of me. It clicked its beetle jaws as it stabbed its two front legs at me.

I ducked, barely avoiding its scythe-like claws—which passed so close they stirred my wild blond hair.

I needed cover.

I spotted one of the dragon statues dead ahead, marking one of the many turns of the driveway, and tried to run faster.

The creature easily kept pace, keeping its balance despite its large size by grabbing and pushing off tree trunks with its extra appendages.

My lungs burned, but I made it to the statue, darting around it just as the creature made another lunge for me.

It was *almost* a miscalculation for me.

The creature was able to adjust its jump at the last minute, so it lashed out *around* the statue with its four arm-like legs.

Thankfully I had taken the turn so tight I almost fell, so its legs brushed over my head.

Even better, the insect-creature had stabbed its front left leg through a small opening between the dragon's back and its half-furled wings. But, when it pulled back, the curving angle of its claw made it impossible to slide back through the hole.

It was stuck.

I almost laughed in my light-headed glee. Finally, my luck was changing!

Not being an idiot, I changed my path so I was headed for the mansion and kept running—I could hear Ellie's hysterical screams, so I couldn't be that far from safety.

I glanced back at the monster, and my stomach curdled when I saw it plant its legs and then yank hard, *snapping* its front leg in half.

Its disembodied, claw-tipped foot slid off the statue and fell with a sickening splat.

The creature dangled its injured leg in front of it, straightened, then scanned the forest.

I sprinted as fast as I could, my heart pounding when I heard the monster's loping gait gaining on me. Rather than look back I stared at the ground, watching my feet and—there! A fallen branch that had lots of dried, shriveled leaves hanging from it.

I snatched it up as I tried weaving around a tree. The insect-creature frog hopped around the trunk, almost landing on top of me.

I held my breath as I snapped my fingers, pulling magic from the air, through my blood, and down to my fingertips, creating a candle-sized flame as my wizard mark burned and surfaced just under my left eye.

The shriveled leaves caught on fire fast, and I jabbed the burning branch up at the creature's head.

It reared back, but before I could scramble away it curled its abdomen under itself, ramming its stinger in my direction.

I veered to the side, dodging successfully, but my legs slipped out from under me.

Before I could scramble to my feet, it wrapped two of its legs around my ribcage and yanked back, making me choke on my own air. Its blade-like claws sliced through my shirt and stabbed into my skin, creating a hot, knifing sensation.

I struggled and thrashed as the monster pulled me along. Rather than carry me, it let me fall to the ground and dragged me backwards over fallen branches, rocks, and stretches of pavement.

"No!" I pulled uselessly on the appendages which tightened around my waist, and screamed when its claws dug in, shedding dribbles of my blood.

Where were those useless vampires? They had to be able to smell my stinky blood by now!

I tried to grab at tree trunks, chipping my nails and skinning my knuckles when the monster effortlessly yanked me free.

It was hard to breathe in my panic, but I tried to shove it down—if I didn't keep a clear head there was no way I was going to survive this thing.

I went limp and tilted my head back, trying to figure out where it was taking me. Just up ahead I saw the statue where the monster had yanked its own leg off.

It was headed in a straight line, seemingly intent on dragging me off Drake land.

If the vampires didn't come before then, I was dead.

I hurriedly calculated its path, my ribs aching as if its claws were resting directly on bone as it pulled me along.

I had one chance. It was going to pass close to the dragon statue…and the monster's severed front claw.

I leaned to the side closest to the statue, waiting for the flash of its claw.

In one smooth movement I managed to pinch the claw between my feet and toss it up at my head. I caught it and stabbed upwards, piercing the monster's abdomen with its own claw, which sliced through its tough carapace.

The monster collapsed on top of me.

Unfortunately, I hadn't planned for its giant-arse stinger, which stabbed my shoulder when it fell.

I screamed as hot, gut-wrenching pain knifed through my shoulder. The stinger must have been coated in poison, because it felt like my blood was boiling in my veins.

The monster dropped me as it tried to stand, endlessly turning in a circle and thrashing through the underbrush as it tried to pluck out the claw I had wedged in its abdomen.

I tried to move, but my vision was turning hazy, and soon I couldn't even scream anymore.

My body felt heavy, and it took a lot of effort to keep breathing.

I thought I heard shouts, but I couldn't be sure because my eyes closed against my will. Something prodded my forehead twice before I lost all feeling and fell into darkness.

CHAPTER SEVEN

Hazel

I woke up slowly, noticing the foreign sensation of sheets so soft they felt like silk, and the curious lack of pain.

Had I died? Was Heaven actually full of comfortable beds and expensive linens? I mean, I certainly wasn't going to complain about it. That actually sounded pretty awesome at the moment. Though I was starting to get hot.

I slowly opened my eyes, wondering if I'd see Mom or Dad first.

Instead I got a face full of red eyes, a fashionably handsome look of distaste, and hair that was so artfully ruffled it belonged on a runway model instead of the head of a vampire.

Oh, I thought, my musings coming to me in a foggy mist. *That's Killian Drake.*

Although my thoughts were complacent, my body must have known better, for a shot of adrenaline tore through me. *Wait... that's Killian Drake!*

I sat up, intending to shriek, but the pain in my ribs stole the breath from my lungs, so it ended up being more of a feeble wheeze.

Killian, seated in a velvet armchair placed at the end of my bed, gave me a clear look of condescension. "I advise you to move with care. Your shoulder wound finally just closed, and it took a dozen fae potions to keep you from dribbling blood like a wounded water buffalo."

I stared wide-eyed at Killian, barely daring to breathe.

Why was the Eminence of the Midwest and the leader of the Drake Family sitting in a chair by my bed?

He wasn't the type to wait by *anyone's* bedside, much less an unimportant kitchen servant. Which meant he was doing this for a reason. What, I couldn't possibly fathom. Hopefully I could bleat my thanks, he'd leave, and I could stew it over in comfortable loneliness.

I awkwardly cleared my throat. "What happened?"

Killian blinked slowly, the red of his eyes so dark they almost appeared black. "So droll and so typical. Do you really not remember the creature that did its best to disembowel you?"

"I remember stabbing it in the abdomen with its own claw." I tried to discreetly roll my shoulders, marveling over the smooth motion that didn't hurt, even though I'd basically taken a dagger wound.

"Yes, rather ingenious for a wizard. Although you did your best to die afterwards and have been out of it for an hour." Killian pointed to a glass chalice filled with a foamy blue liquid. "Drink that."

I squinted at the cup—was it *bubbling?*

"It's an A level healing draught," Killian said. His tone was bored, as if such a potion was nothing significant when, in fact, they cost about a month's worth of the average human salary. "Drink it so you stop wincing over your cracked ribs."

I seriously hoped Killian was exaggerating due to his general irritation with me, but I didn't dare refuse. (Although I had a sinking suspicion this was going to cost me big time in the future. Did he plan to dock my pay?)

I held the chalice with a shaky hand and took a sip, relaxing at the flavor—which tasted creamy, almost like ice cream, with a tangy hint of sea salt.

I glanced up, surprised to see Killian hadn't left while I consumed the potion. That he was still sitting in his chair made the hair on the back of my neck prickle.

Yep. It was final. He had to be here for a reason, and whatever it was, I was *certain* I wasn't going to like it.

I cleared my throat. "It was a fae creature, right? What was it doing here?"

Fae are a little different from the rest of us supernaturals because they have access to...I suppose you could call it a realm. It's much smaller than Earth, and about four times as dangerous, as it's infected with magical creatures—from unicorns to the more frightening trolls. Supposedly elves used to rule this smaller realm, but they died out centuries ago, and the place turned toxic. Not many fae live in that realm anymore, with the exceptions of fae Courts. Nobles can stake their claims given they are the only type rich enough to afford the necessary magical wards that make it possible to stay there.

Occasionally monsters slipped from the fae realm to Earth, but it was pretty rare, and exceptionally weird that it would spawn so close to Drake Hall.

Killian shrugged. "It is called a mantasp—an insectoid monster from the fae realm, yes. Which, *obviously*, implies a fae let it loose here."

I gaped at him. "No way."

He raised a black eyebrow at me. "I suppose you know better?"

"It's against the non-aggression treaty!"

He rolled his eyes. "It's only against the non-aggression treaty if it can be proved the fae actually did it. Given that I do not have a fae on staff capable of discerning such a thing—and no fae would willingly take a job that would rat out their kinsmen—it's impossible to prove."

I felt the cool sensation of the healing draught trigger, and the skin on my ribcage tingled and itched. I awkwardly scratched it as I frowned in thought. "Could it have been the murderer?"

Killian shook his head. "Too flashy. Though it is suspected the murderer is of fae origin as well." He leaned his head back, and the light from an elaborate light fixture above us caught his eyes, revealing more shades of crimson red.

I frowned when I looked around and realized I was *not* in my bedroom in the servants' quarters. This place was way too fancy. There was a chandelier, expensive sheets, and the mattress had an elaborate foot and headboard and was big enough for me to roll across multiple times. *Where was I?* I was still wearing my black dress pants that were part of my uniform, but my slashed white dress shirt had been replaced with a soft cotton t-shirt, and I wasn't certain I wanted to know who had changed me while I was out of it.

The corners of Killian's lips turned up in a slight smirk that boded poorly for me. "Hazel Medeis."

I slightly hunched my shoulders and reluctantly met his gaze. "Yes?"

Killian's smirk bloomed, flashing his fangs which gave a bit of savagery to his otherwise stylish image. "I've taken an interest in you."

I felt the blood drain from my face, and my hands shook under the despicably soft sheets that had swindled me into complacency. "Please don't," I blurted out, then realized how that sounded. "I mean, I'm, uh, not worthy of your...attention."

Killian stood, his height adding to the imposing figure he already made, and ignored my protests. "You successfully fought off a mantasp using only a flicker of magic. If you hadn't been bleeding out like a wounded seal—"

I really was starting to wish he'd stop comparing me to animals—it was hardly reassuring given the current company's diet.

"—you might have finished it off. I didn't know such a feat was possible for wizards—you all are so hilariously useless at anything besides magic." He slid his hands into the pockets of his pants and glanced down at me. "I always thought it might be fun to have a pet wizard capable of harassing the fae."

Relief almost made me flop back on my pillows. He wanted a pet wizard, did he? Then I was the worst candidate for the job. "I am sorry to say, sir, but I am very bad at magic," I told him, doing my best to fake embarrassment and cover up my joy. "I don't have much at all—that's *why* I had to outmaneuver the monster."

I peeked up at him to see if the act was working.

Killian was still, unfortunately, smirking. "I don't believe it." His British accent was a little stronger than usual—I had thought it was so faint because it had been worn away with the passing of time, but maybe he did it on purpose?

"But I'm not lying!" I tried to discreetly edge across the bed, putting myself on the side farther away from him. "I can show you my registration in the Curia Cloisters—I have barely any powers at all. That's not something I can fake!"

Killian gave me a withering look. "Of course you aren't faking it," he scoffed. "Wizards are too stupid to pull off such a conniving and convincing act. No, I suspect your parents had your powers sealed at birth."

I barely kept from laughing. He thought my parents would *seal* my magic? They'd never do that—our family existed to serve the House! As it was, my lack of magic was the greatest threat *to* House Medeis!

"I'm sure you think and were told you have limited powers," Killian said. "But I don't believe it. Your parents were some of the most powerful in their generation, despite the low ranking of House Medeis."

I wanted to snarl at him, but it was true. Even though my parents had been quite powerful—Dad had been considered a genius in his younger days, and Mom had been even stronger than him—House Medeis had a really low ranking among wizard Houses in the Midwest. We just didn't have that much power.

"The statistics that they would birth a dud are astoundingly low," Killian continued. "But there's one condemning piece of evidence that you *do* have more magic, and they knew it."

I pressed my lips together and wasn't able to keep the sourness out of my voice. "What?"

"You." Killian flicked a finger at me. "If you really are a dud, why didn't they try for another child? Or adopt? Even if they adopted outside the family, a second or third child with a sibling bond and strong magic would better cement your position as Adept. Except they knew it wasn't necessary."

I smiled and tried to keep my voice pleasant. "I didn't need siblings because I have plenty of family to back me already."

Because wizards don't stab each other in the back like vampires! A moment passed before I realized that was exactly what wizards apparently did and was the reason why I was even in Drake Hall.

Killian shrugged. "It doesn't matter what you think. I'll take you to the Paragon for inspection. He'll be able to determine if I'm right."

"The *Paragon?*" I squeaked. The Paragon was the top fae representative in America. He didn't rule over the fae—they had splintered when the last of the elves died and had created their own fiefdoms in the different regions. But the Paragon was supposed to be the strongest fae alive, and *all* the fae Courts spoke through him. "You can't involve the Paragon in something like this!"

"I can. He owes me," Killian said. "And given the *delicate* nature of politics, there aren't many fae I would believe to tell the truth. Luckily, the Paragon is an idiot." He sauntered toward the door, oozing arrogance thick enough to make me choke.

I stared—shell-shocked—at his back. For a moment, I was tempted to laugh. All my life everyone had taken my lack of magic for granted. And now Killian Drake—master vampire and tyrant of the Midwest—was raising a fuss about it.

This gave me a shred of hope. When he found out I was indeed a dud, he'd drop me, and I could safely disappear into the mass of servants. That was…if he didn't kill me for delaying him.

Killian snapped his fingers. "Medeis, come."

Knowing I'd only have to bear it until my abilities were affirmed, I swallowed my irritation and slowly crossed the room. My muscles still shook from the exertion of "playing" with the monster, and the creamy taste of the healing draught was turning sour—though that might have been my situation instead of the potion.

Killian swept away without another word, disappearing down the hallway faster than I could walk.

I tried to jog, but my ribs must not have been fully healed yet, because pain stabbed through my side. I clutched my ribs as I tried to figure out which way he'd gone.

"This way, Hazel."

I nearly jumped out of my skin when I realized another vampire stood right behind me. It was the beautiful female who had attended the meeting with him at the Curia Cloisters. She was still in her pantsuit, and her pitch-black hair was pulled back in a no-nonsense ponytail, but her smile was surprisingly warm. "The car is waiting for you." She walked at a *much* slower pace so I could keep up—which was a good thing because she led me through a portion of the mansion I hadn't ever seen, even in my tour of the place on the day of my arrival.

We came to what looked like the front entrance—everything was cast in white and black marble with enough windows to make a greenhouse, and an elaborate double stairway that wound up to the second floor with an elevator crouched just behind it. (A very necessary thing given the size of the place.)

A maid standing at the entrance gawked at me as she automatically pulled a door open for my vampire guide.

I gave the maid a helpless look, but hurried after the female vampire, almost skidding down the stone staircase just outside the door.

A black SUV was parked at the bottom of the teardrop shaped bit of driveway that pulled up next to Drake Hall.

A vampire standing at the front of the SUV opened the back car door for me.

Killian was on the far side of the bench, talking on a silver smartphone as he jabbed his finger at a screen on a similarly colored tablet. "I don't care if the fae are *wistful* for a winter festival. It's a power grab, and they just want to put their magic on display to lull the humans over to their side."

The vampire wanted me to sit *back there*? With *HIM*?! I gaped at the chauffeur vampire and shook my head. "Can't I sit up front?" I whispered.

The chauffeur blinked. "Why?"

"Denied!" Killian snarled into his phone.

I flinched, but Killian didn't seem to notice our conversation, he was so focused on chewing out whatever poor soul was on the other end of the phone.

"If you suggest such a stupid bargain again, I'll have a finger broken every time you mention it. Understood?" Killian continued.

"I don't wish to disturb the Eminence—he's working." I chewed on my lip and did my best to look bashful and concerned.

The vampire chauffeur shrugged. "Sure." He closed the door and opened the front passenger door.

Relieved, I scrambled in and closed the door behind me.

"I'll follow with Julianne," the female vampire said to the driver, her voice muffled sounding from inside the car.

The driver nodded and unhooked a friggin' *sword* from his belt as he circled round the car to his side. "Yes, Celestina," he said.

She smiled at him, then trotted down the driveway to a small, four door car that was—surprise!—black.

The driver slid into his seat, leaning his sword against the dashboard so it was easily accessible, and then fussed with a wireless earpiece in his right ear. "Dragon, taking flight."

I glanced out the window, half expecting a sendoff, and was not disappointed. I saw several other vampires—all visible even in the dark night due to the pristine whites of their dress shirts—step out of the front decorative greenery and bow.

The driver started the car, and we rolled down the driveway, passing by the stupid dragon statues on our way out.

I sank deep into my car seat, feeling numb and tired. I couldn't wait for this all to be over.

When we pulled up to the local public library, I rubbed my eyes as I struggled to understand what was going on. "The Paragon is at the library?" I muttered.

Vampire hearing is a thing, so of course Killian heard me, but what was surprising was he also chose to answer me. "He's hiding." He abruptly ended his phone call. "The Paragon hides wherever he thinks others are least likely to find him. In this case, it does not take a genius to recognize that no fae noble—with their boundless vanity—would ever venture here."

That was pretty rich considering the snobbery of vampires, but I kept my mouth shut and scrambled out of the SUV before the vampire driver could help me.

Our local library is super cute. It's constructed out of brick, and on the front lawn there are a few statues from famous kids' books.

I smiled at the nostalgia of the building, but was almost hit when Killian flung his car door open.

He smoothly exited the car so he could stare down his irritatingly straight nose and gaze at the library as if it were some place beneath him.

(See? Such a snob!)

The nice female vampire, Celestina, exited her car and bowed slightly when she joined Killian on the chipped sidewalk. "I received word that the Paragon is in the back reading room, near the fireplace."

Killian sauntered into the library, Celestina walking just behind his left shoulder.

I nervously shifted my weight from one foot to the next and glanced out over the well-lit parking lot. This was the first time I was off Drake land since the night Mason attacked me.

Would he try to grab me, now? But it was getting late, how would he even find out I was here?

"*Medeis*." Killian's voice was lined with irritation.

I suppose Mason is now a secondary worry to surviving Killian Drake. I scuttled after them, slipping through a slowly shutting door and crossing the front lobby.

Killian strode through the library with what seemed like a sauntering, careless gait—though let me tell you he covered *a lot* of ground because I had to jog to keep up.

"The library will close in fifteen minutes," a mechanical voice announced over the library loudspeaker—not like my vampire escorts at all cared.

We whizzed past the reference librarian's desk, and as soon as we hit the sea of bookshelves that held all nonfiction and adult fiction books, the quiet noises of the library—the beeps of books getting checked out, the crinkle of pages being turned—were muffled and fell off into near silence.

Killian made his way through the stacks with the ease of familiarity—though I suppose he could probably more easily read the labels and use sounds for context clues. But he didn't stop even when we reached the far back wall. Instead he turned and followed the wall until we reached a corner which opened up into a hexagon shaped room.

The focal point of the room was the enormous gas fireplace and stone mantel. Newspaper racks pressed against the walls and were stacked with periodicals and the latest magazine issues. Plush, green couches were arranged in front of the fireplace, and someone was splayed out over the nearest one with a folded-up newspaper spread over their head like a tent. The newspaper barrier did very little to block out the deep and throaty snores curling up from the covered face.

Killian stalked across the room, stopping at the snorer. He leaned over the couch, resting his forearms on the top of it, and plucked the newspaper off his victim. "Paragon," he said.

"What? What?" a simultaneously smooth and grizzled sounding voice peevishly repeated. The snorer sat up, revealing a head of long, silky white hair, and a well-groomed white mustache with whiskers so long they drooped past his chin. Slightly pointed ears and thick glasses with wire frames that almost covered up bushy eyebrows accented the Paragon's wizened-old-man look, as did the wrinkles that lined his face.

The old man peered around the room, grimacing when he looked up at Killian. "Oh," he said. "It's *you*." He sat up and toddled to his feet, brushing his clothes—a dark robe covered with bronze star embroidery and slitted at the elbows to reveal a light blue undershirt—with an unnecessary amount of care. "What do you want now?"

"Paragon, you wound my delicate feelings," Killian smirked. "Perhaps I came to call upon an old acquaintance?"

The Paragon flipped his glasses up and gave Killian a look that could kill. "Save your pretty words for someone who might be susceptible to them. It's too late to try and butter me up, I know you're a weasel." He swatted at his own mustache with annoyance, then squinted at Killian. "You didn't tell any of the fae Kings or Queens that I'm here, did you?"

"I have not," Killian said. "Yet."

The Paragon groaned like a teenager, his shoulders slumping uncharacteristically for a fae of his advanced age. "Then I have to repeat myself: what do you want now?"

Killian folded his arms across his chest. "I need to consult you on a small matter that requires privacy."

The Paragon screwed his mouth into a shrivel. "How small can the matter be if it requires privacy?"

"Now that you mention it, perhaps I *could* call the Winter Queen to join us."

The Paragon rolled his eyes. "You are *such* a sore loser." He plunged his hands into the pocket of his robes and pulled out what looked like a coin purse with a pink unicorn stitched into the fabric. "Hold on." He peered at me through the thick lenses of his glasses. "Literally."

He flicked the purse open, and it was hard to say if everything in the coin purse exploded out, replacing our surroundings, or if the coin purse sucked us inside. All I knew was one moment we were standing in the library, then after a gust of wind that made me shut my eyes, and the feeling of the ground slithering beneath my feet, we were in an entirely different room.

It appeared to be a workshop crossed with…a rec room? A foosball table and a big screened TV were placed next to a bookshelf of books that were probably older than the United States of America. Glass vials filled with rainbow colored liquids were carefully arranged next to a cooking station that was lined with cupboards of ingredients. The biggest part of the room was claimed by a massive wooden desk made out of thick tree trunks and branches supporting a polished wooden tabletop. Three similarly crafted bookshelves were crammed behind it. It seemed to me they were all alive, because as I watched two of the bookshelves sprouted leaves, and the desk grew a flower.

Impressed, I glanced over at the Paragon.

He proudly shook his coin purse and grinned at me. "A pocket realm! Fae magic at its best!"

"This is your office?" I guessed.

The Paragon puffed up his chest and stretched his arms out, beckoning to the room. "Given my role as the top fae representative in America, I travel frequently from Court to Court. Naturally, my work must come with me."

I peered around the office again. "So that means we're in the fae realm?"

"A tiny sliver of it that is under my direct control, yes. Though my office isn't stationary in the fae realm—that would make me too easy for those wretch nobles to find." He made a face, then furrowed his brow and clawed at his mustache when he nearly inhaled a whisker.

Killian plopped down on an elaborately carved chair made of white wood. "Have you finished schooling the wizard?"

The Paragon flipped his glasses up again, this time to peer at me. "A wizard? My, my—I never thought *you'd* keep mixed company, Mr. Paranoid."

"She may be of use to me." Killian glanced at the living desk, which sprouted a chrysanthemum at the corner closest to him. He narrowed his eyes at it, and the flower instantly withered and died. "Which is why I brought her here. She's a Medeis—the last one."

"Ahh, you are Hazel Medeis." Some of his pluck left the Paragon and was replaced with moroseness as he bowed his head. "I heard of your parents. I am sorry for your loss. Wait." He furrowed his brows and glanced back at Killian. "What are *you* doing with the House Medeis Adept? Did you kidnap her? You shouldn't do that, you know. Even if the wizards fear you and let you have her, it's not a good look. Besides, you don't even *like* humans, much less wizards!"

Killian smiled, and the black-red of his eyes seemed to lighten up into more of a glowing blood red. "She came to me willingly.

Some infighting in her House, I believe, but I don't care about that."

The Paragon glanced at me—I couldn't tell if he was looking to me for confirmation, or was checking to see if I was shocked by Killian's careless words.

I wasn't surprised. Killian Drake wasn't feared just because he's good at smoldering. His general disregard for any life except vampires had gotten him a pretty dark reputation. In fact, if he *had* shown interest in Mason and everything that had gone down with House Medeis, I would have turned tail and run for all I was worth. I did *not* want a vampire mucking around in my business—particularly one as powerful and terrifying as Killian Drake.

The Paragon blinked, but kept on staring at me.

I shrugged a bit and edged away from Celestina—the much taller woman loomed over me as she perused the bookshelf just behind me.

"What interests me is her magic—or lack of," Killian continued. "She's awful at magic. Lighting a candle is probably as useful as her magic gets, even though she's a Medeis. Given her pedigree, that seems a bit suspicious."

The Paragon frowned. "You think she's faking it?"

"No," Killian snorted. "Wizards are far too proud—if she really had more power her House would have trumpeted it from the walls when she made Adept. No, she believes she's a near dud in magic. Which makes me suspect her powers were sealed as a child."

The Paragon turned in a slow circle, tapping his fingers together. It took me a moment to realize it was in excitement. "It can be done—though I've never heard of anyone being stupid enough to *want* it. But the wizards have asked us fae in the past to seal the magic of their most dangerous criminals."

The Paragon had a point—if my magic was sealed it was done by a fae. Though wizards have more natural magic since we channel it through our bodies, the way we can use it is limited.

We can bend the elements to our will—like fire, wind, water, you get the point—and fight or defend with raw magic.

The fae are in a similar but opposite position. Since they have to use things to channel magic for them, they can use magic for things like sealing powers, disguises, imbedding a spell in an item, a strain of hypnosis, and so on. They can't react as quickly as a human wizard can, and in a magic fight a human wizard would win over a fae. But outside of fighting—which is more useful since supernaturals hadn't had a large-scale war in decades—fae magic has far more uses.

Like sealing someone's access to magic.

But even though it was possible, the idea that *my* magic was sealed was totally stupid. There's no way my parents would have allowed it—and no one could have done it without their knowledge. (Besides, who *would* have done it? Mason had obviously been planning a long time, but I doubt he had his takeover in mind when he was ten.)

"Perhaps Aphrodite might be able to tell if she's sealed." The Paragon made his way over to a bookshelf behind his desk.

Killian rolled his eyes. "That abomination can't sense magic any better than a fruit fly."

The Paragon gasped in horror. "How *dare* you say such things about this majestic creature!" He turned to a massive, velvet red cushion that was carefully placed on the middle shelf. Resting on the cushion was what I had assumed was a preserved egg from the fae realm—it was a very unusual shade of pink.

But when the Paragon put his hand on it, the egg uncurled, revealing spindly legs, a hairless tail, and a wrinkled head ornamented with ears so big they were almost bat-like.

It took me several long moments to realize the Paragon was petting a hairless cat that had a prominent belly and wrinkle lines that made the feline look angry.

"He didn't mean it, my dear," the Paragon told his...unique cat. "He's jealous of your inherent beauty and great charm."

"I have never seen that cat leave its cushion in its whole life," Killian said. "It has *no* charm to speak of."

"Don't listen to him, Aphrodite." The Paragon scratched the cat under the chin and was rewarded with a deep purr even I could hear.

"Aphrodite?" I cautiously asked.

The Paragon beamed at me. "Aphrodite is a hairless sphinx cat with the bluest of bloodlines and a peerless pedigree! She came from a particularly famous litter of sphinx kittens, for her siblings have been scattered across various realms to bless the residents of the universe!"

"*Mmmert*," Aphrodite said.

The Paragon apparently wasn't anywhere near finished as he beamed at his treasured pet. "Given her great beauty and remarkable family, I knew I had to give her a name worthy of her glory! Inspired by a great number of Renaissance paintings, I settled on Aphrodite."

"*Don't*—" Killian started to say.

"Why?" I asked.

A thin wrinkle connected Killian's eyebrows, expressing his horror.

The Paragon, however, chortled. "Because as it seems Renaissance artists were incapable of creating art in which the goddess Aphrodite was clothed, neither can fur be allowed to hide the greatness that is my feline companion!"

Shocked, I stared at the bald cat. "I...see?"

"Indeed!" The Paragon laughed until his precious cat hooked her claws in his tunic and pulled. "Wait—you must sheathe your claws, Aphrodite. I can't let you ruin this robe, too!"

Killian looked physically pained—or ill. I wasn't sure which, but either way it made my day to see him uncomfortable. "Stop playing with the cat and check to see if she's sealed."

"But—"

"*Now!*"

"Bossy!" the Paragon huffed. He made a face at Killian, then beckoned to me. "Step this way, wizardling." He shuffled across his office, pausing at the far side of the room where a massive, spiraled horn leaned against a wall. He picked it up, grumbling under his breath as he struggled to hold it. "Mutant giant unicorn," he complained as he staggered to a dark corner of his office. "Thing was an abomination. I can only hope it didn't breed like rabbits. Here we go." He maneuvered the horn—which was almost as long as I was tall—so the sharpened point was tilted down, then tapped the ground.

That corner, which had previously appeared dark and dusty, flared to life. Elaborate swirls and circles of stars burned a bright gold on the ground. The light left the circle and traced up the sides of the wall in thick strokes reminiscent of trees, then crawled across the ceiling in another star pattern so the entire corner glowed with magic.

The Paragon slapped his hands on his robe, then pointed to a crescent moon at the dead center of the circle. "Stand in the center, if you please. Yes, right there."

I stood in the circle, still wearing my black pants from my job and the white t-shirt I had woken up in. I curled my toes in my running shoes, smiling at the quiet hum of magic that seeped beneath my feet.

"Check her thoroughly," Killian instructed from his chair. He reached inside his suit and adjusted something in a pocket. "I'm sure whatever it is it's well hidden, or she would have been outed by now."

The Paragon snorted. "What! Did you do the impossible and develop magic powers and a deep understanding of them in the past five minutes? Get bent!"

As I stood in the circle—relaxed and confident in my lack of powers—I watched the Paragon's spry movements. There was something about him...His words were more modern than I'd heard from some werewolves, and his movements weren't just quick, they were liquid—effortless. Was he really as old as he appeared? Fae were capable of deception. He could use magic to cover his true appearance.

"Right, then. We'll begin," the Paragon said. "This *shouldn't* hurt."

Suddenly I was a lot more alert. "*Shouldn't?*"

"Well, I've never done anything like this before, so I can't be certain. Hah-hah!" He sheepishly scratched his cheek.

Alarmed, I shifted and considered edging out of the circle.

In an instant Killian was standing behind the Paragon, his red eyes narrowed on me. He held up a finger and slightly shook his head, his orders clear. I was to stay.

I swallowed as glowing stars from the ceiling started to drop, putting me in a personal star shower. Whenever a star hit me it spattered me with liquid light, which glowed gold and bronze for a few moments before seeping through my clothes and into my skin.

It was warm, but not unpleasant, and I tilted my head back to look up at the ceiling, getting star dust on my eyelashes.

"Hmm. I'm not seeing any reaction yet," the Paragon said.

"Then look *harder*," Killian growled.

"That's not how it works," the Paragon began. "You see—"

"Skip the lesson, and *find* her seal!"

"Fine, fine—no need to be fussy! Just wait—oh!"

CHAPTER EIGHT

Hazel

Lines of light formed, shooting from the little spatters the shining stars had made on my skin. They crossed up my body and congregated at my eyes, giving the world a golden haze.

I felt my wizard mark surface—hot and sudden—but there was extra warmth on my face as well. That extra warmth alarmed me more than the giant unicorn horn or the foreign magic floating around me.

A wizard mark is kind of like a magic-sensitive tattoo that only shows up when we tap into magic. It's usually a pattern of swirls, shapes, or spikes, but more important than the design is the size—which indicates the level of power a wizard has. It's why my single loop was considered shameful.

But you're *born* with your personal ability to hold and channel magic—there's no improving it. There's no changing your wizard mark, so *what was wrong with my face?*

"Yep, she's sealed alright," the Paragon confirmed as he struggled to lean the giant horn against the wall. "In fact, I think I recognize that magic!"

The circle of light faded, then died out as the Paragon strode over to his desk and started rummaging through its drawers.

With the magic gone, the lines of light on my body disappeared, as did the spots the little stars had left, and the warmth of my wizard mark.

I barely noticed—I was staring at the busy Paragon. Surely I had heard him wrong? There was no way I had sealed magic! Numbly, I shook my hair out and brushed off my clothes just in case there was any remaining magic, and stepped out of the circle.

Celestina gave me a brief smile as she came to stand by me. I was actually glad for her nearness. She was tall, and there was something comforting about her big presence after...this.

Killian, it seemed, preferred to hound our host. He planted his hands on the Paragon's desk as the older man paged through a ledger. "What did you find?"

"Ah-hah, yes, here it is!" The Paragon plopped his ledger on his desk and tapped an entry. "It seems my predecessor sealed you himself, Adept Medeis."

"What?" My shock made me clumsy. I almost tripped over my own feet as I crossed the workshop so I could stare at the paper.

Most of the notes were written in the curving script of the language of Fae, but even I could recognize the entry which was dated with the human calendar, and marked with my parents' signatures.

"My *parents* asked him to?" I yelped.

"Seems like it." The Paragon set his glasses aside and peered down at the ledger. "Says here they brought you in when you were still a toddler. According to the report, they asked my predecessor to lock up all except the tiniest bit of your magic abilities."

"I have to sit down," I muttered. There was an incessant buzzing noise in my ears, and the room seemed to move around me.

I had more magic? But my *parents* had arranged for me to have it sealed? I glanced back at the ledger, certain it was a trick. But in addition to their familiar signatures, I saw my father had scrawled a sketch of the House coat of arms next to their signatures, marking it as an official agreement between the Paragon and House Medeis.

Something in my gut rolled, and I felt sick. My legs shook, but I locked my knees and stiffly shuffled until I could plop down in the nearest chair.

"I'm sorry to say it doesn't give a reason why." The Paragon thoughtfully tapped his ledger.

"I don't care *why* they did it," Killian snarled. "What's important is the seal. Can you remove it, or must it be broken?"

"Um," the Paragon said.

"*Um?*" Killian repeated in an icy voice.

I was barely aware of their argument. I bent over, my head hanging between my knees as I just tried to *breathe*.

"It doesn't give any conditions for breaking the seal, or any instructions," the Paragon said.

"Your predecessor was so sloppy he didn't make any notes?"

"We Paragons take *pride* in our work!" The Paragon preened, then almost jabbed himself in the eye when he tried to push his glasses, which were still on the desk, up his nose. "We don't often take private clients, but when we do all is done to their specifications. In this case Rand and Rose of House Medeis signed a silence clause. Only they and my predecessor know the details of the seal, and they are all unfortunately dead."

"If you cannot break it, then remove it," Killian ordered.

"If a lesser fae had made the seal I could, but I'd not risk it on my predecessor's work. He was a wily, shifty old man," the Paragon said, sounding not very Paragon-like. "It's unlikely to work, and far more likely that she'd die—which would do you no good."

Killian growled, and I finally managed to sit up.

I was still shocked—this changed everything in my life for the good, but I was dimly starting to realize what it meant.

My parents had lied to me about my magic for years. They saw me get bullied and picked on for my lack of magic, and they never told me the truth. Even now, when I was an *adult*!

But I also realized that my present situation—with Killian Drake and his "interest" in me—was pretty treacherous, and I *needed* to be aware of what he was saying—or about to do to me.

"How, then, can she remove it?" Killian asked.

The Paragon retrieved his ledger and snapped it shut. "Based on my predecessor's limited notations, it seems that the seal has a condition on it—a requirement she must meet or perform. If she meets that condition, her magic will be freed."

Killian raised one dark eyebrow. "You don't know what the exact condition is?"

"The ledger doesn't say, no."

"Exactly what good are you?"

"That was *hurtful*!"

"You seem to be under a delusion that I care."

The Paragon sniffed and stuck his nose in the air. "I'll see that I remember this whenever you ask me for a favor."

"You have yet to actually be *helpful*," Killian said. "All you did is confirm Medeis has more magic. You can't break her seal, and you won't take the Night Court in hand and get them under control—"

"I am the top fae *representative*, not the fae emperor!"

"There hasn't been an emperor in at least 50 years," Killian impatiently said. "You're as close as it gets."

The Paragon looked like he wanted to rip Killian a new one—he seemed a bit taller and wider in the shoulders than when we first met him, so he probably was wearing a disguise—and as much as I would like to see that, the seal did concern me.

"Could you make a guess?" I asked.

The fae swiveled around to face me and blinked. "Pardon?"

I forced myself to stand and took in a deep breath. I had to handle this—I didn't have my House at the moment, and it was possible the Drake Family would make things worse. I needed to be calm—even though my head still buzzed. "The seal," I said. "Could you make a guess what its breaking condition is?"

"Oh. Well. Stereotypically, if a seal is placed on a person who is *not* a criminal, the breaking condition is that their life is in danger, or that they are being attacked. There's a chance…" He trailed off when he saw my face.

I shook my head. "I've been attacked twice in the last week."

The Paragon glared accusingly at Killian. "Are you doing a crappy job of taking care of your servants?"

Killian folded his arms across his chest with the grace of a panther. "I *did* say she sought me out."

"And they say we fae are evasive," the Paragon grumbled before facing me. "True love's kiss is a popular seal in fae culture, but given your age I'd guess it wasn't yours. Taking into account the secrecy, it's fairly likely the condition was set by your parents, in which case your guess would be better than mine. I assume you know them well, which makes you more likely to guess what sort of condition they would set."

An hour ago I might have agreed, but I didn't know anymore. Did I *really* know my parents? I mean, how could they hide something like this from me? What other secrets did they have that I never knew about?

"Can you tell how much power she has behind the seal?" Killian asked.

The Paragon retrieved his glasses and rubbed them off on his robe. "Want to be sure it's worth the investment, eh?"

"Yes," was Killian's flat reply.

The Paragon glanced at me, but I just shrugged again.

At this moment I'd rather have Killian's brutal honesty in his motives than my parents' kind lies.

"Er, well, I can't be *too* certain," the Paragon began. "But it seemed quite right."

Killian stared at him until he squirmed. "And what does 'quite right' mean?"

The Paragon fanned himself with his ledger. "It means she'll be a capable wizard, should she ever get the seal removed."

AFTER A FEW MORE MINUTES OF talking—which didn't reveal anything more useful or illuminating—the Paragon kicked us out of his pocket realm and dumped us back in the library parking lot. The two Drake Family cars were the only ones in the parking lot given that the library had closed during our hour-long expedition.

By the time we made it back to Drake Hall—this time I rode with the much more pleasant Celestina and the female driver—I was yawning and ready for bed.

Or really, I didn't want to think or feel anymore after the mixed surprise the Paragon had dumped on me, so sleep sounded amazing. I slipped out of Celestina's car when we pulled up to the front door and waved to her as I hopped on the sidewalk and started to follow it around to the back side of the house, where the servant rooms were.

"Where do you think you're going?"

Ice threaded through my blood, and I turned around, almost ramming my nose into Killian's chest. "To my room?" I said.

"I didn't dismiss you." A frown pulled at the corners of his lips—a very dangerous sign for my wellbeing.

"Um," I said with a shocking amount of charisma. "I didn't know you had to dismiss me?" I ended in a squeak, which I hated. Killian Drake was terrifying, yeah, but I didn't want my mannerisms telling *him* just how scary I found him.

Killian snapped as if calling a dog to heel. "Come." He walked off, casually climbing the stairs and disappearing through the front door of Drake Hall.

Celestina, moving so quickly and quietly I didn't register her presence until she stood next to me, nodded at the door. "You better go after him."

"Did I do something wrong?" I asked.

Celestina smiled, her fanged teeth a stark white against the brown of her skin. "Not at all."

I wasn't quite sure I believed her, but I didn't see any way out of it. So, I trotted off after the master vamp.

I entered just as he finished giving instructions to the attentive female vampire who had driven Celestina and me home.

"Size small," Killian said. He glanced back at me, then frowned. "No—make it an extra small."

Before I had a chance to contemplate what important exchange I had just missed, Killian swept down the hallway, and the female vampire trotted off in the opposite direction.

I jogged to keep up with Killian, whose wretchedly long legs allowed him a casual walk for my huffing jog. "Your job description is changing," he announced.

"Yeah?" I gloomily asked.

"You are no longer a member of my staff, but of my security," Killian said.

I let out a loud "HAH!" that actually sounded like a goose honk before I slapped my hands over my mouth. I guiltily looked up at Killian, hoping I hadn't stirred his wrath, but he ignored the sound and kept walking.

"Excuse me...sir." The fitted waist of my dress pants was starting to inch down, making my jog more than a little awkward. "But...House Medeis doesn't train for security."

"I am well aware of House Medeis's pacifistic tendencies and its stupidly optimistic attitude toward fighting," Killian said. "But you signed a contract to *my* Family, and no one else will take you. You either join my security, or face the House Medeis member who threw you out."

What a *jerk*! I knew he only cared about vampire interests, but the total disinterest in his voice as he discussed my *life* really hit it home for me. "I was not objecting to the change in position," I said between gritted teeth. "But I wanted to make sure you knew that there's *nothing* I can do for you that would be at all useful, between my background and the...seal."

I briefly shut my eyes—if only I could easily stamp out the reminder of my parents' lies.

"Obviously, you are useless at the moment," Killian said. "But I've always wanted an attack dog, and I'd rather train it myself than deal with any bad behaviors you picked up previously. It seems to me it will be possible to scare that seal out of you one way or another." His eyes resembled barely glowing coals when he glanced down at me. "Knowing that, the best course is to invest in your training. We will begin tonight."

"Training?"

Given that vampires couldn't use magic, it seemed unlikely a trainer was going to pop out of the woodwork and teach me meditation methods or something.

"Weightlifting, target practice, distance running, and some form of martial arts at the very least." Killian started down a set of austere marble stairs, and I hopped after him, my mouth gaping as I searched for a response. *Any* response!

What I oh-so-charmingly found was, "Target practice?"

Killian looked over my head as we descended the last step. "I'm assuming your pacifist upbringing did not include instruction in sidearms."

"You mean a *gun?*" My voice went high pitched.

Killian rolled his eyes. "As I figured."

I trailed behind him, dazed, but not for the reason he thought. I wasn't shocked about the idea of training with a gun, but rather that a *vampire* was suggesting it.

Vampires are the old people of the supernaturals. They wear old fashioned clothes and are constantly moaning about the past "good ol' days." Vampires are *terrible* at adapting to our rapidly changing world. Heck, I don't think the majority of them even know what the internet is!

That a *vampire*—the most tradition-worshipping race of supernaturals—was suggesting a gun as a weapon rocked my world.

"Here we are." Killian yanked open a solid metal door to what I realized was a weight lifting room.

It was bright due to a bunch of fancy wall sconces that looked like they belonged in a five-star hotel. One of the long walls was comprised entirely of sparkling clean mirrors, the far end was beautifully stained timber, and the other long wall was floor to ceiling TV screens which pieced together to make a beautiful waterfall in the middle of a forest.

The ground was covered with cushy black mats that looked clean enough to eat off, but most of the floor space was covered with fancy weight machines, dumbbells, medicine balls, barbells, and the like.

I gaped at the room. Between the extravagant lighting and sparkling equipment, I was pretty sure most professional sports teams didn't have such nice facilities, which was super weird.

Vampires didn't do *fitness training*. In general, they tended to believe they were inherently superior—mentally and physically.

But judging by the presence of the six vampires who were sweating over their workouts, Killian Drake was not content with his vampires' natural abilities.

Killian tilted his head back. "Rupert."

The vampire who had been doing hanging crunches from a bar dropped to his feet. He trotted across the room, and I recognized his sharp features and red hair as belonging to the less than welcoming vampire I'd met in the kitchens my first day in Drake Hall.

When he saw me, he frowned, but dutifully bowed to Killian. "Your Eminence."

Killian twisted slightly at the torso, glancing over his shoulder as the tall female vampire, Celestina, slipped into the room behind us. "Celestina, Rupert, I have a side project I want you to work on."

Rupert perked. "Yes, Your Eminence?"

Killian flicked his eyes in my direction. "This."

I—or *this* as he called me—pressed my lips together to keep from protesting. (I had the vague feeling that the more Killian knew how little I cared for this plan of his, the keener he would be to enact it.)

Thankfully, I was not alone in my dislike. Rupert gaped at Killian as if he'd grown another head.

"You mean the human," Celestina supplied. "Hazel Medeis."

"Yes," Killian confirmed. "I plan to train her to be an attack dog, but first she needs to be toughened up so she's not quite so..." He glanced down at me. "Puny."

I mashed my lips together so hard it was turning into a demented smile. I dearly wanted to snarl about being puny and managing to hold off the monster the fae had unleashed on *his land*, but that was probably a death sentence.

But my tendency to stick up for myself hadn't been beaten out of me by my fellow wizards, so it was too much for it to go *entirely* quiet, even when faced with the likes of Killian Drake. A sarcastic "woof" slipped out of my mouth before I even realized what I was saying.

Killian raised an eyebrow, Rupert—of course—frowned deeper, but Celestina grinned.

Before I could suffer any repercussions, Celestina saved me by holding out a gym bag. "I brought what you requested, Your Eminence."

Killian took it from her, unzipped it, and riffled through its contents.

Celestina then turned her attention to me. "I am Celestina Drake—First Knight of the Drake Family. I will do my best to strengthen and train you."

The First Knight—the title given to the second strongest vampire in a Family, which pretty much meant she was the second-in-command—and her focused attention was a little unnerving.

I wasn't used to having a model-tall woman who had enough deadly grace to run easily in pantsuits and stilettos smile at me so welcomingly. The tight bun she had her black hair wrapped in couldn't mask its luxurious thickness, and the golden-olive tone of her skin gave her beauty a warmth that the other vampires in the room—equally handsome but cold in their paleness—lacked.

I shifted nervously. "Nice to meet you, Celestina."

Her smile grew, but although her white fangs flashed, the garnet shade of her eyes seemed almost kind. That warmth was dangerous. There was a possibility she used it to lull people into complacence.

I relaxed my posture when she finally removed her gaze, and glanced over at Rupert while Killian Drake unfolded black workout pants from the gym bag. "Rupert," Celestina said. "Introduce yourself."

"Why?" Rupert drawled. "It's a rat-blood."

"Rupert," Celestina snapped. All of her warmth disappeared in a moment, and her eyes glowed red.

Rupert instantly snapped to attention. "I'm Rupert Drake," he said in a flat but speedy voice. He jerked his chin at me. "I look forward to *training* you."

Though he sneered, the speed at which he responded to Celestina's order showed just how powerful she was. (Not that I expected anything less from Killian Drake's First Knight.)

I sneaked a glance at Killian—he was pulling what looked like a white shirt from the bag and seemed pretty occupied. Good.

I gave Rupert the biggest smile I could muster. "That's great. Though it seems I'll have to hope the smell of my blood doesn't upset your senses—which seem surprisingly *delicate* and *fragile*."

Rupert, apparently having the maturity of a toddler, scowled and decided to tattle. "Your new pet is yippy, Your Eminence."

"It is the nature of puppies," Killian said in a dismissive tone. "Some find it endearing."

Celestina cocked her head and studied Killian's face. "Do you, Your Eminence?"

CHAPTER NINE

Hazel

Killian paused, and I held my breath and sweated nervously. "She is amusing—particularly when prodded into yipping," he finally said.

I blinked. "Huh?"

Killian ignored me. "Rupert will instruct you on weightlifting and running. Celestina will be your weapons teacher."

"Why?" I asked.

"Because if I placed you in a room with a weapon and Rupert, I'm not sure you'd survive."

Wasn't that just *awesome*? Though it seemed I was allowed to be mouthy—as long as I didn't push it. That was good news. I had a healthy sense of self-preservation, but when you got picked on as much as I had, you also had to develop a sense of determination, or you'd be crushed by it all.

"Locker rooms are through there," Celestina said, seemingly at random, though she pointed to the two doors at the far side of the room.

"Okay?" I glanced curiously at the door.

Killian held the shirt up against me. "It's too big. She is the equivalent of a purse dog. This is unsatisfactory." He narrowed his eyes at his First Knight.

Celestina slightly bowed her head. "I understand, Your Eminence. I will send someone out to procure her clothes in the proper size. Will this do until then?"

I frowned slightly. "Why are you asking *him* that?"

Killian's eyes were a fathomless black as he studied me in a clinical way. "I suppose."

"Excellent." Celestina swiveled to face me. "You may change in the locker room, Hazel Medeis."

Killian held out the clothes with the languid grace of someone doing a great favor.

I made myself carefully take them and cross the room, waiting until I got through the locker room entrance before sourly muttering, "Oh, I may change, may I?"

"See? Such fun to bait," Killian loudly said with satisfaction.

I jumped at the reminder of vampire hearing—which while not as good as a werewolf's was still obviously much better than mine—and scurried into the women's locker room as quickly as possible.

I hurriedly changed and threw my stuff in a locker, pausing just long enough to wash my hands and make a face in the mirror.

As much as I didn't want to admit it, Killian was right. The clothes were too big on me. The shirt hung down past my butt, and I had to roll up the pant legs. I looked like a kid wearing her parents' clothes. (Plus I only had my black buckle shoes that were part of the servants' uniform, so I looked impressively stupid.)

I sighed and rubbed my tired eyes.

I had no idea what I was doing, and I wasn't sure how I felt about being Killian's new pet project.

This was the opposite of what I wanted to happen, but I didn't have any choice but to go with it and pray the vampires didn't kill me in their ignorance. (Though I was hoping that my seal—which couldn't easily be broken given that it hadn't so much as shivered despite what I'd lived through the past week—held out long enough for the vampire Eminence to lose all interest in me.)

And...a small part of me was aware that this random gym thing was keeping me distracted from stewing over my parents' actions. Which I was actually grateful for. Mason's betrayal was a shock, but perhaps I could understand why.

But I would *never* understand why my parents had me sealed.

Ever.

When I came trotting out of the locker room I was surprised and pleased to see Killian had left.

Celestina stood with her hands on her hips, watching Rupert as he unearthed a set of dust-covered dumbbells that looked like they were about three pounds each. (For reference, three benches down, a male vampire was effortlessly using a pair of 50lb dumbbells while he laughed and chatted with his friends.)

Rupert glanced in my direction as I approached the area he had cleared in front of the mirrors. "I don't think you could look more pathetic if you tried."

I locked my legs. "I feel like you have unresolved anger issues with wizards," I said. "Were you ever scorned in love by a human? Maybe had a *Twilight* fling?"

Rupert's jaw dropped, then his face turned a lovely shade of red that almost matched his hair. "W-w-what?" he sputtered.

I observed with great interest. I had made the guess to be cheeky because I figured it wasn't possible, but based on his reaction maybe I hadn't been far off?

Celestina observed my buckle shoes. "You need appropriate footwear."

"Sorry," I said. "I don't have any here."

She tapped the side of her leg. "Not a problem. I will add it to the list. Now, Rupert will commence with your training. I am merely here to observe."

And probably make sure he didn't kill me—which I might deserve after my little *Twilight* comment.

"Okay." I nodded and tied the extra material of my shirt in a knot at the waist so it wasn't quite so loose. "Thank you."

"Rupert, you may begin." Celestina bowed her head to the red-haired vampire, who had recovered—though his eyes glittered with furious sparks.

"Fine," he said through gritted teeth. He paused, then bowed to Celestina. "You're training her tomorrow in weapons?"

"Yes."

Rupert smiled maliciously. "In that case, we'll begin with the arms. She'll need weight training before she can handle lifting a weapon."

It sounded logical, which instantly put me on my guard. (There was no way he was going to play nice when he made his dislike of me so obvious.)

Rupert pointed to the dumbbells. "Pick those up—and don't set them down until I say so."

Turns out, I was right. Rupert wasn't playing nice at all.

He trained me in weightlifting for about an hour and a half, and for almost the entire time he focused on arms—stopping only to make me do these *awful* squats and lunges when I needed a break.

It was really difficult, but it wasn't until the following morning when I woke up and—even though I was just sitting in my bed—my arms and legs hurt so much I thought the night had been a hallucination and the fae monster had crushed me.

It hurt to move my arms at all, and I had a feeling staircases were going to be murderous if my legs ached this much already.

I didn't want to leave my bed—I ached too much—but the magic in my wizard blood was starting to make me hot and sweaty. I was in the slow and painful process of trying to slide out of bed when my bedroom door abruptly banged open.

I rocketed upright, then fell on the floor with a pain-infused mewl when my legs gave out. I groaned and tried to push myself off the ground, but that used my arms, eliciting another yelp.

"What are you *doing*?" asked a chocolate-smooth voice I was starting to resent.

I peeled my face off the ground and glared up at Killian, who was lounging in my doorway. "Trying to stand."

"No." Killian gazed around the room as though its appearance insulted him. "In here. What are you doing in here?"

I used what little ab strength I had to sit up and lean against my bed, then peered down at my clothes with a frown when I realized I had fallen asleep in my borrowed workout clothes. I tried to brush wrinkles from the shirt. "What are you talking about? This is my room."

"No, it's not," Killian said.

For a moment, I panicked. I wildly inspected the room, confirming it was the plain but clean room in the servants' area I'd been assigned the day I arrived. I was in the right place—that was my blood-stained shirt peeking out of the laundry basket I had shoved in the corner.

"Yes, it is?" I was so confused it came out as a question.

"Not anymore."

"Not my room?" I said, bewildered. After the fae attack, the "surprise" of my magic and my parents'...whatever, the news that this was no longer my room made my eyes sting with tears. I sniffed, aware it was ridiculous to cry over a room, but my life had been one huge upheaval for months, now, and there was something about losing my room that made me want to burst into tears. "Then where will I sleep?" I asked, my voice getting extra squeaky.

"You were supposed to get a new room last night." Killian's

voice didn't lose its silky quality, but he spoke pretty quickly. "Apparently Rupert failed to inform you."

This made me feel infinitely better—not because I actually cared if this was another petty insult from Rupert, but because the dark quality to Killian's voice said he wasn't pleased, and since waking up I had decided that anytime Rupert was in trouble it was a good time for me.

I pressed my palms against my eyes and took a deep breath, trying to shoulder off my wild emotions.

"Celestina has been looking for you for at least an hour as your training was already supposed to have started by now," Killian added.

I ran my hand through my blond hair, trying to detangle the worst of my bed-head snarls as I peered at the alarm clock on the nightstand. "It's noon."

"Your powers of observation astound me."

I squinted at him. "You're up. Why are you up?"

Killian quirked an eyebrow up. "Vampires are capable of operating in daylight hours."

"Yeah. Except they don't usually."

"I expect better from my Family and myself." He abruptly swung out of my room and walked off. "Medeis, come!" He snapped his fingers as if calling a dog.

I wobbled after him, finding it an unspeakably painful process given his long strides and my pins-and-needles legs. "Where are we going?"

"To deliver you to Celestina, and remind her to show you to your new room." Killian left the servants' quarters, entering the more ornate part of the hall, and to my horror started up the first marble staircase he found.

"My new room isn't in the servants' quarters?" I gripped the slippery banister for balance, but this made my biceps burn with pain—which ignited a new dislike of Rupert. (I *hoped* I had the opportunity to bleed around him. The scent of my blood would make him gag!)

Killian reached the top stair and scoffed down at me. "No. We're going to make you sleep outside in the kennels with the dogs. I thought you'd make a charming addition to the pack."

I paused one step down from him. "You have *dogs*?"

"Their presence irritates the local werewolves."

Killian led me in the most meandering, winding path possible to take me up to the top floor, where most of the vampires stayed.

He stopped in the middle of the hallway then dug out a smartphone from his black suitcoat, pressing a speed-dial number. "Celestina," he said when the other end picked up. "I found her... No—she was in the servants' quarters, like an abandoned puppy...Yes."

He turned around to study me, the red of his eyes more visible in the daylight—even though the window shades were, for the most part, down in the whole house. "I've changed my mind for her training today. Get her a sword, then take her for a run." He hung up and glanced at the screen of his phone.

The edges of his lips curled down so slightly it was almost imperceivable, then he glanced at me. "Stay here," he said. "*Right* here—until Celestina comes for you."

He seemed to be waiting for a response, so I nodded as I tried to discreetly massage my on-fire thighs. "Okay."

Killian blew past me and headed back the way we came. A few seconds after he disappeared from sight Celestina casually jogged —as if it were an easy thing to do in high heels—up the hallway.

"Good afternoon, Hazel. This way—I'll give you a tour before we pick out your sword." She offered me a smile, then gestured down the hallway.

"Killian was serious about me getting a sword?" I asked.

"A gun is more efficient, but Killian likes all members of the Drake Family to excel in ranged and close-quarters combat,"

Celestina said. "Though I believe he has a deeper reason for teaching you swordplay."

"Like what?"

Celestina held up a finger. "Hold that thought—here is your new room." She tapped the paper label that read "The Wizard" in fancy calligraphy. "You'll have to wait until after our run to inspect it—we're already late the way it is. You can come back and change into proper clothes when we finish."

"That sounds marvelous." I stared longingly at the door as I thought of showering—I had been too exhausted last night to do more than collapse in bed.

"Sorry—sword and a run first. The Eminence's orders." Celestina winked at me, then strode off down the hallway again.

Now that I knew what I was looking for, I noticed the nametags.

Sigmund, Julianne, Gavino, Manjeet, Katrina, Nikos—beautiful and fancy names that tasted like history were emblazoned on every door. Some were written on fancy paper in calligraphy like mine, others were carved into lacquered nameplates.

When Celestina stopped outside a door, I eagerly checked the nameplate—which was one of the lacquered ones.

"Josh".

I blinked and pointed to the nameplate. "Josh?"

"Yes."

What kind of name was that for a vampire? Was she serious? I shifted my weight on my feet, trying to find a comfortable way to stand. (Spoiler: I couldn't.) "Is he new or something?"

Celestina thoughtfully tapped her cheek. "No. Rather, I believe he is older than I am."

"And his name is *Josh*?"

"He's very strong," Celestina said.

"In other words, his eccentricities are tolerated because he's strong enough to make his power be known. Got it."

Celestina laughed. "You are likely right—though I've never

heard anyone phrase it so succinctly. I think you'll get along with Josh." She opened the door and walked in without announcing herself. "Come in," she called when I lingered in the hallway. "We have to pick out your sword."

"Is it okay to just barge in without his permission?"

"Given our task, of course."

"Is he even awake?" I reluctantly poked my head inside Josh's room.

The walls were packed with weapons. There wasn't a bare patch of wall space—something sharp or dangerous was on every square inch. Crossbows, recurve bows, and quivers were all neatly bolted to the far wall—it seemed like they fit around the wall with the windows the easiest. (The shades to the window were, in fact, pinned to the wall with arrows.) Firearms—like rifles, pistols, and handguns—were artfully arranged together, sharing a space on the long wall with a variety of spears, polearms and what I recognized as sai used by some martial artists. Finally, the other long wall held a collection of swords and daggers—katanas, broadswords, rapiers, dirks, and tons in styles that I didn't recognize. It seemed the swords were his main passion—that collection was clearly the largest.

The furniture was pretty minimal: black leather couches, a poster bed with black-out curtains that hung from its rails, and a bookshelf. It took me a few moments to realize the box that served as his nightstand was actually an ammo box, and suddenly I understood with great clarity why no one messed with Josh.

"Over here, Hazel." Celestina clasped her hands behind her back as she studied the sword collection. "We need to pick a sword that will be appropriate for your height—which might be a bit of a challenge given that you're petite."

"You could give me a large dagger." I stared at the wall with admiration—there was something beautiful about the polished swords.

"No, you need an actual sword," Celestina said. "It will provide you with extra reach, and range for your magic."

I blinked, the spell the beautiful weapons had cast on me broken by my spirit of self-preservation. "What do you mean?"

"Oh, that's right, I never explained. You wizards usually use raw magic, right?"

"We *only* use raw magic. It's our only power."

"Yes, but it is possible to channel it." Celestina selected a heavily ornamented broadsword off the wall, but held it as if it was as light as a feather. "Which means you can channel your magic up the length of the blade. It gives you a weapon to deal with anyone near, but it also allows for more finesse and control of your powers."

I rubbed the back of my head as I eyed the sword she held. "I think I learned something like that in my wizard lessons. But wizards haven't fought like that in ages, and it wasn't ever exactly common."

"It requires mastery of magic *and* your weapon, so I imagine most people wouldn't bother," Celestina said. "Particularly given wizards in general are lazy and don't tend to strive for their full potential."

"We don't all have the same potential," I pointed out. "We're limited by the amount of magic we can channel."

"Not quite the way you think." Celestina put the sword back on the wall. "But you aren't alone in your complacence. Most supernaturals rely on natural talent and don't seek to improve themselves."

Thinking of the expensive weight room in the basement, I guessed, "But not the Drake Family."

"Not the Drake Family," she agreed. "We strive to overcome our weaknesses and strengthen ourselves."

Huh. Suddenly things were making a lot more sense—why Killian got his vampires out of bed during the day, why they had the training sessions, and why his Family was so *feared*. She was right, to an extent. Magical society isn't super big on perfection. In all honesty we're just struggling to hang on as the world changes and magic continues to die out. But apparently Killian wasn't going to take that threat at face value.

This epiphany suddenly made me about a thousand times more nervous about what he had planned for me.

Celestina frowned as she thoughtfully pulled a rapier from its stand.

"Not that one."

CHAPTER TEN

Hazel

Celestina and I turned around to see a vampire standing in the doorway.

Black haired with a vampire's signature red eyes and pale skin, the new vampire also wore what was apparently the Drake Family standard uniform of a black suit and tie...but the sword strapped to his belt was likely a personal addition. There was something about him... He possessed that deadly air that vampires have—the liquid grace that screams predator. But he didn't hold himself the same way as his fellow vampires. He was shorter for a vampire, and his shoulders were slightly hunched, and he seemed *tired,* for lack of a better word.

"Josh—perfect, I could use your expertise in choosing Hazel a sword," Celestina said.

The vampire, Josh, tilted his head. "Ahh, yes. Selecting a weapon of destruction that feeds on the lifeblood of its enemies and sings the sweet promise of death is a careful process—though a futile one given the fragile existence we eke out on this dying planet."

My forehead wrinkled as I tried to sort through the vampire's flowery monologue. *I don't think I've ever heard a vampire talking*...death poetry. *I thought that was limited to especially philosophical humans.*

Celestina merely smiled at him, which meant this was probably another one of his eccentricities.

A few moments passed, then Josh shrugged. "With her lack of training, she'd have an easier time with a crossbow."

"Killian wants her to have a sword. For her magic."

He crossed the room, intently staring at me, then gazed at the weapons on his wall. "In that case, a chisa katana would be ideal for her—lightweight and shorter in length." He brushed a few swords, before choosing a Japanese sword with a black hilt wrap. "This one," he said, almost reverently. "With an original handguard from the Tokugawa era. The hilt is made of wood wrapped in ray skin and braided with silk rope."

Josh selected a scabbard and sheathed the katana, then offered the weapon to me with a slight bow. "I trust you will take great care of it."

I started to reach for the sword, until I realized what this meant. "Wait, isn't this from your personal collection? Are you sure you want to lend it to me?"

Josh shrugged. "It is a gift—unless it is not the right sword for you. Then I will take it back and give you another."

"But...it's yours," I dumbly said. "Isn't there a practice one I can use?" I asked Celestina.

The beautiful vampire shook her head. "I'm afraid not—we weight our weapons. You wouldn't be able to use them. Besides, Josh doesn't mind."

"Indeed," Josh piped in. "It will provide me an excuse to buy a new sword to replace the bare spot on the wall." He smiled in satisfaction—almost passing for cheerful—then practically pushed the sword at me. "It's yours now."

"Thank you." Reluctantly, I took the sword, wincing when my fingers left smudgy prints on the lacquered black scabbard.

"Of course. You will require ties which will allow you to secure the scabbard to your clothes, but what you wear now is too pitiful to even attempt to use." Josh eyed my clothes with clear condescension.

"I sent out for proper attire last night," Celestina said. "Her clothes are in her room if you want to reference her size, but first we have to go for a run."

Josh nodded. "Very well. I will do so."

The dark-haired vampire left his bedroom, leaving Celestina and me behind.

"Does he seriously get to check out my room before I do?" I asked.

Celestina laughed. "You will be afforded privacy should you need it, but you will find the Drake Family does not hide anything from each other."

Why? Because they were actually close, or because Killian was too paranoid of a takeover to let them be?

"Come, we will go outside for your run." Celestina glided into the hallway, waiting only long enough for me to scramble through the door after her.

"We're running outside? Can you do that?"

"I will be carrying a parasol for sun protection, and we will be moving at a slower pace given your human limitations," Celestina acknowledged. "However, it is good for me to be out and under the sun—it gives me the opportunity to work on my stamina and practice operating in a weakened state. We commonly practice under the noon sun." She led the way back to a spiral staircase that, if memory served me right, went all the way down to the first floor.

"Wow. So, Killian has turned the Drake Family into a bunch of Spartans, huh?" When I stepped down the first stair, my legs almost gave out from the stabbing pain in my thighs. I thought going up the stairs was bad. Unbelievably, coming down was so, so much worse.

"Perhaps relatively speaking," Celestina said. "Rather, it is that we are living to our full potential."

I kinda doubted the vampire I had seen in the Victorian outfit at the vampire meeting I'd busted into would see running outside as "living to her full potential." Heck—I don't think *any* of the vampires at the meeting believed that. But this was probably how Killian had become Eminent of the Midwest and had the Regional Committee of Magic in a choke hold. (Killian Drake was terrifying by himself. But knowing he had a houseful of ripped, militant-esque vampires who trained outside in the sun for funsies made him into a person you would *never* cross.)

Somehow I managed to hobble down the stairs and outside, all while carrying my new sword—though it did take me a while.

Celestina, thankfully, didn't seem to mind. It gave her time to grab an umbrella (black, shocker) from an umbrella stand, and check in with a few vampires before escorting me outside.

The sky was a drab and cloudy gray, and there was a breeze that had a bit of a chill to it that made me smile. (Apparently spring wasn't leaving without putting up a fight—a good thing if Celestina intended to make me run a lot, or I'd turn into a sweaty pig in minutes when I combined my magically induced high body temperature with the warm air and a brisk workout.)

Celestina led me to a running path that was covered with woodchips, nodding to the female vampire she had given the clothing orders to last night. "Good day, Julianne."

Julianne smiled and twirled her own umbrella. "Hello Celestina—taking the wizard for a run?"

"Yes. Thank you for picking up her clothes."

"Of course—whatever the Eminence wants!" The vampire—a pretty blond—glanced at me with a small amount of curiosity before she smiled again at Celestina. "Oh—Sigmund left his post about fifteen minutes ago—he wanted to get a fresh blood pack since we got a delivery about an hour ago. And Ling is holding a firearm practice right now which those of us who aren't on duty are all attending."

Celestina waved her off. "Thank you for the update."

Julianne bowed. "I will leave you to it, then, and wish you well!"

Celestina turned back to me. "Now," she began.

"Let me guess," I said. "I have to carry my katana while I run." I'd been eyeing the area, which was suspiciously free of benches or sword stands.

"Exactly," Celestina said with some surprise. "You are smart for a wizard!"

"Wizards aren't stupid."

She looked unconvinced, but said nothing more as she indicated to the tree-lined path. "We'll take this circuit. It's the shortest—only a single mile."

"Oh, well, if *that's* all," I said.

Celestina laughed. "I imagine it will seem long at first. But don't worry—I can monitor your breathing with my hearing. If you need a break, we will walk. It will do you no good to push your body into an injury."

"That does actually make me feel better," I admitted. "As long as you actually know human breathing patterns?"

"I am familiar, yes. Shall we begin?"

I stared down at my sword. If my parents could see me now, what would they think? I then remembered what they'd done, and silenced the thought.

"Yeah." I had to crane my neck back to meet Celestina's gaze. "Starting sounds great."

I switched my grip on my sword—getting more smudges on it —then rolled my shoulders back with determination.

Celestina nodded in approval, then trotted off—*still* in her high heels—at a tolerable jog. Well, a jog for me. Judging by how little her sun-blocking umbrella bobbed, I'm pretty sure it was a fast walk for her.

My arms had settled into a dull ache even though I toted my sword. Speaking of which, can I say I was so glad Josh decided to give me a smaller katana? I can't imagine how terrible it would have been to drag one of the bigger ones around. But my thighs *burned*. Like, there was a distinct possibility I wasn't going to be able to haul my rear upstairs to my bedroom once this was all over.

I wasn't wheezing much—which surprised me until I realized it was probably due to all the sprinting and running away from potential bullies I did. But the pain from weightlifting had me scrunching up my face and limping along. "Shower," I reminded myself. "Think of the shower."

Celestina made an amused noise as we left the shady lane and the path meandered toward the back of the property. "Motivating yourself?"

"Yeah," I said. "Is this the way to the pool?"

"Not quite. This path doesn't go that far back..." She trailed off as she gazed out over the lawn, her dark brows bunching together in a look of concern.

"What is it?" I asked.

Celestina slowed down so she was barely moving as she carefully surveyed our surroundings, her red eyes tracing over the back of the mansion, the gardens, and the trees a little off to the side. "I smell something that doesn't belong here."

"What?" I jogged a little farther, then slowed to a walk as I studied her face.

"Death," she said bluntly.

I wondered about that—vampires were technically dead, after all. But I wasn't about to ask such a rude question, plus Celestina looked legit worried, so I started scanning the area as well.

Celestina left our jogging path, making for the trees.

I trailed behind her, adjusting my hold on my sword so

Celestina could grab it if she needed to—perhaps the fae had dumped another monster off?

Celestina ducked under a low hanging tree branch, froze, then muttered under her breath in Spanish.

She yanked her cellphone out of her suitcoat and pressed a speed-dial number.

I peeked around her shoulder, freezing when I saw a pair of booted feet poking out of a bush. It was a body.

My skin turned clammy, and I thought I could detect the faintest whiff of blood. Somehow, I didn't think the owner of the feet was as lucky as I had been. My stomach protested, and I rapidly backed away.

"Your Eminence," Celestina said to her phone. "The murderer struck again, and I believe I found his latest victim."

Two hours later I was showered, dressed in a suit that fit me surprisingly well, drinking tea from a real bone china teacup...and surrounded by vampires.

We were located in a meeting room—or the at-home, vampire-version of a meeting room. A long wooden table that had dragons carved into its legs stretched through the center of the room, but as big as it was, it still wasn't large enough to fit all the Drake vampires who were present. The unseated vamps stood at the edges of the room, their eyes glittering ruby red in their fury. The room was as lavish as the rest of the mansion—expensive paintings hung on the wood paneled walls, and the marble fireplace probably cost a fortune—but I found it a little off putting because it also lacked any windows and was so dimly lit I could barely make out the flower pattern of my teacup.

A male vampire exchanged shouts with a female vampire, and Celestina stood in an attentive position at the door, holding a handgun aimed at the floor.

I sank lower on my rickety chair and tried to make myself as unnoticeable as possible. The meeting had only started ten minutes ago, and there had already been a lot of slamming fists on the table so it cracked ominously.

It turned out the body Celestina and I found belonged to Layton—a Drake vampire, and the first victim from Killian's lineage. Unsurprisingly, the powerful Family was not taking the news well.

"We must take action," Rupert declared. "Layton was killed on Drake Family land. That's reason enough for us to declare war!"

"Declare war on what?" asked a male vampire with chestnut hair. "We have a serial killer on the loose—other Families have had losses as well."

"And they have been too lazy and incompetent to find the murderer—or murderers—themselves," a female vampire hotly said. "We cannot afford to hope they will shake themselves out of their apathy—our race will die out before then. We must find the murderer and mete out justice—for Layton's sake!"

"Might I remind you, we've also lost a servant and two blood donors," Josh said. He leaned against the wall, nonchalantly studying the bare blade of a dagger that he balanced between his fingertips.

"Obviously." The female vampire rolled her eyes. "There has been collateral damage. But it is inexcusable that we lost one of our own in a time where every vampire is needed to assert our power, and turning new vampires is nearly impossible!"

I bristled at the implication and started to shift in my chair, before I remembered who I'd been placed next to and froze.

But I was too late. Killian—seated at the head of the table, with me directly next to him, though I had voluntarily scooted against the corner of the table—glanced over at me.

I kept my eyes on the teacup and pressed my lips together.

Why was I even *in* this meeting? Killian meant to make me into a soldier, but this was Drake Family business. I absolutely didn't want to be here—but Celestina hadn't given me much of a choice. As soon as my hair had dried enough that it wouldn't soak the collar of my suit, she had dragged me here and forcibly served me tea before the other vampires had arrived.

She probably had been ordered to by Killian, given my spot, but I understood even less why he would want me present.

Killian blinked slowly, and kept staring at me as the heated discussion continued.

"Obviously the murderer is backed by the Night Court," Rupert said, naming one of the biggest local fae Courts. "For too long they've threatened us and opposed our movements in the Regional Committee of Magic. It's time we finally teach them a lesson."

There were murmurs of agreement from the other vampires.

"The Night Court," Josh said, his voice simultaneously speculative and wistful. "The darkest of fae Courts who embrace the breath of death into their lives."

The female vampire standing on Josh's other side, sighed. "That lacked sense."

Josh morosely studied his dagger. "For those who do not share the burden of life, yes."

The vampires all stared at him for a moment, before collectively turning the discussion to a new point.

"If the others would help us, we could get this murderer much more quickly," said one of the vampires I'd seen at the gym.

"They said they would help," Julianne—the vampire who had reported to Celestina right before we found the body—sourly said. "The problem is they won't prioritize it."

"And they never will," a vampire snorted. "Everyone is too concerned with holding onto their own power—that's why the wizard is here."

I felt like a bunny in a bear den when the vampires all shifted their glittering red eyes to me.

Though my heart pounded and my survival instinct screamed

at me to run, I carefully set my teacup down and did my best to look angelic.

It seemed to appease them, and they looked away.

"The other members of the Committee don't help us out of concern for themselves." Rupert slammed his fist into the table with enough force to make my teacup rattle. "They're *happy* to see us struggle. It's why they won't try and rein the Night Court in even though they *must* be behind all of this!"

I frowned at my teacup as I listened, not sure how much I liked hearing all of this. (But I didn't think trotting around Drake Hall in ignorance was great for my health, either.)

"Hazel." It was the first time Killian had spoken since sitting down, and it brought an instant and smothering silence to the room.

I hid my hands under the table and made myself meet his eyes. "Yes?"

"What do you think?"

Agog, I stared at him.

What did I *think*? What did it matter what I thought? Why was he asking me this in the middle of a heated discussion I had no right to be a part of!

My heart beat faster and faster, and I finally understood how it was possible for wild animals to die of fright. "What do I think about what?" I asked in a surprisingly calm and solid voice.

Killian motioned to the table. "The discussion."

I stared at him for a few moments longer, waiting—and hoping—for him to laugh at his own joke.

He didn't.

He was serious.

Whhhhyyy? I never wished for powers of telepathy as much as I did then. Why, why, why was he throwing me under the bus? If I said the wrong thing one of his little minions was sure to kill me —at bare minimum Rupert would give me a weightlifting workout spawned from Hades, and I'd die in my sleep.

I cleared my throat. "I think the pattern over the last few decades has been that the various magical races will keep to their own. I wish it was different, but it's the way things have become—as I've learned." I paused and sucked in a breath before I made myself soldier on through. "I think what's most worrisome is that the murderer is going after vampires *and* those they associate with—servants and blood donors, too. The killer isn't doing this just out of political motivation, or they'd choose their targets more carefully. Besides, everyone wants to avoid getting the humans worried. The more humans killed, the less likely you'll be able to keep this out of the public eye, and this will have a domino effect on *everyone*."

I glanced around the room and was met with thoughtful and surprised gazes. Celestina gave me a faint smile, and Josh a nod of approval, but everyone remained silent. I snuck a peek at Killian—who was still staring at me.

"And?" he said.

He wanted me to keep going?

I frantically pulled my stray thoughts together, trying to come up with a conclusion that would get me out of this. "It means whoever is doing this doesn't care about that possibility," I said. "Humans greatly outnumber us and are more than capable of killing us off in masses. So I guess a serial killer is possible, unless..." I wanted to suck my neck into my shoulders, but I made myself sit straighter instead. "They're doing this on purpose—killing the servants and blood donors—to make *you* look weak."

Killian smiled at me, and the smothering silence finally evaporated.

"Obviously," Rupert grumbled under his breath. "We've known that from the beginning."

"But to have a wizard see it, too, can only strengthen our hypothesis, given she is coming at it from an entirely different viewpoint," Celestina said.

This spawned thoughtful looks on most of the vamps present.

Killian finally straightened in his leather chair, going from languid to predatory in the blink of an eye. "Regardless who the murderer is, they are almost certainly sent by the Night Court. The Committee has turned a blind eye to the Night Court's antics for too long—they don't care how many laws the Night Court breaks as long as they only hassle the vampires. But that's fine—it's their prerogative." His eyes were black in the dim light as he smiled, revealing his elongated fang teeth. "But I will make them feel pain, too. At the next meeting, I will strike down the request for land usage submitted by the local fae Courts and werewolf Packs."

"What did they want to use land for?" a male vampire asked.

Killian shrugged. "They wished to turn it into a land preserve that werewolves and fae could use for magical purposes. But it doesn't matter. They won't get it."

The vampires laughed and grinned. The mood of the room was still pretty grim and tense, but they clearly found joy in subverting the others' plans.

I pressed my lips together more tightly and stared at my teacup.

I could actually sympathize with the vampires—possibly for the first time in my life.

House Medeis holds life as precious, and while we're somewhat infamous for banning killing—even in self-defense—I understood the horror of what was going on. Someone was picking off innocent people—and vampires. It wasn't during battle; it wasn't even in an official *fight*. It was on Family land—a place that should be safe. (Well...safe for them.) No matter what politics were going on, killing innocents was *never* okay.

But I didn't like Killian's plan to get rid of the park. Not because I felt strongly about the park—though I did recall it was something the werewolves had been excited about for a while—but because it wasn't right to use his position on the Regional Committee as a way to extract revenge.

I couldn't argue, though, that no one else cared about the murders. But cooperation between the races wasn't common. Too much blood had been spilled, and too many wars had been fought for us to really cooperate.

I moodily picked up my teacup.

Nothing seemed fair or right. Killian's vengeful tendencies were too much. But I couldn't say the peace-loving ways of House Medeis were totally right either, or I wouldn't have been sitting here with sealed magic, hiding from my own House.

But it didn't matter for now. All I could do was hang on and try to survive—both the vampires and whoever was committing all these murders.

Which is why I didn't dare breathe a word that, given how easily the murderer/serial killer seemed to slip Drake Hall's defenses, there was a possibility it was an inside job. Because even if it was a valid thought, I was pretty sure the vampires would take offense and possibly react with violence.

CHAPTER ELEVEN

Hazel

A week passed, and there were no new murders.

My life mostly revolved around exercising and taking Epsom-salt soaks in the giant bathtub of my private bedroom. (That was, perhaps, the only major positive in this: the huge room upgrade. My bathroom was the size of my bedroom back in House Medeis, and if I had a death wish I could ransack it for serious money between the soap dispenser that was leafed with real gold and what I suspected were real rubies welded into the giant mirror frame.)

I wasn't seeing much improvement in the physical fitness area, but Celestina assured me I would soon. I *was* able to hold my sword in the sword forms now without my arms shaking. But that meant giving credit to Rupert for the weightlifting, something I was morally opposed to.

"Switch to a defensive stance next," Josh instructed. He circled, keeping a critical eye on my movements. "For as inevitable as the final kiss of death is, I imagine you desire to fend it off for as long as possible."

Josh had taken over my sword training for the past two days, during which I'd come to learn a lot about him. For instance, he wasn't judging my lack of fighting abilities—though I wish he was—but rather just being...Josh. I'd never met a vampire as morose and fixated on death as Josh before. (I mean, vampires are *immortal*. If anyone thumbed their nose at death it was vampires. Josh, however, didn't seem to agree.)

I maneuvered my body so my sword pointed down, but was positioned in a way that would protect my stomach.

"An excellent choice," Josh said. "This stance in particular is helpful against werewolves, who are prone to going for the guts of their victim—though the smarter ones will focus on your neck."

"Fabulous," I said. "Something to look forward to."

"When you add magic to your sword stances, you'll find you are much more capable of fighting than you imagined." Josh stopped in front of me with his hands clasped behind his back. "Magic is something of a cheat code when fighting."

"Oh yeah," I said. "Totally. That's why everyone is scared of wizards."

Josh tilted his head as he studied me, his forehead wrinkled. (I think I confused him about as much as he confused me.) "Very well, it seems you require a demonstration. Take up a kata—overhead cut."

A kata is a Japanese sword form—sort of. It's really a set of choreographed movements, but since I was a total newbie to the art form the only kata I had learned were pretty limited in length. They all have fancy Japanese names, but Celestina had decided it wasn't worth trying to teach me when she laughed so hard at my initial attempts she almost impaled herself on a wrought-iron fence.

The stance Josh ordered me to use was actually super difficult. You hold the sword above your head, then cut down directly in front of you. There's way more to it—balance and pressure play a huge role in it—but it was tough for me to do with as many repetitions as the vampires liked to give me because it required holding my sword steady *and* lifting it above my head, things my chicken arms had a difficult time doing.

Josh waited until I had completed the motion twice before interrupting. "Hold," he said when my sword was shoulder height. He drifted closer and tapped the blade of my sword with a finger. "Put a spark of your magic there."

I blinked. "Not my hands?"

"Correct. It might take some practice, but try to isolate your magic to the sword blade—not the hilt."

I pulled at the magic that freely floated around the air, channeling it through my blood and into a usable state. Since I had so little this was pretty hard, and I was grimacing before I'd even managed to produce a spark. But it was even harder to make the magic manifest on the blade, not my hands. It took about five minutes, then a tiny spark of blue magic flickered on the edge of the blade.

Josh waited a minute before the magic stabilized, then nodded. "Good. Now continue."

I gritted my teeth as I continued with the kata, raising my sword above my head and then swinging it down. It was hard to keep my magic flowing and wrapped around the sword like tiny sparks of electricity.

"I believe your lack of magic will be a boon as you learn finesse." Josh folded his arms across his chest and nodded in satisfaction. "It should be easier to maintain control over your spark of magic and learn how to control it with your movements as opposed to struggling with a great deal of magic and spending most of your concentration on keeping the amount right. Here, try on this dummy."

"Celestina said I shouldn't practice on dummies—I'm so weak I might hurt my arms on impact," I gloomily said.

Josh forcibly made the dummy—a creation of hardwood lined

with cut lengths of tire rubber—bow its box-shaped head at me, then stepped back. "It won't be a problem this time."

I approached it—moving slowly so I could more easily keep the spark of my magic going. I adjusted my feet into the proper stance, then raised my sword above my head and dropped it down in the practiced cut.

The spark of my magic flared on impact, burning through the layer of rubber as if I was cutting through butter and digging into the dummy's wooden shoulder. The smell of burnt tire filled the sword studio, but I stared at the mutilated dummy, shocked at my own success.

"You'll get better as you expand your sword stances," Josh said. "I've been researching the possibilities, and it seems to me that you could use a sword to point and direct your magic. I don't understand why fighting with weapons fell out of fashion with your kind. It's much more efficient."

"That's amazing." I stared at my sword with new eyes. "It's that powerful, even with magic as small as mine."

Josh shrugged. "You are layering your magic—however thin it may be at the moment—over a deadly weapon with an edge that is fearsome on its own. It's expected."

"Josh!"

We turned around to see my "favorite" vampire—Rupert—standing at the other side of the sword practice studio, his jaw clenched.

"Must you teach the wizard here and stink up the rooms?" he growled.

Josh blinked. "The burnt rubber smell should fade soon."

Rupert rolled his eyes and pointed to me. "I meant *her*! Her rat-blood reeks."

Josh shrugged. "That seems like a personal problem. You should meditate on it—lest the void will take you."

Rupert curled his lips back in an almost werewolf-like snarl.

(Vampires usually liked to be much more refined.) "Your bizarre words have been tolerated long enough. I'll—"

Before he could utter his threat, another vampire smacked him on the back of the head. "Enough with that—or haven't you learned your lesson? You don't want to tangle with Josh."

I wasn't certain I heard the other vampire right, so I glanced at Josh.

He looked especially benign today in his black workout pants and bright orange t-shirt that had a video game logo on it.

But he was apparently stronger than Rupert? Interesting...

"Don't touch me." Rupert ran a hand through his short red hair. "You might be too frightened to challenge him, but I will."

I adjusted my grasp on my sword, but I didn't dare lower it yet. Last time I let the tip touch the ground Celestina made me carry my sword on a pillow for half a day. "Challenge?"

"He means to fight me for my position in the Drake Family," Josh said in the same tone of voice he used to announce the kitchen's dinner menu.

"Oh. What's your rank?"

Josh adjusted the dummy. "Second Knight."

"*For real?*"

"Yes. I don't have a hope of ever achieving First Knight," Josh said. "No one does. Celestina is a beast to fight. I lose more weapons to her brutish fists in our friendly matches than I ever do in field combat." He sighed. "So many delightful weapons forever broken..."

I slightly shook my head. "Wow. Staying here is definitely going to make me deal with all of the stereotyping I apparently do."

It did make me pause for another reason, though.

Why on earth did Killian Drake have his top two underlings playing nursemaid to a wizard? Given that I was such a total beginner, any of his vampires would be more skilled and able to teach me the basics. But he'd chosen Celestina and Josh. (And Rupert, but I suspected that might be an underhanded maneuvering on Killian's part for some complicated reason I didn't want to understand.)

"Regardless, the rat-blood should be trained in a different part of the house," Rupert continued. "Heaven knows she stunk the whole place up when the mantasp monster nearly succeeded in killing her."

"She's Killian's new pet," another vampire said in a steely voice. "She goes wherever he wants her to."

"He doesn't care where she is," Rupert said. "That's why he dumped her off. He's probably just using her for bait anyway."

He swiveled to stare at me.

What a puke. If my wild speculations were right and the murderer really was an insider, I'd bet Rupert was the one—not because of his terrible personality, but because he just seemed to hate *everyone*. Obviously, he had some buried issues.

Several long seconds passed, and Rupert still didn't look away from me.

"Oh, sorry, were you expecting a reaction or something?" I asked. "Because he's Killian Drake. I'm realistic enough to know he *only* ever brought me in because he thought he could use me in some way."

Josh nodded approvingly.

Rupert curled back his upper lip, showing off his fangs.

"Don't pick fights with the wizard," the steely voiced male vampire ordered. "It only makes you look stupid."

"Because I refuse to subject myself to the rat-blood's stench?" Rupert scoffed. "Please. The rest of you are too soft. I can barely stand to be in the same room as it. It speaks to the quality of your abilities."

A female vampire sighed and rolled her eyes. "This is why everyone knows you're adopted," she said, dryly. "Drake vampires have too much pride to throw temper tantrums."

"Careful," another vampire warned as he eyed the female.

"More than just Rupert have been brought into the Family externally."

"And *all* of us have enough sense not to argue in front of the wizard," a tall, willowy male vampire said. "Enough."

He must have been high enough in the pecking order to command their respect, because they all fell silent—Rupert included. (Though he cast me a dirty look—as if his big mouth was my fault.)

Josh seemed unbothered by the tense mood. He studied the clock on the wall with the same meditative scrutiny he gave life. "We have tarried too long; it's already sunset. Come, Hazel. It's time for your evening run."

My magic had faded while I was pre-occupied listening to the fight, so all I had to do was slide my chisa katana into its scabbard with a click that was so, so, *so* satisfying after a long practice. I tied it to the weighted belt Celestina had gotten me, then followed Josh out of the hallway.

I waited until we reached the stairs that would take us out of the basement before I risked prodding Josh. "What were they talking about?"

"To what are you referring?"

"Being adopted into the Drake Family." We reached the top stair, and I was pleased I hadn't lost my breath while scurrying up the steps and talking. (Maybe I *was* improving!)

"Oh. Rupert was originally part of a European vampire lineage—the Cotelleon Family. Killian formally adopted him into the Drake Family several years ago when everyone in the Family—excluding Rupert—was killed for colluding against their regional committee. Many of us here in Drake Hall are not actually Drake vampires, turned by Killian, but adopted from other Families." Josh led me through the front door and outside into the purple of twilight as he casually dropped his truth bomb.

Killian allowed other vampires to join his Family? It seemed strangely generous for him—though I suppose it was for his own race, not another. "And Killian willingly took Rupert in?"

"Yes." Josh made his way around the house, choosing what running path we'd go down. "Of course, it meant he inherited all Cotelleon land and resources with Rupert's adoption."

Ahhh. There was the manipulating and selfish Killian Drake I knew.

I actually sighed in relief that I wasn't so far off my mental picture of the Eminence. "I see."

Josh selected one of the longer paths—or rather longer for me. (Celestina told me there were trails that wove several miles through the Drake Family's apparently vast acreage.)

This particular path wound toward the wrought-iron fence that encased the entire property, following it as it divided Drake land from the neighboring property and made for the road at the front of the hall.

The moon was bright in the sky, and only the smallest sliver of sun was left, so I kept my jogging pace brisk. If I didn't finish in time it was going to be totally dark, and the likelihood that I'd trip on something would rapidly multiply.

We'd been running for only a few minutes when a hideously loud, shriek-like bray shattered the silence.

I skid to a stop. "What was that?"

Josh peered past the fence. "I believe that was the neighbor's donkey."

I tried to process this information. "Wait, you guys know your neighbor?"

"Indeed. The dogs are rather fond of her because she gives them biscuits. They slip through the fence and run off to her house when possible—though sometimes the aforementioned donkey chases them away."

It seemed weirdly domestic that the Drakes had problems with their dogs—which I still couldn't quite wrap my head around—going to visit the neighbor. (A donkey-owning-neighbor, no less!

It just seemed like something Killian wouldn't normally tolerate living next door to him.)

"You have caught your breath, so I believe it is time to move on," Josh said.

I nodded and started running again, staying silent as I mulled on the peculiarities of the Drake Family.

I happily noticed that my lungs didn't burn much—maybe I was right about the stairs and my stamina was increasing?—but my sword started to feel *really* heavy around the time our jogging trail ran parallel with the road and looped near the front gates.

The gates were more for visual appeal than actual defense. Each gate was cut in the shape of a roaring dragon, and there were plenty of spots where you could wriggle through it, or the wrought-iron fence that separated Drake Family land.

My steps were getting heavier as I trudged along, so when Josh stopped, I assumed it was an air break for me. "Thanks," I panted as I kept walking.

Josh, however, was statue still. He stared past the gates, and something *in* him moved.

The hair on the back of my neck prickled as my instincts made me shiver and I finally understood how Josh came to be Second Knight in the Drake Family. I cleared my throat. "What is it?"

"Intruders."

I blinked, and Josh had his cellphone in his palm, dialing a number with a careless swipe of his hand as he stared at whatever had his attention. "Intruders," he repeated.

I casually shifted closer, trying to hear the other voice, but vampire hearing is so good they must set the volume on almost silent, so I couldn't make anything out.

"Two," Josh said. "A wizard and a werewolf."

I squinted in the direction he was staring and could just make out two figures standing in the middle of the road just beyond the gates like a pair of idiots waiting to get hit. It took a moment, but

I saw the suitcoat and the distinctive orange shade of the tie, and I realized at least one of the figures was a House Tellier wizard. Which probably meant the other person was the werewolf.

I stiffened. There was no way either of them was the murderer who was out on the loose—not many werewolves hunted alone, and those who did were carefully watched, and it would take *a lot* for a wizard to be able to take out a vamp. Plus, the wizard just *happened* to be from House Tellier?

Not likely.

He'd probably been sent by Mason—though I had no idea where the werewolf fit in all of this. Slowly, I untied my sword from my waist and considered sliding it from its scabbard.

"I assume they're here for your wizard," Josh said, still talking on the phone. "Do you wish for me to dispatch them, or…?"

"No, I'll handle it myself," Killian said directly behind me.

I was actually pretty proud that I didn't jump at his abrupt arrival—another sign of improvement! (Or maybe living here had shot my nerves and adrenaline?)

"You think they're here to spy on me?" I stepped aside as Killian adjusted his fancy gold cufflinks (dragon shaped, of course).

"Unless you have a secret boyfriend, or two." Killian smirked.

"The wizard is House Tellier," I said. "They helped Mason with his coup."

"Are you certain the whole thing wasn't a lovers' quarrel?" Killian was almost purring.

"Mason threatened me with marriage, or the death of my House," I said flatly.

"Very well. I'll take care of it." Killian frowned and adjusted my arms so I held my sword correctly.

"Yes, Your Eminence," Josh said.

"Wait. Take care of it? What does that mean?" I asked.

Killian ignored me and jumped the fence. He was a smudgy blur in the blue shadows that were slowly taking over, so I actually only knew he went over because I heard the rattle of the gate. Moments later he was out in the road with the House Tellier wizard and the werewolf. He had them both by the throats—the werewolf was pinned to the ground with a foot and the wizard he held up so the wizard's feet dangled in the air.

I didn't even know how he did it so fast. There wasn't a scuffle, Killian was just *that* overwhelming and moved like quicksilver.

Killian's gaze wandered from the werewolf to the wizard, and his eyes started to glow an eerie, bright red. "You thought you could intrude on *Drake land*?" His voice was dangerously smooth, like a sword slicing through meat. "And escape with your lives?" He smiled savagely, his white teeth flashing in the darkness.

The werewolf and wizard made choking noises, their thrashing becoming increasingly more frantic.

Killian's smile hadn't dropped, and there was something...*wild* in his eyes.

The hair on the back of my neck prickled. I sucked my neck into my shoulders and scooted closer to Josh. "He's going to threaten them and tell them to get lost?"

"Not at all," Josh said. "He's going to kill them."

"*What?* But they aren't doing anything!"

Josh shrugged. "It's their mistake."

My thoughts whirled so fast in my head I could barely contain them. "Hold my sword." I thrust my sword into Josh's hands, then sprinted to the fence. I wriggled between the spokes on the gate —one of the benefits of my small frame—and popped out on the other side. "Killian, *wait*!"

Killian shifted slightly to watch me as I ran to join him. The wizard wriggled in his grasp, his feet kicking, but I could tell he could still take shallow breaths—same thing applied to the wolf that was clawing at Killian's foot. Though Killian must have been putting more pressure on the werewolf. He was red faced, and the muscles in his neck were popping.

"You can't kill them," I said when I finally reached him. "They haven't done anything wrong."

"They're loitering on Drake land." Killian's voice was as frosty as winter. "That's reason enough."

"They didn't even make it past the fence!"

Killian shrugged casually, holding the struggling wizard above his head as if he were merely stretching. "If I kill them no one will be around to say otherwise."

"But that's wrong!" I argued. "They didn't try to kill or hurt anyone."

Killian lifted an eyebrow. "I had hoped you were intelligent enough to realize they are here to spy on you and take news back to the traitor that threw you out. Perhaps I overestimated you?"

"I know why the wizard is here," I said. "But I still don't want him dead."

"You're from House Medeis." The ice in Killian's voice was starting to mellow to a bored tone, which was good for the werewolf, the wizard, *and* me. "You don't want anyone dead, no matter what atrocities they commit," he continued.

I opened my mouth to argue, except he was correct. Based on the rules of House Medeis, if—no, *when*—I reclaimed House Medeis, Mason would be handed over to the Wizard Council to be judged. Even if he *did* kill a member of my family, at worst he'd be exiled. Which wouldn't be much of a hardship based on his relationship with House Tellier.

But that was a dilemma for a different day. "Maybe, I don't know," I finally said. "But I know killing them would be wrong. Can't you just question them and send them on their way?"

"You want me to spare *both* of them?" Wrinkles appeared on Killian's forehead, dispelling the last of the fearsome coldness.

"Please," I repeated.

CHAPTER TWELVE

Hazel

Killian stared at me for several long moments, the glowing red of his eyes gradually dimming. "Fine," he flatly said. He immediately dropped the House Tellier wizard, who hit the road with a painful thump and a gurgle. Killian purposely stepped harder on the werewolf before moving to stand next to me. He stared down at the werewolf and wizard as if they were bugs he'd found in his home. "Tell your leader if he sends any more goons here, they will be slaughtered. Hazel Medeis is under the Drake Family's protection. Understood?"

The werewolf was massaging his throat, but he nodded frantically. The wizard moaned as he peeled himself off the ground, but he nodded so hard I thought he might snap his neck.

"Leave, before I change my mind," Killian said.

The wizard scrambled to his feet and ran down the road, heading for a car parked on the curb. The werewolf was a little slower, loping behind him.

I exhaled—exhilarated by my win—so I barely registered when Killian reached into his suitcoat.

He slid out a handgun, inserted a magazine, aimed, then fired. His shot grazed the werewolf's shoulder, making him howl in pain—though he didn't run any slower.

"What did you do that for?" I squawked.

Killian shrugged and removed his handgun's magazine. "Principle."

I pressed the heels of my palms into my eyes.

"I didn't kill him," Killian pointed out. "I didn't even wing him." He sounded almost regretful about that.

I needed to get him away before he decided to blow up their car for the fun of it. "You are unbelievable." I marched for the fence. "Thank you," I added when I was close enough to brush my hand across one of the dragon gates.

Killian waited until I was through before he jumped the gate with an athleticism I had to admire. "Don't make it a habit."

"Mercy doesn't become you?" I asked.

Killian tilted his head back, and a shadow of the cruel vampire returned. "I have no use for mercy."

"We'll see about that."

Killian lifted an eyebrow again—I was starting to recognize it as a sign of both disbelief and amusement from him. "Josh," he called, "how is it my wizard is overly opinionated?"

"Her ignorance makes her daring." Josh held out my sword for me, which I took with a smile of thanks.

"What, no prophecy that as a wizard I'm closer to death, and it unhinges my inhibitions?" I joked.

"That is also likely true," Josh agreed. "I thought I would be sensitive to your lifespan and refrain from mentioning it."

I snorted.

Josh bowed to Killian. "How do you wish for us to proceed if we see any wizards in the future?"

"Question them," Killian said. "If they are sent by someone, immediately kill them." He ignored my squeak of anger. "If they ask to see Hazel, let them, but stay within range." Killian glanced down at me.

The last orange light cast by the long-gone sun had faded, but the moon was bright, so I could still see Killian's speculative look pretty easily. "What, you think I'm going to start getting visitors?"

"Possibly," Killian said. "Now that it is confirmed you are under my protection, any allies you have that are brave—and stupid enough—may come."

I bit my lip as I thought of Felix and Momoko. "You might be right," I admitted. "Thank you."

Killian shrugged. "Continue with your run," he said. "The time it took you to get from Josh to the road was abysmal." He was gone before I could say anything more, running so fast he made a slight breeze.

I indignantly held my katana to my chest. "He just can't say anything nice, can he?"

"He doesn't have to," Josh said. "Are you ready?"

I puffed out my cheeks then nodded. "Yeah...Thanks."

"Into the blackness of the night, which perhaps mirrors the color of my soul," Josh morosely said.

"You have got to get out more."

SEVERAL DAYS LATER, in the late afternoon, I found myself the unlucky recipient of Killian's attention as he scrutinized me in my suit—which had already been adjusted by a tailor after what I thought of as the "murder meeting."

Apparently, the tailor hadn't done a good enough job, because Killian was looking me over with the critical eye of a mother-in-law as he lounged on a leather couch. "You look like a child dressed up as a secret service agent," he finally said.

I tapped my foot—my favorite part of the outfit given they

were reinforced leather boots that cut off at the ankle—on the mosaic tiled flooring. "I can't help my height."

Killian sighed and slightly tilted his head back. "It's going to be a pain trying to make you look even half as fierce as you should."

"Is that why you make all the Drake vampires wear suits?" I asked.

"No. Increasing your fierce factor is something *you* need given that you have the appearance of a puppy. My vampires are intimidating in their suits, but for an entirely different reason."

I rubbed the back of my neck as I thought. "It sets you apart, but it also shows how *aware* you are of modern times and conveniences. Is that why everyone has smartphones?"

I didn't expect an answer, but Killian smirked. "Precisely. Given my kind's terrible habit to be complacent and spend most of their time complaining about change, the stark difference in *my* Family is unsettling." The smirk fell from his face, and he abruptly narrowed his eyes. "You don't have a phone."

"Nope," I said. "I had to leave it behind when I ran."

"You'll need one."

"What, so I can call Celestina if I get lost on the running trails?"

"No, because eventually we'll have to take you out on a test run," Killian said. "And it's imperative that you are able to communicate."

I tugged on the lapel of my black jacket—which was actually quite comfortable, though it was going to be a beast to walk around in when the true heat of summer hit. "It's still tough to run over a mile at a time, and you want me to go out to a fight?"

Killian shrugged. "You need to get used to blood and death," he said. "I can't have you whining every time an enemy is slain."

"If you traumatize me, I'll just whine more," I warned him.

A dangerous light lit up Killian's eyes, making the black depths show just a hint of red. "Traumatize...now that is a thought." He sat up on the couch, resting his elbows on his knees, and stared at me.

I forced myself to stand still and boldly meet his gaze. (If I squirmed, I had learned he just pushed harder.) I didn't have to like it, though. I wasn't sure what was worse—weight lifting with Rupert or hanging around Killian like a pet.

Killian stood and glanced at the window—which had a gauzy curtain drawn to block out the brightest bits of sunshine that managed to peek through the dull gray clouds. He'd probably heard something, based on the slight quirk of his eyebrows. (I was coming to learn that his eyebrows were the gateway to his moods, and thus studied them hardcore.)

"Where is Celestina?" I asked. "She usually comes to get me right about now for practice."

"She's out for the afternoon," Killian said.

"Oh, on a mission?"

Up went one of Killian's eyebrows, signaling his amusement. "Mission? We're not an intelligence agency."

I let my arms hang at my sides. "Mission sounded better than asking if you sent her out to go intimidate and rough up some people."

"We're not the mob, either," Killian scoffed. "But in this case Celestina requested time off."

"Good for her," I truthfully said, though it ruined my escape plan. "Are we done making fun of my suit yet?"

"You have somewhere more important to be?" Killian asked in a deceptively mild voice.

"Nooo," I reluctantly said.

His smirk was back, and he sauntered closer to me. "If you are so bored, we could go downstairs and engage in a practice match. It's about time you started having play fights."

"*No!*" I said with a lot more fire. "We can make fun of my suit!"

Killian made an amused sound at the back of his throat. "You don't need to worry. You could *never* touch me or any Drake vampire this early in your training."

"I am not *at all* worried about hurting you." I shook my head for emphasis. "But I'm pretty sure I'll get killed by accident."

"Have a little faith."

"I prefer to be a skeptic, thank you."

Killian chuckled, but was turning toward the door. I didn't understand why until I heard the knock. "Come in," he said.

A female vampire opened the door and bowed deeply to Killian. "Please excuse the intrusion, Your Eminence, but two wizards have approached the gates and requested an audience with your wizard."

I furrowed my eyebrows so much it made it hard to see. "Seriously?"

"Yes," the vampire said simply.

"Bring them into Drake Hall. If they are indeed Hazel's friends, they can use this room," Killian said.

The female vampire bowed, "Yes, Your Eminence," and disappeared, leaving the doorway empty.

Killian adjusted his tie, then glanced back at me. "Scream if you need help."

"You're not staying?"

"For *wizards*? No. Don't take too long." Abruptly, he left, leaving me alone—in my *suit*—to wait for the maybe-friends-maybe-Mason's-cronies.

When I heard footsteps, I knew it had to be the wizards—most of the vampires were as quiet as cats, except Rupert who stomped when he was angry, which was most of the time. I poked my head into the hallway, and I felt the tension, anger, and frustration I'd been carrying for weeks instantly start to fade. "Momoko! Felix!" I bolted from the parlor and tackled my closest friends, squeezing them in a tight hug. It was the only way I could assure myself they were okay.

Momoko laughed and threw an arm around me, but Felix silently dragged me closer.

"You're okay," I said, the relief raw in my voice. "I didn't know—I had no way of finding out what happened!"

"We're fine," Felix said.

"We're more worried about you," Momoko added.

I released both of them and stepped back. I could barely look away, I was just so relieved to see them. Unfortunately, it looked like the past few weeks had taken a toll on them as well. They didn't have any *visible* wounds or bruises, but Momoko seemed a little pale, and even Felix's Awesomely-Good-Looks were dulled a bit—he had dark circles under his eyes and his hair wasn't as glossy as normal.

I barely remembered to call out a belated "thank you!" to the vampire who had brought them in before I grabbed Felix and Momoko by the wrists and tugged them along. "Come on—tell me everything."

I left the door cracked—I didn't want the vampires to think I was hiding anything, and it hardly would have mattered with their hearing anyway.

"You first." It was Momoko's turn to grab my wrist and drag me over to the leather couch Killian had previously perched on. She sat down and pulled until I did as well, and Felix plopped down on my other side.

"But—" I tried.

"Spill it, Hazel," Felix ordered.

I gave in and told them a brief version of all that had happened since I had arrived—though I only alluded to the vampire murders as I didn't think Killian wanted the details spread.

"And Killian hasn't asked for anything in return?" Momoko asked when I was finished.

"He said he plans to use me as an attack dog," I pointed out.

"Yeah, but to have his second and third best vamps train you?"

Felix ran a hand through his blond hair, momentarily ruffling it. "There's got to be an angle we don't see."

Momoko pressed her lips together. "You'll be careful. The Drake Family is ruthless. Killian might be biding his time until you can take House Medeis back."

I winced at the thought. I'd gotten a little lax since Killian seemed to find my complaints and observations amusing, and I'd gotten to the point where I considered Celestina and Josh friends.

Not that I doubted either of them (Killian, however, was shady as hell) but they had their loyalties, and I had mine. One day I wanted to take House Medeis back, but I didn't want Killian to be involved in that. I didn't want him to have control over me, either.

"But you have more magical abilities, wow," Felix said. "That's a lot to take in."

"Is there any chance the Paragon was lying?" Momoko asked.

"No," I flatly said. "He has no reason to lie to me, and there's no possible way he's under Killian's thumb. He's the *national* fae representative. Killian's power base is here in the Midwest."

Momoko shook her head. "I can't believe your parents would do that to you. They loved you, and they just let you suffer when you were bullied?"

"You two were there for me," I reminded her.

"Yeah, but I know you still ran into problems as an adult, and you wouldn't tell Felix or me," Momoko said. "Your parents had to know that, too. So why would they lie to you?"

I stared at the ground and shrugged. "I don't know. All I can think of is that I didn't know my parents as well as I thought."

I would have cried, but I'd run out of tears weeks ago. I had turned the issue over in my mind thousands of times, trying to find *some way* to put a positive spin on it, but there wasn't. My parents had majorly messed with me, and now they were gone, and I couldn't even ask them *why*.

"We're sorry, Hazel." Felix leaned into me.

"It's fine." I cleared my throat and sat straighter. "But now I want to hear about you guys. How is everyone—and how's the House?"

Felix grimaced, and Momoko collapsed back into the couch.

"It's bad," she said. "But now that we know you're safe, it's better."

"For real, guys." I bit my lip. "Has Mason...*killed* anyone?"

"No." Felix shook his head. "He's busy trying to keep us under his thumb and the House in some semblance of working."

"Ever since you left it's been throwing a *fit*," Momoko said. "It hasn't weakened any more—I think out of sheer spite. Even though it's been cut off from its Adept for weeks, just yesterday it locked a visiting House Tellier wizard in the basement."

A rush of warmth and affection for my home hit me. "I'm glad it's fighting."

"Oh yeah," Felix snorted. "It will keep making Mason miserable. It's why he didn't send anyone after you sooner—though we're grateful he did, it's how we found out where you were."

"*Everyone* heard how Killian Drake almost killed Langhan—that's the House Tellier wizard who spied on you—and the werewolf mercenary Mason had hired. It really freaked Mason out that Killian personally kicked them out. Did you really stop him from killing them?" Momoko asked.

"Yeah," I said, somewhat hesitant to own up to it.

"That's really weird," Felix bluntly said. "Killian Drake is incredibly powerful—there's no reason why he should listen to you."

I shrugged. "I don't know what to make of it either."

"We're glad you found a safe place," Momoko said. "House Tellier told Mason they wouldn't send anyone to try and reclaim you as long as you were inside Drake Family lands, and Mason knows he can't send any of *us* after you, so I don't think he can hurt you."

"Does he know you two are here?" I asked.

"Nope." Felix shook his head. "He thinks we had work shifts today at the library."

Both Felix and Momoko were set to graduate from the local college in fall, so in the meantime they worked part-time at the local library, along with Felix's sister-in-law, Leslie.

"Our parents sent us out to find out how you're doing," Momoko said. "Everyone is going to be relieved."

Felix studied my suit with a disturbed look. "Maybe?"

"You guys still haven't given me a straight answer, though. What is Mason doing to the House? Not the building, but our family?" I stood up so I could face both of them and stare them down.

"We're...managing," Felix said.

"He's used magic on a few of us," Momoko admitted. "But since you left, the threatening stopped—though he has us wearing magic-blocking bracelets." She held up her wrists, showing off the unassuming silver bands that hung from her wrists.

My mouth dropped open. "How can he do that? It *has* to be illegal!"

"It would be," Momoko sighed and dropped her hands in her lap. "Except he says we're wearing them for training purposes—which *is* allowed."

I made a sound of outrage.

Magic-blocking bracelets were mostly used on wizards and fae who broke the law. But wizard Houses occasionally used them for punishments and training—we had a pair or two lying around House Medeis in my parents' day. But purchasing enough bracelets to cuff all the wizards sworn to House Medeis should have done more than raise a few eyes, it should have set off some alarm bells.

"The Wizard Council can't possibly believe he's got cuffs on everyone in House Medeis all the time for *training* purposes!" I scoffed, naming the wizard subcommittee that over-saw regional wizard issues.

"They're turning a blind eye." Felix balled his hands into fists. "We've sent emails and text messages out to the other Houses—they still won't help."

"At least since we're wearing the bracelets he doesn't have to physically subdue us—though he won't let anyone leave the house unless it's to go to work," Momoko said.

That was the silver lining, I suppose. Keeping their magic blocked was cruel, but if it meant he wasn't hurting them, and if it gave them a little more freedom, that was better than the alternative.

I rubbed my forehead. "If you have the bracelets he can't expect you to fight back, so he's not torturing you or anything...right?"

They exchanged glances, instantly raising my hackles.

If they were trying to decide how much to tell me, that meant it was a lot worse than they were letting on.

"It's getting worse the longer it's taking him to seize control," Momoko finally said.

"The Wizard Council have announced they're not going to move to stop him—they called it an 'in-house' issue that should be solved by those of us in House Medeis—which is ridiculous since they *know* House Tellier is helping Mason," Felix bitterly said.

"But! He's hit a wall." Momoko grinned mischievously. "Your parents' human lawyers. The firm won't proceed with the will without you there—they actually had the police come and threaten to arrest Mason when he came to their offices to try and convince them to give him all the papers and the signet ring. He had to leave because if he got arrested *then* the Curia Cloisters would certainly get involved because of the bad publicity."

I placed my hands on my hips. "You said your parents are covering for you...so you're planning to go back, aren't you?"

"We have to," Momoko said. "For the good of the House."

I slightly shook my head. "But if things get worse—"

"We can't go anywhere else, Hazel," Felix said. "House Medeis is our home. We want to stop Mason. You're safe, which is the highest priority. We can ride everything out from there. You just need to stay safe—and maybe see if you are sealed after all."

Momoko nodded and forcibly smoothed her jeans with her hands. "Felix is right. We'll be fine—it's not like *we* can help Mason take over the House."

"Yes, but—" I started.

Felix mulishly tucked his chin, and I could tell we were about to have an argument, when the door banged open behind me.

"Wizard," Killian said, his voice like melted chocolate. "You've wasted enough time visiting. You need to continue your training: I have an experiment I want to try."

I warily looked up at the vampire. "Experiment? With *training*?"

"Don't worry your head about it." Killian glanced briefly at my friends before writing them off in under a second. Without waiting for a response, he grabbed the collar of my suitcoat and dragged me behind him.

"Bye, guys—*don't* risk yourselves for the House," I called to them as Killian towed me to the parlor door.

Both Felix and Momoko stared at me with open shock, their mouths dropped.

"Tell everyone I love them—oh, and do you think you could maybe bring my cellphone and wallet if you can sneak out to see me again?"

Felix appeared at the doorframe as Killian hauled me down the hallway. "Can't do it," Felix called. "Mason went through your room and confiscated all your stuff—phone and wallet included."

"Why is he always so thorough? Ugh! In that case, I'll call you on the Drake Hall phone line when I get a chance. Be safe!" I had to shout louder as Killian dragged me farther from the parlor. "Could you *wait* a moment?" I tried to maneuver so he didn't strangle me with my shirt collar.

"No."

I rolled my eyes. "I'll walk, just let me go."

Killian gave me one last tug, then abruptly released me so I almost lost my balance. I quickly recovered and hurried after him, trying to adjust my coat back into place. "What's the training? More weightlifting?"

"Not this time." When we reached a staircase, Killian led me up rather than going down below to all the training rooms.

I followed in silence until we reached the second story. "Thank you for letting me talk to my friends."

He started climbing the set of stairs that took us up to the third floor. "I didn't do anything."

"No, but you allowed it, and you didn't have to. I appreciate it." I was mildly confused when he had us keep going past the third floor and climb the stairs to the final floor—where more of the vampires lived. I would have said it was where the top ranked vampires were, but since Josh was on the third floor with me, that couldn't be true.

Killian elegantly shrugged, looking a bit like a model—which seemed despicable to me, but magic, and supernaturals as an extension, by its very existence made things *not* fair, so whatever.

I studied Killian's back, trying to gauge his reaction. "I'm guessing you don't care about Mason or what's going on with House Medeis?"

"Definitely *not*," Killian scoffed. He led the way down a hallway, stopping to open a door to an empty bedroom. We marched through it, and Killian opened the glass patio doors to a small balcony.

It was already pretty dark outside because of the clouds, but I still saw a bunch of vampires standing outside, carrying the special sun-blocking umbrellas they have *everywhere* in the mansion.

I peered over the patio ledge at them, mildly confused. "I don't get it, how am I supposed to train up here on the patio?"

"Remember, I said we're experimenting in your training," Killian said in his velveteen voice.

"Yes," I cautiously agreed. "What do you have—*planned*!" I yelped when Killian scooped me up with an alarming amount of finesse. It was a weird sensation. No one had picked me up like this since I was a teenager, and because he tucked me against his chest I was a lot closer to his face than I wanted to be. In fact, I was now so close that I could see the deep red color of his eyes had flecks of black, which is what made his gaze so much darker than any of his underlings. "What are you doing?" I demanded. I didn't know what to do with my hands—the adrenaline surge said I should grab onto his jacket and cling for life, but instinct told me that would be a horrible idea. Despite my panic I did notice that Killian was *cool*—temperature wise, I mean. I was starting to get jealous—I was sweating again—until Killian chuckled.

"I just said." He spoke in that deceptively light tone I didn't like. "Experimenting."

And then he tossed me over the side of the patio. As if I was a bad apple he was casually throwing away.

CHAPTER THIRTEEN

Hazel

I screamed as I fell four flights, my eyesight turned blurry from the wind, then something hit me with the force of a train, and I briefly lost all my air.

When I could finally see—and breathe—again, I realized Celestina was holding me much the same way Killian had. "W-w-where?" Bewildered, I looked around. Celestina was standing on the ground floor, just under the patio. She must have caught me when Killian threw me.

"You're safe, Hazel," Celestina said in a cooing, calming tone.

"I am *not* safe," I wheezed as she slowly set me down. I took a few staggering steps, then glared up at the patio.

"Did your magic break free?" Killian called down in a careless tone.

"You could have *killed* me!"

Killian leaned against the patio ledge. "That was the point. I wondered if a traumatic event would unseal your magic."

"I was attacked by a mantasp!" I shouted. "That would have counted as traumatic if that's all it needed to unseal me!"

Killian shrugged. "It was worth attempting."

"*No,* it was *not!*"

"Also," Killian continued as if he couldn't hear me, "I was bored."

"You can't toss me over a patio because you're *bored*!" I hollered.

"I'm starting to understand that—your yelling is more unpleasant than boredom."

"GOOD!"

Killian's smirk—its charm inescapable even from several stories away—re-appeared, and he beckoned to me. "Come back up here."

"NOT ON YOUR LIFE!"

Killian's laugh echoed across the mansion grounds as I turned, still irate, to Celestina.

She met my scowl with a slight smile. "I would never hurt you," she said.

"Yeah, super convincing after you let him throw me off a balcony."

"I knew I could catch you," she assured me.

"Uh-huh." I peered up at the tall vampire, and some of my defensiveness left me as I realized Celestina had her thick black hair down for once. "Did you get your hair cut?"

"Do you like it?" She turned in a circle, a beaming smile turning up the volume of her vampire beauty.

"It's gorgeous."

"Thank you!" she said. "Now, shall we go upstairs?"

I groaned. "Doesn't he have better things to do?"

"Yes," Celestina agreed. "But it's not often he has something amusing. Come—this time he won't drop you over the side."

"No, instead he'll just dangle me by my ankle."

"Your words—they hurt, my wizard," Killian lazily called down in a voice as sure and smooth as ever.

"You're as convincing as a cockroach right now, Killian. Try again," I sourly said.

Killian laughed some more as I reluctantly followed Celestina inside.

Internally, I stewed.

Not over Killian dropping me off the patio—that's pretty standard for what I'd expect from him.

But there was something about this...it didn't really feel like Killian was trying to weaponize me. He seemed to be having...*fun*. And weirdly, I was grateful for the hassle he was willing to go through to see me safe.

But was I just being stupid? Or was Felix wrong; could I really make friends with these vampires—as deadly and dangerous as they were?

SINCE I'D BEEN MOVED to the floor the vampires lived on, I'd also been...*encouraged* to eat dinner with them. Breakfast and lunch I had in the kitchen with the other staff members, but the few times I had tried skipping dinner, Celestina showed up to drag me off to the dining room.

It's not what it sounds like.

Yeah, they insisted on keeping the lights dim so I could only tell about half of what I was eating. But the vampires didn't just sit there swirling blood in wine glasses—though, for reference, they were served blood in either frosted or heated mugs depending on their personal preference—they actually ate some human food.

Celestina explained that they didn't get much nutritional value out of it, and they couldn't taste a lot. (Spicy food was insanely popular with them simply because they could actually taste the heat.) But they had dinners usually about five times a week because they craved food, and it was an excellent "bonding experience" for the group as a whole (dead serious, those were her words). Only about half of the vampires attended at a given night—sometimes more, sometimes less—but no matter how many were there, everyone sat at the longest banquet table I'd ever seen in my entire life.

It wasn't a "bonding experience" for me. I was always ignored, and my presence was barely tolerated. Even though I'd been at Drake Hall for weeks it still felt that way.

So, the day after Killian had flung me off the patio, I followed my usual schedule and arrived to dinner as early as possible, sitting at a chair in the corner of the long-arse table so I was out of the way. I was contemplating my mashed potatoes as I wondered if the banquet table thing was left over from dinner parties in regency England, or some other time.

How old was everyone anyway? Killian Drake was a mystery, but I wouldn't put it past him to have been strutting around England when King Arthur pulled the sword from the stone, which meant his offspring could have easily lived through historic England.

"You," Rupert sneered when he entered the dining hall and caught sight of me.

I moved from my mashed potatoes to the pork roast the kitchen staff had slaved over. "Yep. Sorry if you were expecting someone else. Wizards don't have shapeshifting abilities."

"Why does Killian insist the *animals* eat with us?" Rupert bemoaned. "We are creatures of taste and class."

"Could your taste and class get moving? You're blocking the door," the steely voiced male vampire rumbled.

Rupert sidled out of the way and took up a spot at the opposite end of the table.

I shrugged and ate my pork roast as more vampires filed into the room, rapidly filling the seats at the table.

"If you cannot stand to be near the wizard, why don't you just leave?" Julianne, the blond-haired female vamp who worshiped the ground Celestina stood on, asked Rupert with a slight glare.

Rupert narrowed his eyes at her, ignoring the kitchen staff who set a plate full of delicious food in front of him. "Is that a challenge?"

"Rupert, stop being a pain," a very proper male vampire ordered as he cut an asparagus spear into equal, precise pieces.

Rupert coldly eyed him. "Know your place, weakling," he sneered.

With a flash of metal, Julianne tossed her steak knife at Rupert in a move my human eyes were barely able to discern.

Rupert caught it with a flash. He bared his fangs at her and flicked the knife. It embedded in the backrest of her chair, just above her shoulder, with such force I wouldn't be surprised if the tip of the knife poked through the other side. "Apologize," he demanded.

Julianne glared at him. "No."

Rupert flung his steak knife, and it might have hit Julianne, except Josh raised his fork, deflecting the dinnerware so it fell with a clatter. He didn't even look up from his plate while he did so—rather he seemed to be mourning his mug.

"I was hoping for a wine with tonight's meal," he said.

"Wine makes you sick," Steely Voice reminded him.

Josh sighed. "Ahhh, yes, but such pain might be worth the momentary reminder of what mortality felt like, with all of its inhibitions and dim knowledge."

"Thank you, Josh," Julianne said.

Josh waved her off. "Think nothing of it."

I studied the table and stifled the desire to shake my head. The Drake Family was a unique mixture made mostly of power and violence, but it had a swirl of affection somewhere in there. I didn't think other vampire Families threw steak knives at each other over dinner and then chatted about wine. But what did I know?

I buttered my roll and was content to be quiet and eat.

"I enjoyed your performance the other day."

It took me several moments to realize the sentence was directed at me. I looked up and down the table before I met Steely Voice's eyes.

"You have an admirable set of lungs," he added.

"...thanks?" I tried.

"Oh, your screams were *such* fun to hear!" Julianne gushed.

I tried for a smile, but I'm pretty sure it was more sarcastic than genuine. "I'm so glad I could provide amusement."

"You know, that's true." A male vampire plopped in an open chair across the table from me, and studied me with a curious look that was pretty unnerving with his red eyes. "I don't know that I've ever seen the Eminence laugh like that. Have you, Celestina?"

Celestina appeared at my side, taking the spot directly next to me. "Not very often, and not for a long time." She smiled down at me. "Though I don't know how he could have not laughed given your...*unusual* vocabulary."

I wrinkled my nose and set my fork on my plate with a loud clatter. "You said you wouldn't let me get hurt, and then he hung me off the side of the balcony on a rope like a piñata!"

"At least he didn't dangle you by the ankle as you feared he might," Celestina offered. "And you were never in any danger. Those on the ground were prepared to catch you."

"I was hoping you would fall," the vampire across from me said. "You make a different sound when falling from when you just dangle."

"Do I?" I sarcastically asked. "How very unexpected."

A few of the vampires showed a sliver of fang or exhaled a chuff of amusement.

Which meant Rupert, of course, couldn't let it pass. "I am surprised, Celestina," he said. "I would have thought you'd hate the wizard."

Celestina took a sip of heated blood from her mug. "Why?"

"She is the recipient of the Eminence's attention. Is that not enough?"

Celestina smirked. "Quite the opposite. I'm thankful."

Now it was my turn to be surprised. "Really? I would have thought this would be a big pain in the butt for you."

"Not at all." Celestina shook her head, and the glossy curtain of her hair swished. "I think it's good for the Eminence to have a hobby—particularly one he can laugh over."

"Of course," I grumbled into my mashed potatoes—which were flavored with flecks of fresh parsley. "Anything for the Eminence."

Celestina patted me on the shoulder. "It isn't an entirely selfless desire. I was finally able to get my hair cut for the first time in a decade. Ever since he made Eminence, he's worked every moment of the day. I have hopes he'll play with you more, and maybe I can go get a manicure."

The vampire sitting across from me had yet to touch his food (he and all the other vampires were served noticeably *less* than me) and instead nursed his frosted mug of blood. "That is a profound thought."

"If he spends too much time with his new hobby it might hurt the Family," a female vampire farther down the table nervously said.

Julianne pressed her lips together and gave the other vampire a flat look. "Do you *really* think the Eminence would *ever* neglect his duties, or let the Drake Family image be tarnished by slothfulness?"

Even though she had addressed the question to the female vampire, just about everyone, even Rupert, shook their heads.

"It's a good stress relief for him," Celestina said.

I eyed her as I ate my last forkful of potatoes. I had labeled her an ally, but this was a gentle reminder that her priority was, obviously, the Drake Family. Still, I could have done without being seen as a stress management device.

Celestina continued, "Even before the murderer was on the loose, he worked relentlessly, researching the cause for all the failed vampire turnings and attempting to rally other vampire Elders from their deadly apathy."

I wrinkled my forehead in confusion. *What is she talking about? Deadly apathy?* The failed turnings weren't a shocker—everyone knew vampires, shifters, and werewolves were slowly dying out. But what did the leaders of the other vampire Families have to do with anything?

"Which brings to mind—who should take the Eminence his evening blood?" Steely Voice asked.

"Was there a new blood delivery today?" Josh asked.

"Yes, it came in late. I saw the delivery girl leaving when I came up to dinner," Julianne said.

"Excellent, we should try to give him extra, then," Celestina decided.

"Why?" I asked.

Celestina considered the question. "The Eminence is particular about his blood," was the non-answer she finally gave.

"That tells me nothing," I said.

Celestina smiled mysteriously, and I grunted and went back to my food.

"Why don't we send the wizard?" the male vampire who'd sat across the table from me suggested.

"Hard pass." I stabbed some asparagus, assuming that was the end of the matter.

"It's an honor to be chosen to go." A cold beauty enveloped Julianne for a moment as she stared at me. (It was then that I realized maybe dinner really was a bonding experience for the Drake Family.)

I took care to chew, buying myself a moment to come up with

a respectful response. "All the more reason why it shouldn't be me," I said. "I'm just the wizard."

"You're also entertainment," said the vampire across from me —who I was *really* starting to wish had ignored me like everyone else used to before I was dropped off the patio. "Given the murders, it is more important to keep the Eminence amused than to secure additional honor for ourselves."

I almost choked on my ice water and glanced at the other vampires to see how they would correct him.

Unfortunately, they all looked thoughtful.

"Perhaps it's a good idea—for tonight, at least." Steely Voice folded his arms across his chest—he was pretty broad shouldered and muscled for a vampire.

Desperate, I looked to Josh, hopeful that my instructor might get me out of this mess—the *last* thing I wanted to do was deliver blood packs to Killian. Even though there was no chance he was going to bite me—my blood reeked as Rupert liked to constantly remind me—if Killian was hungry it wasn't a good situation to be in. Josh was my last hope for deliverance.

The black-haired vampire met my gaze. "The joy of life can defang the bleakness of eternity," he "helpfully" said.

"But—" I started.

"It's settled, then," Celestina said. "Hazel will deliver the Eminence his blood—though I will go with her to show her where to take it."

The Drake vampires nodded, and the decision was made despite my opposition.

But as long as I lived in Drake Hall, I had to do what the vampires decided, which is why I found myself standing outside the door of Killian's office half an hour later, bearing a silvery tray weighted down with chilled blood packs.

I reluctantly knocked on the door while glaring at the blood packs. (If they tried to make me do this again, I was going to give him all the nearly expired pouches!)

"Enter."

I rolled my shoulders back and bumped the door open. "Celestina and the others sent me up with your dinner."

Killian didn't look up from the document he was reading. Rather, he gestured for me to step inside.

I tiptoed in, but didn't bother hiding my inspection of the place.

The room was all Killian—incredibly, or perhaps restrictively, tidy with every book in place and every paper sorted into a folder or stand. Bookshelves austerely covered the walls, filled with what looked like some priceless volumes of magical books, but one of the gorgeous shelves also held a flatscreen TV, a tablet, and a laptop. It created a sort of jarring combination of history and modern tech, but that's really what Killian was, and why he was so dangerous.

Killian finally looked up from his paper. "Am I to assume there is some method behind my underlings sending *you* here?"

I set the tray on his impersonally bare desk. "Not one I understand. They seemed to think you need to be entertained—though I'm not sure what they expect me to do."

Up went the edges of Killian's lips in that mocking almost-a-smile. "Given your unique personality, to be amusing all I imagine you have to do is exist."

I pressed my lips together, making them thin. "It's not like I go around doing stupid things."

"No," he agreed. "It's your propensity to hiss and puff up like a startled kitten when prodded."

"I still don't understand why you insist on training me if you think I'm so harmless."

"Even when properly trained to the point of being deadly you will *still* resemble a troubled kitten or puppy," Killian said. "It is due to your nature rather than your fighting abilities."

I turned to study Killian's collection of technology, but I

watched out of the corner of my eye as he snagged a blood pack from the tray.

He stabbed the pack with a pointed straw, then sucked it straight from the pouch.

Killian leaned back in his hair, his eyes at half mast, the straw fixed at the corner of his mouth, and he looked *irritatingly* like a model in an advertisement, which wasn't fair. I'd much prefer he linger in dark corners of the room and look like he was planning something evil than showing off his appearance. He was only stunning because it gave vampires a natural advantage over easily swayed humans who would most likely be stunned at their smile.

Unfortunately, I stared too long with my eyes flicked back in an unnatural position, and he caught me staring.

"What is it?" Killian asked.

"Nothing." I resolutely stared at the TV screen.

Killian darkly chuckled. His chair creaked when he stood, and though I didn't hear his feet on the beautiful maroon carpet, I could *feel* his presence behind me. Nothing could hide such a deadly aura.

"I don't believe you." He was so close his presence loomed behind me, and I could see in the TV reflection he was half leaning over me. "Are you disgusted? Frightened?"

I paused for a moment and wondered if he was right. Was I scared?

My heart wasn't pounding any faster than usual even though he was right behind me. But I'm pretty sure my sense of danger was starting to go screwy after living with all these vampires. I still watched Killian with the same kind of intensity I would give a tiger—respect, distance, and the wish that there was a glass wall between us.

I turned around to face him, and couldn't help the laugh that bubbled past my lips.

Killian had appeared dangerously attractive leaning back in his chair with his blood. But now, standing above me, pouch in hand, he more closely resembled a giant kid sucking on a juice pack.

"Enjoying your juice box?" I asked through another snort of laughter.

Killian raised an eyebrow—I *thought* in amusement. "It is odd that most people would be disgusted by the contents of the pouch, but you laugh at it."

I coughed, getting myself under control again. "You're a vampire. What else are you supposed to drink? Besides, you didn't kill anyone to get it, the delivery service dropped it off, and I know they pay their blood donors well."

Killian studied me as he drained his first pouch. He backed up—keeping his eyes on me—and tossed the pouch in the trash before reaching for a new one. "You are one of those awful people who follows a moral code."

"*Everyone* follows a moral code."

"No, everyone is too busy trying to figure out what shades of gray they can get away with manipulating or pulling before they get in trouble," he scoffed.

"That might be how vampires are, but wizards aren't like that."

"Yes, I imagine that's true given the way wizard Houses are just *lining* the driveway, seeking to be your political allies," he dryly said.

I dropped my eyes at the reminder.

"You are a rarity." Killian leaned against the edge of his desk. "A supernatural who actually does as they say. It makes you both weak and incredibly powerful at the same time. That's why you are dangerous. And once you have your magic, I imagine that's going to be more obvious."

I decided to risk looking at him again. He was finishing his second pouch, draining it more slowly than he had the first. "I'm surprised you drink packaged blood," I said. "Isn't fresh blood from a donor supposed to make a vampire stronger?"

Killian sucked the last of the blood from the package. "It is," he said. "But I will *never* drink from a blood donor." He tossed the package out and added, "Most of the Drake Family consumes packaged blood only."

"But...why? Isn't it a status symbol to have blood donors? And if it improves your abilities I would have thought you'd be all over it."

Killian halted, and the cruel, cold creature inside of him surfaced. It was in the heartless curve of his smile and the flinty look in his eyes that now glowed redder and underlined the paleness of his skin. "I don't drink from a donor because I'm not like you. I know just how much gray makes up the world, and how easily we betray others."

It wasn't an answer that made sense, but the white of his fangs was a bit unnerving, and I was starting to regret I asked. I needed to snap him out of it. "Okay." I fought the desire to back up when he stood straight and sauntered toward me, drawing close enough that if I moved my arm I'd brush him.

"How fascinating—you really aren't afraid," he murmured.

"It's not like you could drink from me," I said. "Actually, I could stink you out of this room with a papercut."

"Why do you sound as though you have thought about this?"

I threaded my fingers together and slightly widened my eyes in my best innocent expression. "I've considered seeing if I could make Rupert gag."

There. The feral thing that had risen inside him started to sink back into his bones. He stood taller instead of crowding me, and his terrifying smile became more of a smirk. "It seems to me it wouldn't be wise to overly irritate your weightlifting instructor."

"I don't think he could be any more of a crank, so I might as well have some fun with it. I hope you have a good reason for keeping him around because that guy needs to learn how to *chill*."

Killian's smirk became more pronounced. He folded his arms

across his chest and leaned closer—a very different sort of heat rising in his eyes this time. "And what do you mean by *chill?*"

I gave Killian the side eye and took a pointed step away from him. "I wish you'd stop testing me."

"But it's such fun!"

"For you, maybe."

"You don't seem scared now, but you do appear uncomfortable."

"Want me to bat my eyelashes and sigh over you so we can *both* be uncomfortable?"

Killian's smirk deepened. "Try it."

This, of course, meant there was no way I'd do it. The more I thought about it the more I doubted Killian could be *made* uncomfortable. Any female stupid enough to cast doe eyes at him probably got bulldozed. I opened my mouth, intending to share the recent development with Killian, but was interrupted by a loud, piercing scream.

CHAPTER FOURTEEN

Hazel

Killian was at the door first, ripping it open and pausing in the doorway. He already had his dagger out by the time I joined him, poking my head into the hall.

I didn't see anyone, but I thought I could hear faint sobs.

"What's going on?" I asked.

Rather than respond, Killian grabbed me by the collar of my shirt, pushed me back into his office and shut the door in my face, his quiet footsteps retreating down the hallway.

I stared for a moment or two—did he really think I was a pet that would follow non-verbal commands? Oh, heck no! I wrenched the door open and tilted my head, following the faint sound of crying. It wasn't soft sobs, but something closer to hysterics with painful cries mixed in.

I followed the noise down a flight of stairs and into a back hallway. A woman in a maid uniform stood at an open doorway, her shoulders shaking as she tried to hold in her sobs. Past her I could see Killian talking with Celestina and Josh.

Killian turned around and gave me an annoyed look when I

thumped closer, but he didn't say anything to me and continued his chat with his First and Second Knights.

I placed a hand on the maid's back and patted her. "What's wrong? What happened?"

The maid slumped against the doorway and pointed inside the room.

It was a bedroom—one of the vampire ones because it was fancier, though it lacked photos or personal items. I scanned the room before I saw the body positioned by the open window. It was a woman—she looked young, maybe just a few years older than me, and her eyes were open, but I could see from the doorway that she wasn't moving.

Another murder victim.

I wanted to close my eyes, but I made myself swallow and study her. I would have expected the victim to be a vampire given the location, except she wasn't wearing a suit, or any of the fancy workout clothes the Drake vampires lived in, so chances were she was human. The room didn't look disturbed, so she couldn't have fought whoever killed her, unless they moved her afterwards. But she didn't have a mark on her, either. Not even a drop of her blood had been spilled—which was probably done on purpose, or the vampires would have scented her out earlier. I didn't recognize her, and she wasn't wearing a servant's uniform, so she was most likely a blood donor.

She was a regular human—*employed* by supernaturals, not even a member of it.

And now she was dead.

It wasn't fair. She hadn't done anything wrong. As a human, she shouldn't have been pulled into whatever stupid feud had egged the murderer on. None of it involved her.

My throat ached with the tears I would have shed if I hadn't cried myself dry already. I was vaguely aware of the vampires that rushed up and down the hallway as they searched the house for her killer, and I slowly curled my hands into fists.

Celestina slipped out of the room—running an errand for Killian.

I licked my lips. "Celestina."

She paused just in front of me. "Yes?"

"Will the Regional Committee of Magic really not help when innocent humans are killed?" I asked.

Celestina didn't even have to think about it. "This is not the first human victim we've had, and they haven't been inspired to help yet. They are happy to have something bother the Eminence."

I glanced back at the deceased blood donor.

Celestina patted my shoulder, then continued on her way.

I barely noticed; I was etching the blood donor's face into my mind.

I was weak and subject to Killian's whims, but the blood donor's death had triggered something in me. I wasn't going to sit by and let this sicko get away with this. Feeble as I was, maybe there was something I could do to help.

Because this was wrong. And it had to stop.

I LINGERED in the hallway for about an hour, hoping I would naturally get swept up into the unavoidable vampire meeting the Drake Family would hold to discuss the blood donor's murder, but it never happened.

I did find out her name—Michelle Farrow—and I wasn't going to forget it. Ever.

I also found out her suspected cause of death was strangulation or suffocation—no stab wounds, bite marks, or magical spells had ended her life.

No other information was forthcoming, and eventually it got too late. When I found myself fighting to keep my eyes open, I knew I had to call it a night.

But I set my alarm with the plan to get up early and ask Celestina what the vampires had discussed.

Unfortunately, Celestina was out when I woke up. So was Josh.

This meant there was only one vampire I felt comfortable approaching—though I did consider asking even *Rupert* before I dragged myself to his office.

It was kind of dangerous. I hadn't purposely sought him out ever before—and there was a faint chance he may punish me for daring to.

But there was no way I was going to give up so easily. This was for Michelle, for everyone who had come before her, and the desire to keep anyone from coming *after* her.

I took a deep breath, rolled my shoulders back, and knocked on the door of Killian's office.

"What is it, Wizard?" Killian asked through the door.

I bolstered my courage and poked my head in. "Hey." I studied him—and most importantly his eyebrows—trying to get a handle on his mood.

He was seated behind his desk, wearing a suit like always. It was possible he'd been awake the whole night and hadn't yet slept, but I couldn't tell. His face didn't show any extra signs of concern or frustration.

But he also hadn't started smirking or making fun of me the moment I entered either, which might mean he really didn't like me seeking him out after all, or that the murderer situation had killed off his already twisted sense of humor.

He raised an eyebrow at me—not at the angle that meant he was amused but the one reserved for impatience—and stared.

I tugged on the sleeves of my suit. "Did you find out anything more about the murderer?"

"Why?"

I tried to come up with a believable explanation before giving up—he'd never believe me anyway. "Because I want to know."

Killian leaned back in his chair and studied me intently

enough to make me shift my weight from one foot to the other and back again.

"It's a vampire matter. Do you really wish to be involved?"

"It's not a vampire matter—whoever is doing this killed humans. That means it involves *all* of us."

More staring ensued. It felt like somehow Killian was trying to peer into my soul.

"Strictly speaking, there are no new leads," he abruptly said. "We found no signs of forced entry; no intruders were detected. The murderer is using fae spells—there's no way they could move undetected through the house and not be caught. But it seems that for the same reason the murderer themselves cannot be fae. The Drake lands are warded against most spells. A fae couldn't cross the property line without raising the alarm."

"It's likely what you thought: someone who has fae support?" I guessed.

A sharp nod. "But we have no physical evidence, and no leads to follow. Though we have concluded that Drake Hall has been compromised, or this wouldn't happen—which is a worst-case scenario because if it *is* compromised it might be a fae after all."

I absently flicked my ponytail over my shoulder. "Nah, can't be."

A muscle twitched in Killian's cheek. "I didn't know you had become a master of home security." His voice was practically a purr, and a chill ran down my spine at the show of his temper.

"I'm not," I said, doing my best to keep my voice calm. "But I am a wizard."

The angles of Killian's face seemed less severe as he straightened in his chair. "And?"

"As a wizard I can detect all magic," I reminded him. "I mean, even though I don't have much access to magic, I can totally feel it when someone uses magic. I might not know who it is and where they are, but believe me—you can't miss it. It's like someone electrifies the air."

I was rambling. No—not only was I rambling, I was schooling *Killian Drake* on magic 101. There was no way he didn't know this—I glanced at the Eminence, who was staring at me, this time with *both* of his eyebrows raised.

They hovered at an angle I wasn't wholly familiar with—which made me panic a little. What did it mean?

"Can you discern between fae magic and wizard magic?" Killian asked.

"Yeah. Fae magic has a sort of floral feel to it. Wizard magic is tangier and more electric."

I had thought about the killer a lot while I'd been wasting time the previous night.

Since I hadn't felt even a spark of fae magic throughout the evening of the murder—there wasn't even a faint whiff of it in the room—it had occurred to me that my wild guess of an inside job maybe wasn't so far off.

How else could the murderer stalk through Drake Hall and disappear so easily without the help of magic?

I was still pretty reluctant to trot this idea past Killian—I wanted more information first, particularly about Rupert.

He was adopted, and he made it plain he didn't respect most of the Drake vampires—including the Second Knight—or humans, so the slaughter didn't seem out of character for him. But besides a general gut feeling I didn't have much to go by.

Killian stood in a liquid movement that was unnaturally graceful, jostling me from my suspicions. He turned his back to me and rested a forearm against one of his bookshelves as he broodingly leaned against it.

I had what I wanted—the update on the murderer—so I peered over my shoulder to start plotting out my exit strategy.

But I was blocked when Killian crossed his office in the blink of an eye and set his hand on my shoulder.

I didn't scream as I might have a month ago, but I did jump a little—mostly because he got right up in my face, and his hand was delightfully cool. (I was pretty hot since I had opted to wear my stuffy suit in an effort to placate Killian so he'd be more likely to share information.)

He was bent over so he could stare into my eyes. This close I could see the deep red of his iris. Not to get all poetic, but his eyes strangely reminded me of red stars set in the black velvet of the night sky.

"I don't trust you," Killian announced.

His closeness was really upping the 'danger-danger, this is a predator,' factor, so I had no choice but to resort to humor. "How shocking. You always seem so gullible."

One corner of his lips turned up in the hint of a smug, satisfied smirk. "We'll draw the murderer out."

I waited for him to continue, but he didn't, so I had to ask, "How?"

He finally took a step out of my personal space and stood upright again. "You and I will leave Drake lands, unescorted," he said. "If the murderer has a political motive, they won't be able to miss the opportunity."

"Did you say 'you and I'?" I asked. "And 'unescorted'?"

Killian's voice was silken with his self-satisfaction, but I think I preferred his frustration to it because he sounded equally dangerous but now focused on *me*. "You're the ideal target: weak, fragile, and defenseless."

Mulishly, I put my hands on my hips. "Well, when you put it that way."

"The murderer won't be aware of your training. And in your current state, compared to a vampire you *are* easy to kill."

I stretched my arms above my head as I tried to think.

I wanted to figure out who was behind the murders, and I'd already decided to get myself involved. The danger didn't bother me so much—though if anyone from House Medeis heard about it, they'd undoubtedly throw a fit. (The House comes first and all of that, but humans were dying, so I'd put our entire society before the House for this occasion.)

But the idea of wandering around with Killian without any other Drake vampires? Yeah, that part didn't thrill me.

"Do we need to go out together?" I asked. "Can't you just send Celestina and me out for a girls' day or something?"

"Not if we want the murderer to take the bait before they kill someone else," Killian said. "Eventually they will attack you—you are too tempting of a target to pass. But it will take time for them to decide that killing you would negatively affect us if you are only seen with the Family and not me personally."

"You want the murderer to think that in getting me, it will be a direct attack on you?" I wrinkled my brow as I stared at the Eminence of the Midwest. "Do you *really* think you can be that convincing and get this sicko to attack me on one outing? Because everyone knows you only care about vampires."

Killian's entire demeanor transformed. He went from standing tall and smirking to prowling closer to me. There was that odd gleam in his eyes again. "Oh?" His voice dropped to a rumbling purr. "I don't think it will be that difficult." He tenderly brushed my cheek, which made me shiver. "All we have to do is make it seem that there's...*something* between us."

One of his hands glided around my waist, stopping at my mid back, and he scooped me into an embrace. His other hand slid under my chin and gently pulled up so I had to look up at him. "Don't you agree?" The seduction act dropped when he grabbed me by the cheeks like a grandma pinching a baby.

Smooshed against him as I was, I was able to confirm his entire body was pleasantly cool. (Not fair! Vampires got the looks, the speed, *and* a pleasant body temperature? I call foul play!)

"Why would we do that?" I asked through squished lips. "We'd *both* be miserable!"

Killian released me, though he didn't move away. "I'm willing to suffer a little for my own amusement."

I eyed him. "Your reputation won't take a hit?"

He hardened abruptly, his expression turning flinty and his smile threatening pain. "I'm enough of a monster, no one will dare to *question* it."

I felt the truth of this in my bones, so I sucked in a deep breath. "Okay?"

He blinked, the darkness draining from his eyes. "Hm?"

"I'll play bait."

"...are you certain?"

"Yeah." I brushed my slacks off to give me something to do. "This can't keep going on."

He slightly narrowed his eyes. "It's wrong?"

I nodded.

Killian rolled his eyes. "See—a regular paragon of virtue. Disgusting."

"It's working to your advantage right now, so I don't think it's anything to complain about."

"Whatever," he sourly said. "You've taken all the fun out of it."

"When will we go?" I asked. "Tomorrow?"

Killian appraised me, his eyes traveling over my small frame. "A week."

"Do you think we have that long?"

"Yes, because I'll make our outing known publicly tomorrow when I send Celestina out to order a dress for you and make reservations."

I nodded and awkwardly swung my arms. "Okay. Sounds good."

Killian returned to his desk and sat on the very edge. "In the meantime, I expect you to train with diligence. An extra week might be the difference between life and death."

"Got it. I guess that's my cue to go get changed." Not knowing what else to do, I nodded to him and headed for the door.

"Hazel."

I paused in the doorway and turned around, surprised by the use of my name. "Yeah?"

Killian stared at me, the only sounds in the whole office was the rhythmic tick-tock of a grandfather clock in the corner and my breathing. "Be extra diligent in practicing your magic with your sword," he said.

"Will do." I slipped out of the doorway, almost positive that wasn't what he was going to say. But I didn't know what else he could possibly bring up. It wasn't until I was halfway down the hallway that our conversation finally caught up with me.

Wait—he said he was ordering a *dress*? Just how fancy is the place he's taking me?

CHAPTER FIFTEEN

Hazel

About a week later, I found myself teetering down the stairs in heels trying to juggle my sword and a black clutch stuffed with a book to give it extra heft. (I was willing to go, and I expected Killian would *probably* protect me, but there was no way I was doing this without my own weapon.)

The sun had already set, but the air was hot, so I wasn't cold in my sleeveless cocktail dress. I was pretty sure the humidity was going to ruin the fancy braid a nice maid had helped me tame my hair into, but thankfully I was wearing waterproof makeup, so I wouldn't look *too* rough if I stayed outside long.

I had calculated everything about my look to strive for maturity—the smoky eyeshadow, the heels that added a bit to my height, and thankfully the dress was a sophisticated wrap style. Normally I didn't care a ton about how I looked, besides being presentable. But I wanted to find that murderer—or at least help uncover a lead—and I *didn't* want to do this a second time. If I had waltzed out to meet Killian without the extra prep, I was pretty sure I'd get mistaken for a high school student, so I had to do whatever I could to make our act believable.

Thankfully, when I explained my plan to Celestina, she was all over it. She'd gotten me the makeup and the heels—which I was actually pretty comfortable in. (It helped that she made me jog laps around the mansion in them during the past five days.)

I was pretty happy with my overall look. The dress was gorgeous—it was an opalescent dusty blue color that had hints of white depending on the way I turned. It looked great with my blue eyes and reminded me of a bright afternoon sky decorated with wispy clouds—but I didn't want to know how much it cost. I was pretty sure just seeing the price tag would be enough to make my kidneys shrivel.

The only downside to my outfit was that I hadn't taken the time to ponder how I was going to secure my sword to my waist…

By the time I made it down the last stair, the solar lights that were stabbed into the flower beds at the front of Drake Hall had winked on.

A line of three SUVs were pulled up, but only one driver stood at the side of the car, his hands clasped behind his back. The other two were still in their cars.

The vampire driver bowed to me as he pulled the side door open, revealing a leather interior, and Killian who was lounging on the bench seat, talking on his cellphone. "I *want* the Magic Committee to know about tonight. It will give them something new to think about and hopefully confuse them, which will give me the opportunity to finally pass that law further restricting the Unclaimed in our region."

Yeah, no way was I sitting back there with a scheming Killian.

I pressed my lips together as I studied Killian, then risked a sneaky glance at the driver—whose face held the expression of a stone as he waited for me to climb in. It was a different driver—this one had darker hair and was wider through the shoulders. Hopefully my act would work on him as well.

"Oh, I think I'll ride up front with you." I smiled brightly and placed my hand that held the borrowed clutch over my heart. "I couldn't *possibly* risk distracting the Eminence when he has such important work to do."

The driver furrowed his eyebrows, and it looked like he was going to refuse me.

"Although," I sighed mournfully and switched tactics. "I won't be able to see him from the front seat very well, and he looks so handsome!"

That did it. The slight wrinkles on the driver's forehead smoothed, and he slammed the door shut—probably thinking he was saving his leader from a vapid admirer. He opened the front door and held my clutch for me while I climbed in and balanced my chisa katana on my thighs before closing the door.

He was in the driver's side, buckling his seatbelt and starting the car in the amount of time it took me to inhale.

The drive into Magiford was longer than I remembered, but it made sense given the massive amount of land Killian owned.

Magiford was the magic powerhouse of the Midwest. Located halfway between Milwaukee, Wisconsin and Chicago, Illinois, it was at a perfect location due to its proximity to the large cities and Lake Michigan. The magical community decided to set their headquarters in Magiford rather than a larger city because it already had a strong magical community present, but also because we didn't want to step on any human toes or make them think we had plans to take over.

It was quite small—no skyscrapers to boast of, though there are big office buildings and lots of old architecture. But I loved it anyway, and I knew the city like the back of my hand.

Or I *thought* I did, until the driver pulled into the warehouse district.

"Yeah," Killian said before abruptly hanging up.

I watched in the rear-view mirror and waited until he looked up from his phone before asking, "Where are we going?"

Killian frowned. "What are you doing up there?"

"Sitting?"

He pushed his eyebrows together, looking a bit like a model in an anguished pose. "Why didn't you sit in the back?"

Because you're in the back! "I didn't want to bother you," I modestly said.

He curled up his top lip, revealing a white fang.

Guess he didn't buy that excuse!

"Where are we going?" I repeated, trying to distract him.

He leaned back, lounging sideways across the bench seat. "An exclusive restaurant—you have to be a member to get through the front doors." He lost interest in me and gazed through the tinted windows.

"I'm surprised you didn't want to take the limo today—wouldn't that have been more eye catching?"

"I never ride in the limousine."

I actually twisted awkwardly in my seat so I could peer back at him. "What? Then why is it always in front of your motorcade?"

"Image," he said. "And it acts as a draw to bring enemies out of the woodwork. I find it useful to watch them."

The SUV slowed to a crawl, then stopped directly outside a warehouse that bordered the business district.

I hopped out while the driver opened Killian's door and squinted in the flickering light of the streetlight directly above me. I surveyed the cracked sidewalk and the graffitied metal warehouse. "This is totally not suspicious or sketchy at all," I said.

"Given that Club Luminary is for the refined and influential, I didn't imagine you would appreciate it." Killian straightened his suitcoat. "And you cannot bring your sword inside."

I clutched my sword to my chest. "Why not?"

"Club rules."

"I'm just supposed to be *defenseless*?"

"That is the general idea, yes." Killian smirked. "Though the no-weapon rule does little to hinder the truly powerful. We can be lethal without...*tools*."

I grumbled under my breath as I set my katana in the passenger seat—now doubly thankful for my book-stuffed clutch. Though hopefully the staff wouldn't search me, or they might ask me why I felt the need to carry a copy of *The Abridged Dictionary of Useful Latin*.

Killian exchanged a few murmured lines with the driver, then sauntered away, heading straight for the super sketchy warehouse. "Come on, Wizard."

"This fancy place is seriously in a warehouse? That seems unsanitary." Grit scratched the bottoms of my heels, and I switched my clutch to my right hand—my dominant hand which would make it easier to bludgeon with—as I hurried after him.

"Just wait," Killian advised. He yanked a metal side door open —which squealed in protest—and stalked into the inky blackness.

I cast one last look outside before following him in.

A little light made it through hazy windows at the top of the wall, so I could see the warehouse was completely empty, except for a rusted-out car and a headless broom. Killian followed the wall to the far side of the warehouse, then pressed a red button.

Part of the wall slid open, revealing an elevator car with a velvet carpeted floor, spotless mirrors, and wood paneling. I followed Killian inside a little less reluctantly and tapped my clutch against my thigh.

"Are you ready?" Killian asked once the doors closed behind us.

"Yeah. It's close enough to the truth it won't be a stretch," I said.

After a lot of deliberation, Killian decided we should act like I was a prized pet he was showing off. It would fit his image and most recent actions, and it was sort of true—my importance was just being highly exaggerated to make it seem like Killian would actually *care* if I kicked the bucket.

I glanced at my reflection and was pleased to see the braid was holding. "I think the biggest danger is that *you* go too overboard. No one will believe that you care for me as a person."

"They won't?" Killian smirked and tilted his head back.

I'd realized my mistake and scrambled to fix it as the elevator beeped. "It's not a reflection on your acting skills, but how things are!"

The doors slid open, and Killian's smirk deepened as he offered me his arm.

I gulped, but took it. My only choice was to join Killian in leaving the elevator and hope that catching the murderer was such a priority he'd play nice rather than risk blowing our act.

I raised my chin and prepped myself to put on my 'smitten wizard' act, but the air of the club caught me completely off guard.

I don't know exactly what I had expected—maybe a stereotypical club with loud music that pulsated with overly-obnoxious lights, expensive drinks, and the pervasive smell of BO and perfume.

But this place was an entirely different sort of club.

Settled on top of the warehouse roof, and divided off with glass walls and windows that I bet were *heavily* warded, Club Luminary was a blend of European decadence and modern convenience. It appeared that the club was built like a wheel to allow the best views of the city and countryside, and the center hub was where the kitchens, the granite-topped bar, and restrooms were located. The ceiling was tiled with stretches of skylights and stained-glass windows that paid homage to the various races. The most beautiful, in my opinion, was the stained-glass forest that showed wolves peeking out from behind glowing trees.

"Your Eminence." A woman dressed in black bowed to Killian. "If I may show you to your table; right this way."

Killian and I followed the hostess to a table which was, naturally, set under the stained-glass skylight dedicated to vampires.

(There was a castle on it, a silver orb that was probably the moon, and—of course—red-eyed men and women dressed in the height of Renaissance fashion.)

We passed a few tables of werewolves and three wizards seated in their own section. Beyond our table was a cluster of fae, and they, the werewolves, and the wizards watched with obvious attention as Killian pulled my chair out for me, then seated himself.

"Your server will be with you promptly. Enjoy your evening." The woman curtsied this time, then glided off.

"She's human," I realized.

"Club Luminary management staffs the place with humans—so politics aren't swirled into service and no one is...*tempted*," Killian said. "A fae and vampire own the place—we *do* get along with the fae outside the Night Court," he said when I raised my eyebrows.

I wasn't sure I believed him, but pushing it wouldn't further our act. So I tried to sneakily peer at everyone while smiling adoringly at Killian. I didn't know anyone present, but I recognized them as the movers and shakers of the Midwest. Heck, these people were far above my parents, and they had been highly respected!

When I got around to inspecting the fae, I realized they were clustered around a single male with white hair and a long mustache. "The Paragon is here."

"Yes." Killian idly inspected the cutlery—probably trying to decide which would be most useful to stab someone. "Even he isn't wily enough to avoid the Courts forever."

Our waiter—a human male—swept up to take our orders. Killian ordered a specific blood type for himself, and a five-course dinner for me.

It was a good thing my only real job was to smile adoringly at Killian—like a besotted idiot—because I couldn't have done much else when I saw the string of numbers that my dinner cost.

I dearly, dearly hoped this dinner, the cost of my dress, my suit—and heck, my workout clothes—weren't all being recorded for me to pay back at a later date, or I was in big trouble.

"Something wrong, Pet?" Killian inquired in a dangerously dark and smooth tone.

"Nothing at all," I squeaked.

Killian's look of indifference settled into a slight smirk, and he leaned forward, just before the Paragon pulled up a chair to our table and plopped down.

"Am I glad to see the two of you," the Paragon said. "I've been stuck here an hour already—and they made me change out of my panda slippers before they dragged me here!"

"Good evening, Paragon." Killian accepted the wine flute of blood our waiter delivered. "It seems the representatives from the various Courts have finally caught up with you?"

"Oh, it *seems*, does it?" The Paragon snarled and ruffled his mustache. "You better not have tipped them off."

"I would never," Killian said in a flat and unconvincing tone.

"Why don't you just leave the Midwest?" I asked.

The Paragon sighed deeply. "Can't," he said. "Fae business."

"How terrible," Killian said. "Now buzz off. You are ruining our dinner."

"You have a strange sense of humor." The Paragon eyed the white wine a second server set in front of me.

"It's not humor," Killian said. "I brought my wizard out to enjoy her company, not look at your dusty face. Go away."

The Paragon snorted. "You've never enjoyed anyone's company since the day you were born."

"Perhaps you are right." Killian's unnatural stillness combined with the iciness of his voice made it hard to sit demurely in my chair.

I fought my survival instincts and reached across the table to set my hand on his forearm. He was stiff, but he didn't shake me off. I squeezed his arm, then leaned back, grateful the experience hadn't ended in bloodshed. "I still have to thank you for your help, Paragon. I never would have known my magic was sealed without you."

"No trouble at all." He glanced at Killian, seemingly realizing he'd stepped on a landmine of sorts. "I'm glad I could be of assistance. Have you had any luck in breaking the cursed thing?"

"The seal? No. Though it is not from lack of trying," I said with some acid in my voice.

By now Killian had relaxed marginally and once again returned to leaning back in his chair, the mocking light back in his eyes. "Don't look now, Paragon, but here comes one of your *constituents*."

The Paragon groaned and hung his head as a male fae with silvery hair and copper skin approached our table. He was dressed in a robe of black and dark purples and blues, and had a circlet—or if I was being unkind, a tiara—threaded through his hair. Going by his clothes, I'd say he was a Night Court fae.

"Good evening, Your Eminence," the fae said in a voice that sounded as dark as the night.

Killian showed no signs of hostility. If anything, he seemed even more relaxed, and a frightening smirk played at the edges of his lips. "Good evening, Ira."

"Might this be the wizard you accepted into servitude?" the fae, Ira, asked.

"I am surprised you heard of her."

"Surely you expected the community to talk. Allowing her to pledge servitude to the Drake Family and bring wizard drama into your domain is rather out of character for you."

Killian shrugged. "I will do much for the sake of my amusement. Hazel Medeis—Adept of House Medeis." He extended his hand to me expectantly.

Awkwardly, I reached out to take it, and he tugged me out of my seat so I stood next to his chair.

"She's no servant." Killian slid his thumb under my palm and tapped me, reminding me to slip on a stupid look of admiration. "Rather, I've taken her on as a pet, you could say."

I smiled as big as I could at him and leaned a bit closer, attempting to appear over-eager. (Good heavens, I hoped House Medeis's reputation didn't suffer too badly for this show. Ugh.)

Ira made a noise of surprise in the back of his throat. "You're keeping a pet—an animal that requires affection to survive? And you believe she will survive? It seems you have become overly optimistic—perhaps the stress of your powerful role has changed you."

Killian shrugged. "I have a use for her. Given time I'm sure she'll be terrifyingly adept in magic and fighting. Wizards have the capacity to be stronger than fae, given their war-like magical abilities. It appeals to me."

"Perhaps, except it would seem you'll never be able to take full advantage of her blood," Ira observed. "Even if you coaxed her into putting her faith in you, you could *never* trust her that much, blood-stalker." Ira smirked. "And given her current level of abilities, it seems she'll merely be fodder for gossip for some time—if not always."

"Ira, stop picking childish fights." The Paragon abruptly stood up. "Everyone in the city knows the fae have enough trouble of their own—the only thing you're going to get by poking the bear is your hand bitten off."

"But, Paragon, we fae are only allowed to speak the truth." Ira made a show of widening his dark eyes and motioning to Killian and me. "What I've said cannot *possibly* be offensive if it is the truth."

The Paragon rolled his eyes and pinched the bridge of his hawkish nose. "This job stinks. Why can't I quit?" he muttered under his breath—though I don't know that the vampire or other fae were bothering to listen based on the way they eyed each other.

Killian stayed seated—probably a show of power—but raised

an eyebrow at Ira. "I was unaware that the Night Court had a reason to fear the idea of my having a pet wizard. She won't attack except on behalf of my Family, after all. Unless...*you* are subverting Drake Family interests?"

Now it was Ira's turn to roll his eyes. "What could the Night Court have against the Drake Family?" he simpered.

It was about then that I felt it: fae magic.

Fae magic has a really strong floral scent that always makes me feel like I'm drinking bathwater that's been liberally dosed with roses and bubble bath. It was subtle—which meant it wasn't a fighting spell, but probably something subtle like persuasion magic.

"You really think you can hide it after all of this?" Killian asked.

"You imply we would break the laws of the supernaturals? With what proof?" Ira said. "You dishonor the Night Court!"

I glanced back at the fae who were still seated at the table where the Paragon had abandoned them. They were watching, but the floral feeling wasn't coming from them. Which meant it was the Paragon—unlikely—or Ira. I let my senses stretch toward the night fae, and sure enough I felt a concentration of floral scent. He had a hand planted on his chest, but I'd bet anything a magic-embedded medallion was under his palm, hidden by his clothes.

"He's using magic," I announced.

Everyone in the restaurant was still, and I slowly raised my eyes so I could meet Ira's gaze. "Forgot I was here, did you?" I smiled—it was brittle, but my meaning was clear. "That's fine, though. I'm with the Eminence all the time now, so I'm sure you'll remember in the future."

My threat—though *completely* unfounded—was clear: a wizard was throwing her lot in with Killian Drake, which would substantially change things as long as I wandered around alive.

Ira's expression turned icy. Rather than explode with anger, he seemed to draw all his emotions in so he resembled a stone, but there was something to his eyes—a promise of pain and blood.

I tried to keep my expression pleasant and hoped he couldn't tell how nervous I was, but between the tension of the room and my natural body temperature I was starting to sweat.

Ira—as unreadable as darkness—opened his mouth.

"Ira, boy, you've been bested by the wizard." The Paragon smacked the night fae on the back so hard, Ira stumbled. "Now drop that neat little persuasion spell you have, or club management will get cross with us. Come on." He started to shuffle away, then glanced back at Killian and me. "I'd thank you in the future if you didn't purposely bait my constituents," he dryly said.

Killian shrugged. "They have to learn to leave my wizard alone."

The Paragon made a "hmm" of disbelief, but swept off, a glowering Ira reluctantly following him. Another fae dressed in similarly colored robes scurried up to Ira. They exchanged whispers before the other fae—also most likely of the Night Court—fluttered off, disappearing through the elevator doors.

Noise slowly returned to the club—the quiet clink of dishes, the faint hush of conversation, and the rattling of ice as a bartender mixed drinks at his station.

I let out a deep breath and sagged slightly. We'd made it.

Still holding my hand, Killian stood. With the same confident elegance he did everything, he slid his free hand between my shoulder blades and pulled me flat against his chest. He released my hand only so he could brush my cheek with a gentleness that really made me regret opening my big mouth in the elevator.

"Is this really necessary?" I hissed into his chest.

"After the show you just put on? Yes. Be thankful, I could have pulled you into my lap." His breath tickled my ear as he bent over me so he could whisper. "But I thought you might club me with that purse of yours if I did."

I released a strangled laugh, relaxing a little more at the

thought that I could actually hit him. My heart slowed to a regular tempo, and I was grateful for the coolness Killian radiated—doing more to cool me off than the restaurant's AC.

"You did well." Another brush of my cheek, and Killian released me. He sat back down in his chair as if all of this had been the most natural thing in the world, leaving me to totter back to my seat.

I cleared my throat as I sat down. "Well. That was…" I struggled to find the right word.

"Invigorating?" Killian suggested.

"Not at all what I was thinking, but sure. What now?"

Killian looked downright smug as he picked up his glass of blood and swirled it, his fangs flashing. "Look pretty and enjoy your food, Wizard. That's all you need to do, now."

THE ORDER WAS EASIER SAID than done.

The food was fantastic, of course—probably the best I'd eaten in my life. But eating while Ira scowled at me the whole night wasn't excessively fun. The dessert course got my mind off of everything, though. (They gave me a salted caramel chocolate tart, fruit meringue, and cafe au lait gelato, so it would have been pretty hard *not* to love it.)

After the meal I was overall pretty content, and by the time we left, I was happily zigzagging back and forth, swinging my clutch as I hopped off the elevator.

"Excuse me, Your Eminence, a moment of your time?" One of the waitstaff had rushed down what looked like a set of emergency fire stairs, catching Killian just outside the elevator.

Killian slid his hands into his slacks. "Yes?"

"Club Luminary offers our sincerest apologies for this evening…"

Not sensing any magic, and swiftly losing interest, I continued ahead through the dirty warehouse, making a straight line for the door that opened out onto the street where our SUV waited.

I was hoping if I got out there and buckled into the front seat before Killian followed, he'd forget to order me to sit in back with him.

I walked past the rusted-out car, then felt the sizzle of wizard magic.

CHAPTER SIXTEEN

Hazel

Pinpointing it behind me, I switched so I held my clutch by the edge and whirled around.

A female wizard had snuck up behind me. She held sparking fireballs in each hand. "Surrender, Hazel Med—"

I slammed the edge of the clutch into her throat, choking her. The fireballs evaporated from her palms, and she toppled like a log.

As she went down, she flung a bolt of electricity. I jumped over it—though the landing made my feet hurt, and one of the heels almost slid out from underneath me.

She tried to jab me with an icicle, but I dodged it and—following the endless martial arts drills I'd practiced—kicked her in the gut.

I let my clutch dangle from my wrist by its strap, then slammed a foot down on her stupid robe, pinning her in place. "This! Is Why! You should! Have let me! Bring my! *Sword!*" I shouted as I pummeled my clutch into her head again and again.

When she sagged listlessly, I stopped smacking her and studied her clothes.

Unlike House Tellier and House Medeis, she was dressed in a robe of periwinkle blue. Only one House in the area wore that shade of blue—House Rothchild. "It can't be," I whispered.

Somewhere behind me, a man roared. I turned around, but I could tell I was going to be too late. He was right behind me, supporting an orb of spark-spitting lightning and wearing the same color robe as the woman.

I braced myself and blinked, and my vision was abruptly filled with the back of a black suit.

Killian stood in front of me, casually holding the wizard's arms as if this was a common occurrence. "I issued a warning," he said—the red of his eyes glowing unnaturally in the shadows of the warehouse. "It was the only warning you're going to get." He threw the wizard so hard, the man flew halfway across the warehouse and dented the metal wall on impact.

I winced, then turned back to the female wizard—who was still dazed on the ground. I squatted down next to her, inspecting the House crest sewn on the robe. Yep, it was definitely House Rothchild. But why? They had been my parents' allies! Even more troubling, they were a heck of a lot more powerful than House Tellier. Their wizards all packed a lot more magic in their blood.

Which is why it was an equally shocking realization that I had just beaten down a House Rothchild wizard, using just my training and a book-padded purse. "Oh my gosh," I said, thunderstruck. "Killian is right. We *are* easy to fight off!"

"You don't say!" Killian's velvety voice was a hair's breadth from a snarl.

I rushed to get between Killian and the wizard. "Don't kill her!"

"I don't intend to," Killian coldly said. "She needs to be questioned—and she'll have to be alive for that. But Manjeet and

Leonardo will take care of it. We're leaving." He grabbed me by the wrist and tugged me away from the woman.

Already two vampires I recognized as belonging to the Drake Family stepped through the open side door. Killian only had to flick his eyes at the woman. Both of the vampires bowed slightly, then glided up to her. I didn't get to see any more—Killian towed me out of the door before they reached her.

The SUV was waiting for us, and I knew better than to aim for the front seat when Killian slid in, still holding my wrist. I scrambled after him, and it wasn't until I had my seatbelt in place that Killian let me go. I glanced at the warehouse as the driver appeared in the driver seat with his vampiric speed and started the car.

Someone had turned on the lights inside the warehouse—light glowed from the dirty windows near the top. But even in the shadows of the night I could see the dent where Killian had thrown the male wizard.

The wizard was dead—there was no doubt in my mind about it. But I wasn't really sure how I felt. As a part of House Medeis, I knew I should have abhorred his death and Killian for doing it. But Killian *had* made a public announcement when I had previously asked for mercy—even Momoko and Felix knew about it. And still, the wizards had attacked me.

And while my parents had followed the rule of no killing and avoiding physical fights to the letter, they had lied to me my entire life. Where exactly did that leave me? Uncomfortable, and wishing I didn't have to think about any of this. So, I decided not to—for the moment.

"You know, I can finally see I'm really improving!" I almost clapped my hands in glee. "I think I get discouraged because the only people around for me to compare myself to are vampires—which I'll *never* be able to beat even if we manage to unseal my magic. But tonight showed me just how much better I am now!"

"With enough training, you'll be able to fight on even ground with the average vampire," Killian said.

I didn't believe that, but I suspected Killian didn't care if I believed it or not, he was going to attempt to make me into a stalwart warrior capable of kicking butt. After tonight, I had no complaints about that!

With the adrenaline surging and the glee of having won —*without* magic—making me ride high, I figured now was as good a time as any to drop the bomb I'd been sitting on. "Have you considered if the murders could be an inside job?"

Killian glanced at me. "I assume by your bizarre shift of conversation, this is something you've been thinking of for a while?"

"Maybe—yeah."

Killian stared out his window. "The Drake Family is loyal to me."

"I don't know about that, because let me tell you not all of them are happy."

He raised an eyebrow as he studied my face. "You suspect Rupert?"

"I'm not saying it's him, buuuuut..."

"You suspect him because you dislike him."

I leaned forward against my seatbelt so I could pluck my chisa katana from the front seat. "But he's definitely capable of it."

Killian was still for several moments, then shook his head. "It's not anyone from my Family. I looked into that possibility after the first casualty in Drake Hall, before you arrived," he said. "The Night Court is absolutely behind it."

I shrugged. "If you say so."

I wasn't surprised by his refusal—I actually thought he'd instantly reject me instead of thinking it over for even a moment. But I'd done what was right and spoken up. I'd just have to keep an eye on Rupert—and my senses open in case it really *was* a fae sneaking in and out.

"What do you have in your purse?" Killian asked, drawing me from my thoughts.

"It's called a clutch, and it's stuffed with the biggest book I could fit in it."

"A rather eccentric weapon, but one that Club Luminary could not feasibly refuse. Good thinking."

"Thanks! Do you think tonight was a success?"

Killian shrugged. "It's difficult to say—I'm not sure how desperate or gullible the murderer is."

I nodded slowly and pushed back against the bench seat.

I suspected that our display had gone well—not in the club, but in the attack. The supernatural community was just chock full of gossips...and I suspected that by morning everyone important would know how Killian Drake had protected me—his supposed pet wizard he was training up—and then dragged me from the warehouse by my wrist.

Undoubtedly, he'd done it to protect his investment, but there was a pretty good chance that everyone else would ignore that truth and make us into something else...hopefully it would be enough to bring the murderer knocking.

Which meant I intended to never let my katana out of my sight until the creep was caught, and I had better take my training as seriously as ever.

I WAS FEELING marvelous when I jogged into the gym two days later. Celestina had sent me outside for a warmup run, and I was happily chortling because I was jogging at a faster pace than when I had first started my training. I really was improving!

"Finished," I told Celestina as I came to a stop in front of her.

"Great job." Celestina waved Josh down—who was holding my chisa katana for me on the other side of the gym. "Let's get started, then."

I caught sight of her nails—which were a dainty shade of blue with pink dahlia flowers on her thumbs and pinkies. "Did you get your nails done?"

"Yes!" Celestina eagerly held her hands out for inspection. "I went to a shop while Killian was wining and dining you. What do you think?"

"They're so pretty! I love them!" I appropriately cooed.

"Are we admiring nails?" Josh handed me my sword as he peered over Celestina's arm.

"Yep," I said.

Josh cleared his throat and said in a much more enthusiastic and slightly higher pitched voice, "Wow, they are so totally gorgeous! You're a queen, and they absolutely suit you!"

I stared at him as Celestina almost jumped with her joy.

"What?" Josh asked. "I can mimic girl talk—though I am limited in my vernacular."

Before I could ask—because Drake Hall was *not* a hotbed of modern phrases and girl talk, which begged the question, how had he learned it?—Celestina clapped her hands. "Okay! Since you so easily defeated that female wizard, we've decided you're ready for a bigger challenge." She swiveled and pointed to the area cushioned with thick mats the vampires used for sparring. "Starting today, you'll be in mock fights with some of the other Drake Family vampires while Josh and I coach you from the sidelines."

I squinted at the beautiful vampire. "You're kidding, right?"

Celestina patted my arm—I wasn't sure if she was trying to be encouraging or consoling, which made me more than a little nervous. "Not at all. You've progressed marvelously in your basic training. It's time we work on your foundation in fighting."

I scrunched my nose up. "You're awful. I take back all the nice things I said about your nails."

Celestina laughed. "You might think this is unfair, but if we can get you used to the physical aspects of a fight—the dodging, using weaponry, and general battle strategies and assessment—when you do finally unseal your magic, you'll be a major threat."

"I believe," Josh chipped in, "the proper term is 'a badass'."

It sounded appealing. I was starting to think my seal couldn't be broken given everything they'd already put me through. But that only meant this training was even more important. If I could take down a wizard with my skills, if I improved enough I might be able to take out Mason even *without* magic.

"Okay." I took a deep breath and nodded, rocking forward onto my tiptoes. "Who am I fighting?"

"Rupert," Celestina said.

"Are you *insane*?" I hissed—not caring if the red-haired vampire heard me as he finished what was probably his 400th pushup over on the maps. "He hates me! He's going to kill me!"

"He will do no such thing," Celestina said.

"Isn't there anyone else?" I craned my neck, peering around the gym—only two other vampires were present at the moment, but maybe someone would come down soon?

"We selected Rupert because he knows how to hold back," Josh said. "Which will go much farther in assuring your wellbeing than whether your opponent likes or dislikes you."

"And Josh and I need to watch and assess your skills and natural movements," Celestina added. "It will help us capitalize on any strengths you have that we don't know about, and figure out what weaknesses you need to shore up first."

"First, meaning you assume I'm going to have a lot?" I asked.

"Undoubtedly," Josh happily said. "You are a kitten facing off with a tiger."

"That's just *fantastic*," I muttered.

Celestina laughed. "You'll do fine." She dropped an arm over my shoulders and moved to steer me in Rupert's direction, then abruptly removed her arm as if my skin scorched her. "Sorry."

I waggled a finger at her. "If you think I'm going to forgive you this fast for sticking me with Rupert, have I got some bad news for you."

Celestina flipped her dark hair over her shoulder. "No, I was apologizing for my casual manners."

I furrowed my eyebrows, trying to follow her logic. "What is there to apologize over? We're friends."

"You don't mind?" Celestina asked.

"Nah, why would I?"

"Most find a vampire's touch...unsettling, because we're rather cool to the touch," Celestina said.

"Oh. I actually like that you guys tend to be cooler, since us wizards run hot," I said. "But it doesn't matter."

Celestina laughed and let her arm drape over my shoulders again. "The Eminence did a good thing the night he picked you out."

"What, am I a puppy now?" I stretched my arms out in front of me, reassured by my katana's familiar weight.

Rupert rolled his eyes as we joined him on the mats. "Can we get this over with? I have better things to do than waste my time taking the wizard's feeble attacks."

"Yes, thank you, Rupert, for taking on the role of attacker," Celestina said. "Hazel, we'd like you to push your magic through your sword and use it during the fight."

I snorted. "And what, singe his hair?"

"When you have more magic power you can use the same attack patterns, but the magic will be much more potent, making you far more powerful," Josh said. "This is an ideal way to begin practicing, so we don't have to worry about you accidentally injuring yourself or others."

"I can't hurt myself with my own magic." I settled into a guard stance on the mats, holding my katana horizontally. I tuned out Celestina and Josh, and focused on Rupert and the beat of my own heart.

He tried to circle me, but I kept my footwork sharp and

pivoted so I faced him. I pulled magic from the air and through my blood, feeling a smidgen better when the faint sparks of my magic encircled my katana and I felt the burn of my small wizard mark.

He moved to slug my gut. I moved my katana to block, but it was a feint, and he instead hit my shoulder.

It hurt, but it was a much gentler impact than I expected. It seemed he really was going to play nice.

Encouraged, I dropped my shoulders and concentrated, blocking a kick to my right thigh with my katana before I thrust my sword at his open right side.

With his vampiric speed he dodged easily, but he attacked with the slowness he'd first adopted.

Eventually we fell into fighting patterns I recognized—Josh and Celestina had been drilling them into my head since my first week of training. Rupert landed several jarring hits—at least a few of them were going to leave bruises, but it was almost enjoyable.

It wasn't until he drew so close I couldn't use my katana that I realized something was wrong.

The fight—which had previously been back-and-forth by the book—swerved with his close distance, making me stumble.

I tried to get my katana up, first feinting a jab at his throat with the hilt of the sword before swiveling, but Rupert grabbed it mid-air.

"You're getting cocky, *rat-blood*," Rupert said. He leaned in so close I could smell the faint trace of hot blood on his breath—though even with such close quarters he kept his hand wrapped around my katana.

The blade dug into the skin of his palm, and drops of blood dripped between his fingers. He ignored it. My magic fizzed around his fingertips, but besides the occasional jump of his arm —moving from the electricity—it didn't seem to bother him.

I gritted my teeth, and my arms shook as I fought to keep my sword up. "Aww, we're still using cute nicknames, huh?" I was *really* wishing I had more magic right about now—I could fry Rupert like a bug instead of just annoying him with tiny zaps.

Rupert snarled like a caged animal. He effortlessly ripped my katana from my grasp and flung it away.

"Rupert!" Celestina called. "What are you doing?"

I tried to back up and retreat, but Rupert stayed on me.

"Rupert!" Josh shouted.

I tried to angle myself in Celestina and Josh's direction, but I only took one step. In that time Rupert pushed in closer and jabbed with his fist, landing an explosive hit to the side of my head. I toppled, and instantly everything went black.

CHAPTER SEVENTEEN

Hazel

My ears rang, and when I tried to open my eyes the world swirled madly. Somewhere in the blurry distance someone shouted.

I groaned, and something soft moved under my head as I tried to remember why I had collapsed. The fight abruptly flooded my memory. "That *jerk*!"

I tried to sit up, but everything hurt, and the spinning made my stomach queasy.

"Here." Celestina supported my back with her knee as she passed me a potion.

I recognized it as another fae healing draught. This one had a faint fruity flavor that was a little tart—like kiwi. I chugged it. The first swallow almost made me gag, but as soon as it hit my stomach I started to feel better.

My head still rang, and I could still hear yelling, but finally everything started to focus.

"You *disobeyed* my orders!"

That sounded a lot like Killian, but that was impossible.

Killian would never raise his voice like that, and the British accent was way too strong. Though the tone was certainly flinty and icy enough.

"What's going on?" I finished the bottled potion then wrapped my hands around my head, grateful for Celestina's support.

"It's the Eminence." Celestina's voice was hard to gauge—it was guarded, but also had a flicker of something like worry.

"What, did he come to peer at my prone body and sneer about fragile wizards?" I asked.

"No. I think he's going to kill Rupert."

"*What?*" I dropped my hands and sat all the way up.

I'd been carried off to the side of the gym, but Rupert and Killian stood on the mats where Rupert had knocked me out.

Rather, Killian stood on the mats. Rupert was dangling from Killian's grasp, his feet hanging in the air.

"That trigger-happy tyrant." I struggled to my feet, briefly losing balance when the room bulged like a fishbowl. I shook my head, trying to clear my vision.

"You'll stop him?" Celestina asked.

I took a few tottering steps before I got my feet under me. "Someone has to!"

As the fae potion pumped through my veins I switched from a walk to a mad scramble, quickly closing the distance between me and the rage-filled Killian.

Every muscle in his body was stiff with anger. The planes of his face were hard, but his voice whipped like an icy wind and filled the room. "I said the wizard was to be *untouched*." His fangs were more prominent than usual, and the red-black of his eyes had hardened into something closer to obsidian. "And yet you still attacked her. You should know quite well what I do to those who don't follow my orders."

I swear I could hear the vertebrae in Rupert's neck as Killian squeezed harder.

The red-haired vampire dangled helplessly from Killian's grasp. His face was turning a dark shade of purple, twisted in a horrible grimace. Though he gripped Killian's wrist he didn't try to attack the Eminence.

"You hit her with enough force to knock her unconscious!" Killian shouted.

"And I'm awake now, how about that!" I hurried onto the mats, sliding to a stop just short of Killian.

Killian peeled his eyes from Rupert and studied me.

I tried not to visibly gulp as the blackness of his eyes promised death and froze me where I stood.

Rupert gurgled, reminding me of the situation. I forced a shaky smile to my lips. "Do you want to put him down now?"

Killian looked back at Rupert, holding him effortlessly in the air. "You're going to ask for mercy."

I took a deep breath. "Yes."

"Even though he hurt you."

"We were in a mock fight," I said. "And it's not like he was trying to kill me—I'd be dead if he was."

Actually, I would have died in my first week of training. There were hundreds of ways Rupert could have killed me when I reported to him for weightlifting, and he could have more easily made it look like an accident. The thought nagged me for a moment—if Rupert was the murderer like I thought, he'd already had ample opportunity to kill me and hadn't. Did that just mean he had a bigger plan in mind, or was he innocent?

"He disobeyed an order."

"Yeah, so exile him or something—you don't *kill* him!" I argued. "A fae potion fixed me right up, so he didn't even hurt me *that* badly." A part of me couldn't believe I was arguing on Rupert's behalf, but I didn't want him to get killed because of me.

"For something as fragile as you, the line between death and injury is a fine one," Killian grimly said. "In accordance with your ridiculous House Medeis beliefs you'd argue for him even if he killed you."

"No, I wouldn't..." I trailed off when I realized it was true. If Rupert had killed an innocent in cold blood—not just me—I wouldn't raise a finger.

And that totally went against everything House Medeis taught. But it didn't feel wrong...

Rupert writhed in Killian's hand and choked.

"Killian, you're going to kill him!" I said, panic really starting to sink into me.

Killian watched Rupert with disinterest. "That's the point."

"But—he's from the Drake Family. You..." I trailed off when I realized Killian wasn't listening.

I had to do something!

I hoped with every corner of my heart that I wasn't going to die for what I was about to do. I barreled into Killian, smacking into his chest, then stood on my tiptoes so I could reach up and place my hands over his cheeks, pulling his head down to look at me. "Don't do this, please!"

I wish I could have thought of something more impressive or thoughtful, but I don't think it would have moved him anyway.

A stifling silence blanketed the gym, broken only by Rupert's wheezes. Killian stared down at me—his eyes still the bottomless shade of black that threatened to envelop me.

"Fine." He dropped Rupert.

The vampire hit the ground with the grace of a sack of potatoes, and immediately drew in a deep, coughing breath.

I dropped my hands from Killian's face and took a step back.

Killian turned on his heels and strode away.

I glanced back at Rupert, who was curled up, holding his neck as he tried to breathe again.

Chances were he'd hate me more if I stuck around to chat, so I hurried after Killian.

I paused at the gym door—I was supposed to be training now—but Celestina made a shooing motion, so I followed Killian out.

Killian didn't even glance down at me when I joined him, jogging to keep up. "What is it? You got the mercy you wanted."

"Yeah. Um, are you okay?" I asked.

Killian halted, then looked down at me, his eyebrows furrowed as he stared at me in clear confusion. "What?"

"You were really upset," I said. "I mean, all he did was clock me one in the head."

"He disobeyed me."

"Yeah, you said that, but it seemed like a pretty extreme reaction."

He blinked slowly, like a cat. "I require my Family to be obedient—and I wish to keep you compliant and easy to manipulate. Rupert threatened both of these things."

"Killian." I rolled my eyes. "If you are trying to keep me compliant, I have got some news for you."

He stared down at me for a really long moment, then the corner of his right lip quirked up slightly. "You are a strange creature. Not long ago you accused Rupert of being the murderer, and yet today you spoke up on his behalf." He gently cradled my left cheek in one hand, then pushed back my hair on my right temple, inspecting the area where Rupert had hit.

"I don't get it either," I admitted. "It just felt wrong."

"And of course you must strive to live by mere feelings." His voice contained an ounce of bite that actually made me feel a bit better.

"It's not feelings so much as a moral code," I said.

Killian slightly shook his head. "You virtuous idiots disgust me."

I folded my arms behind my back as I tried to figure out what to say. "Thank you. For listening."

Killian shrugged slightly. "Don't make me regret my decision."

I squawked in irritation. "How am *I* supposed to affect Rupert?" I demanded.

Killian laughed and sauntered off, moving at a much slower and relaxed pace.

Whatever had bothered him was gone.

I watched his back disappear down the hallway, then turned around with the intention of going back to the gym and getting myself an icepack from the freezer. Even with the fae potion I was probably due for a headache in a few minutes, so it was key I prepared. (And hopefully Josh or someone else had dragged Rupert out of the gym by now.)

As I trotted back, I had to wonder...had Killian really come down so hard just because Rupert disobeyed an order? Or was he —as unlikely as it seemed—concerned for me?

As soon as the thought formed, I laughed. It was so hilariously impossible; I was a little embarrassed I even thought it. Killian Drake was a killing, political machine. There was no way he'd ever come to *trust* me, much less care for me.

Ruefully, I shook my head as I re-entered the gym, where Celestina hugged me and proceeded to shove another fae potion down my throat. By the end of the day, I'd mostly forgotten about the incident, except for the implications it might have on my suspicions of Rupert.

―――

Unfortunately, in the week that followed another vampire was murdered—the leader of the Flores Family. Despite the vampires pooling their resources—aka their spies—the murderer still hadn't been tracked down. (Apparently this time Killian had gone so far as to hire a werewolf to sniff out the area, but she insisted she only smelled vampire, which soured the vampires on hiring additional outside help.)

The murder doubled the intensity of the air around Drake

Hall, and dinners were now a grim affair. I didn't see much of Rupert either, but Celestina wouldn't tell me if he was still in trouble or not, she just reassigned weightlifting duty to another vampire—Gavino, whom I privately called Steely Voice.

He was pretty nice, *and* he told me Rupert was still alive and a part of the Drake Family, so I wasn't too torn up about the switch.

Everyone was really on edge, which was why I was surprised and more than a little confused when, about a week and a half after my fight with Rupert, I found myself slathered in suntan lotion and floating in the mythical Drake Hall swimming pool.

It was beautiful, of course. The pool was enormous, and it wasn't just a lap pool but had two legit waterfalls taller than a human, a big slide, and a spa that I could climb into from the pool. The surrounding patio was just as extravagant with stone tiling and lots of comfortable patio furniture arranged under huge umbrellas that were lined with the same sun-proof lining the vampires used on their personal umbrellas. The pool was fenced in with hedges and a few delicate trellises that were covered with ivy to provide additional sun coverage. One of them even spanned the deep end of the pool.

I should have expected the pool would be gorgeous—couldn't have anything less than perfect for Killian Drake, including a swimming pool he apparently didn't use—but I was still more than a little surprised as I floated in the warm water and squinted in the early afternoon sun. I paddled until I had successfully turned around and was facing Killian.

He—along with eight other Drake vampires—was sitting under the shade of the umbrellas. Or rather, Killian was sitting. Everyone else was standing at attention.

"What are we doing?" I asked the master vampire.

Killian took a long drink of his blood pouch—which he was again drinking like a kid sipping a juice box. It would have added to the weirdness of the afternoon, but it irked me to see he somehow still looked stylish. "I already told you. We're testing to see if the seal on your magic is water soluble."

I struggled to adjust myself in my inner tube, but when I was tempted to shuck it off Killian gave me the evil eye, so I kept it on even though I knew how to swim. "I might regret this, because this is probably the most enjoyable '*test*' you've put me through, but are you for real?"

Killian was stretched out on a lounge chair, looking indolent and cool even though it was really hot and he was still wearing his black suit. "Would you rather we return to flinging you off buildings? Or perhaps running you until you collapse?"

I pressed my lips together. "No."

"Then shut up." Killian went back to his blood pouch.

Disgruntled, I paddled around the pool, returning to my own thoughts.

Rupert was still bothering me. As little as I liked it, I didn't think he was the killer. I wasn't stupid: he was a jerk, and he obviously hated me. But he hadn't fought back when Killian nearly killed him.

If he was really the murderer, there's no way he wouldn't have fought for his life. But who else could it be? I didn't know about the other murder victims, but I was almost positive the slayings that took place on Drake land were an inside job. Who else could get in through all the layers of security? And I wasn't so quick to write off the werewolf's complaints about only smelling vampires. But I also didn't know who out of the Drake Family it could be.

I'd met nearly all of them, and I got the feeling they all would walk through fire for Killian.

I thoughtfully glanced up at the other vampires who stood around the patio, searching for...I don't know what.

All of them were stiff. I didn't think it was the sunlight—I'd seen them *running* in the afternoon sun before—but probably the situation with the murderer. Neither Celestina nor Josh was present—I was pretty sure they were heading two separate investigations looking into the murder since Gavino, aka Steely Voice, had taken me running and done some basic sword drills the previous day instead of them.

They—the vampires, not just Celestina and Josh—needed to lighten up. They were all grim, and it wasn't a good look on them. (Heck, even their stereotypical deadly expressions were better!)

A plan started to hatch in my mind, and my impulsive side won out, so I paddled over to the side of the pool. "Killian."

He'd been swiping through his cellphone, but when I called he looked up. "What?"

"Come here, please?"

I couldn't judge the expression in his eyes because he wore sunglasses, but the lack of movement in his eyebrows told me he wasn't amused. "No."

"But I have a question."

"Go bother Gavino." He went back to looking down at his phone.

I pressed my lips together and wiggled in my slippery inner tube as I tried to plot. What would get him over here? I planted my palms on my inner tube and lifted myself up, trying to sit on the edge, but the plastic ring was slippery, and I flipped over, going face first into the water.

I laughed when I resurfaced and was encouraged to see Killian had lifted an eyebrow above the curve of his sunglasses.

"I'm sorry, did I disturb you?" I asked, completely unrepentant.

His eyebrow stayed up as he sipped his blood pouch.

I watched him as I kicked my feet on the surface of the pool, splashing water and making a lot of noise.

"You are a pest." Killian set his blood pouch and phone down, then sauntered over to the edge of the pool. "What do you want?"

"Vampires can get wet, right?" I asked.

Killian shed his sunglasses so he could properly stare at me.

"Do you *really* think I'd have a pool on my property if that wasn't the case?"

"I'm just checking," I sniffed.

"You should know your vampire lore better than to think such an idiotic thing." He rolled his eyes and squatted down so he could lightly cuff the back of my head, which was exactly what I wanted him to do.

The water was almost chest high for me, so I was able to jump pretty high and latch my arms around Killian's neck. I then pushed off the pool wall, attempting to drag Killian into the pool.

I was shocked when Killian actually tipped forward and fell in, plunging into the water with me—I kind of figured I'd just hang from his neck like a monkey and get a laugh out of the other vampires. But I realized the miscalculation in my plan when I finally put it together that I'd pulled the tall vampire down *on top* of me. And there were more than half a dozen over-protective and ultra-loyal vampires hanging around just feet away, and while they would enjoy me making an idiot of myself, there was a possibility they might see this as an attack.

CHAPTER EIGHTEEN

Hazel

Killian planted his feet before he could smash me into the bottom of the pool and stood, dragging me up through the water since my hands were still clasped behind his neck.

Since he was so much taller than me, the water was just a bit over his waist, which meant most of me was out of the water since I still hung from his neck. Water drizzled off his face as he stared at me—his suit soaked through. I shook my head and twisted, scanning the Drake vampires for signs of aggression. It didn't look like they'd moved an inch, thankfully.

"Well," I laughed nervously. "Wasn't that funny? So...goodbye!" I let go and did my best to run through the water to make my escape.

"Not so fast." Killian caught me by the wrist and dragged me back.

"It was supposed to be a joke—I didn't think you'd actually let yourself fall!" I babbled.

Killian ignored me and juggled my wrist so he could take off his black suitcoat, which hit the patio with a wet splat when he tossed it.

"I am really, truly, very sorry. I repent, 100%," I said.

He ran a hand through his dark hair—looking more like a model in an ad than waterlogged like I did.

"I'll run laps," I offered when he finally looked back at me. "To show how sorry I am."

He reeled me in like a fish and pinned me against his chest, then wordlessly walked toward the opposite end.

Oohh, he was going to throw me in the deep end—which was no joke; it went down at least eight or nine feet.

Immediately I changed tactics and wrapped my arms around his neck, clinging to him in the vain hope I'd be too slippery to pry off as Killian drifted into water that was about shoulder height for him—which meant I wouldn't be able to touch the ground without dunking my head underwater.

"I'm sorry, it was a miscalculation—a boo-boo," I said.

"Do I appear to be angry?" Killian mildly asked—his chest vibrating slightly as he spoke.

"No," I glumly said. "But that's only because you're about to get your revenge."

Since I was leaning into Killian—which meant our heads were side by side—I couldn't see his face, but I could *feel* his smirk.

I wasn't about to be swindled into letting him go, so I squeezed even tighter. "I really didn't think you'd let yourself fall in," I grumbled.

"It seemed harmless." Killian positioned himself so he was under the shade of one of the trellises—which cut the intense sunlight. "And you looked thoroughly pleased with yourself at the moment."

I didn't relax my grasp, but the stiffness left my body. "I didn't realize until you were in the water that my actions could possibly be misinterpreted."

"As what? An attempt to baptize me?" Killian snorted.

"No, you—or your backup—could have thought I was trying to attack you!"

Killian laughed. Not his scary laugh that was deep and dark, but a lighter sound that made his chest buzz and lasted a couple of seconds.

I didn't think I'd said anything that funny, but as I adjusted my grasp on his neck—this time grabbing a fistful of the collar of his white shirt, which was almost transparent in the water—I glanced at the other vampires.

Their stance had actually relaxed, and I saw a few of them had the *tiniest* of smiles tugging at their faces—making them look a lot more...well...*alive* than I'd recently seen them.

"Hazel Medeis," Killian said when he finished laughing. "You are, first and foremost, a virtuous idiot. You would never attempt to attack me in my own home, much less at my own pool. Out on the streets if I was already in a fight, perhaps. But you're far more likely to sell off information about me to the highest bidder."

"What? I would *not!*" Outraged, I loosened my hold on Killian so my arms were no longer wedged around his neck and I could lean back and peer up at him.

Killian's smirk was back. "Not even to secure allies for House Medeis?"

"*Especially* not then," I stressed. "If I can't keep Medeis running without breaking trust I don't deserve it."

"You would abandon your friends and family to the dubious care of your cousin?"

"I never said that!" I frowned at Killian. "But if I go around sneaking and lying, I won't be any better than Mason."

"As I said: a virtuous idiot." Killian shifted his hold on my waist so I was more secure and not in danger of tipping back if I let go of his neck.

I studied his face, frowning slightly as I traced the set of the muscles around his mouth and the jaded look in his eyes.

"What is it?" His smirk took on an indolent look. "Captivated by my fathomless charms and smashing good looks?" He moved his hand up my back and tugged me closer.

I switched my grasp to the front of his shirt collar and planted my palms on his upper chest so I could resist. "No, thank you," I said sourly. "Your severe pride is incredibly off-putting."

"Even if it's true?" He tugged harder, almost making my elbows buckle.

"Stop it," I fussed.

"What, don't you wish to try and turn me to the path of the righteous with a soulful hug?" He was outright grinning now—which was a bad sign for my health. "Not many could resist me, and it's your duty as a woman of great virtue." Though his tone sounded honest, there was just enough sarcasm in his words to let me know he still thought I'd sell him out—or stab him in the back—if the chance arose.

"I'm hurt you would think I'm that stupid," I said. Despite my false bravado, being this close to him was starting to make my heart pound harder, and my fingers were registering that the muscles beneath my hands were pleasantly cool in the beastly hot summer air. (No judging—he's sinfully gorgeous!)

"Virtuous idiots are not known for their intelligence."

I kept my eyes on the sky—which was way safer than watching water drip down Killian's arrogantly straight nose. "If this is your idea of hitting on me, I'm pretty sure you're going to be forever alone," I grumbled.

"You think I can't hear how fast your heart is beating?" Killian asked, his voice turning silken—another bad sign for my health. "Now it is my turn to be hurt."

"My heart always beats faster around you because I never know what torture you'll inflict on me next," I complained, telling a convenient half-truth since I'd rather die than let Killian know I was *very* aware how attractive he was.

"You bring up a valid point." I peeled my eyes from the sky to gawk at Killian, and almost immediately regretted my decision since his hair had already started to dry, giving him a roughish look he didn't usually sport.

I wasn't so far gone, however, that I forgot his worrisome declaration. "I did?"

"Yes." Killian's smirk was almost radiant. "If difficult, physical feats don't break your seal, perhaps it requires a gentle touch."

I froze in his arms, my eyes bulging.

Killian gently pressed his forehead against mine, invading all of my senses. "I think we ought to experiment."

I stammered for a moment, trying to find a sufficiently sassy reply, before I decided that to keep my pride, a sacrifice was necessary.

"Hard pass, thanks!"

Using his chest like a springboard, I jumped from his grasp, plopping into the deep end of the pool, effectively dunking myself. I surfaced with a sputter to the sound of dry chuckles. It took a few moments of dog paddling toward the side of the pool before I realized the vampires on guard duty were laughing.

Some were only grinning, a few were laughing, their stances greatly relaxed as they slightly shook their heads. The biggest of them all was actually crouched on the ground, his back facing me as his shoulders shook with silent laughter.

It seemed that I had achieved my goal in lightening the atmosphere. Satisfied, I boosted myself onto the pool edge—gleeful that I was able to do so with relative smoothness, all thanks to weightlifting!

"You're leaving?" Killian called. "Don't you want to come back for a heated embrace?"

"*No!*" I firmly said, a blush warming my cheeks.

Killian leaned his back against the side of the pool, resting his arms on the edge. "Embarrassed is a good look for you," he called out to me.

I grabbed my towel and wrapped it around me. "Go drink a blood juice box!"

"Now you're concerned for my health—how absolutely touching! Behold—the honor of a virtuous idiot."

"I hope you get sunburned!"

The relief in the tense atmosphere at Drake Hall was temporary. By the following day everyone was grim-faced again—though Celestina and Josh were around a little more.

Four days after the pool incident, Celestina took my training back. She worked me hard, but I was pleasantly surprised when she suggested we finish with a snack in the kitchen.

She pulled out a bag of chips, a package of Oreos, and some fresh strawberries—all mostly for me. She ate a strawberry but just sipped at a mug of heated blood while I pigged out on the Oreos.

She let out a huge sigh after she drained the last of her mug, and leaned back in her chair.

"Tired?" I asked.

"Not physically, but I suppose I am mentally fatigued." She offered me a half smile and traced the rim of her mug.

"Any updates on the murderer—or any leads?"

Celestina shook her head. "We're following up on a few more crime scene leads, but the facts simply don't add up. It seems the murderer *occasionally* uses fae magic at the site of the murder, but we haven't been able to detect a pattern to the use, and we haven't been able to prove that it's even a fae perpetrator."

"That's rough." I made myself drink my glass of water before I could ask her if she had considered any vampire suspects.

"There you are," Killian said.

I jumped in my chair, dribbling water down my chin, when Killian abruptly appeared at my side, having soundlessly crossed the kitchen.

He looked at me the way a dog owner looks when their dog has been rolling in the mud. "I ought to get you a collar or a bell."

"Microchipping is an option," Josh said from just beyond Killian's shoulder.

"They don't do that to humans!" I snarled.

"Not even to wizards?"

"No!"

"Pity." Killian turned his attention to Celestina. "Are preparations complete for the meeting?"

Celestina bowed her head. "Yes, Your Eminence."

"And you are ready to leave?"

"Whenever you are, Your Eminence."

Josh circled around the table during this discussion and picked up my unopened bag of chips, inspecting the label.

"What meeting?" I picked the green top off a strawberry.

"Tonight the Midwest vampires are holding another meeting in the Curia Cloisters to discuss the murders." Killian slightly exhaled—which was about the equivalent of a child throwing a temper tantrum for him. "It is with the hope of discussing new security measures that could be taken to stop the murderer, but given the disappointing level of intelligence found in some of the vampire Families, I don't expect a positive outcome."

"It will give you an opportunity to remind them the Regional Magic Committee has finally ratified the new law limiting the Unclaimed allowed in an area," Celestina said.

I blinked. "Wait, Unclaimed are vampires that don't belong to Families, right? Why would you do that to your own people?"

Josh set the bag of chips down and unsheathed his broadsword, much to my confusion—though neither Celestina nor Killian showed signs of concern.

"It's precisely because they are my people that I want to limit the Unclaimed," Killian said. "The Midwest can have as many Lone Wolves running around as the werewolf Pre-Dominant wants. I will not allow vampires to gamble with their own lives and live without a Family, risking their necks, when they could provide support and strengthen our numbers when we already have difficulty turning new vampires."

Judging by the way Killian narrowed his eyes, this was an issue he'd been fighting for a while.

I ate my strawberry as I digested his argument. It was valid—a vampire running around without a Family backing it was an easy target, especially given the feuds between races these days. And vampires, werewolves, and shifters in general were having a harder and harder time repopulating these days. But it seemed pretty high handed and tyrannical since it sounded like Killian was trying to cut off their options and *force* Unclaimed to join a Family despite their wishes.

"Between the new law and the discussion about the murderer, the meeting is likely to go late, so there will be no training for you tomorrow," Celestina said.

"Okay." I eyed Josh as he inspected his bare blade.

"Most of the Drake Family vampires will attend the meeting, but a skeleton crew will remain behind to ensure the safety of the Hall," Killian said.

Josh picked up the bag of chips and artfully sliced through the top with his sword before sliding it back in its scabbard.

"Did you seriously just use your sword to open a bag of chips?"

Josh ate a chip. "What use is there in a sword if not to cut things?"

"Isn't that, like, dishonorable to the blade or something?" I asked.

"Nonsense," Josh said. "It is my homage to the blacksmith—they have created such a stunning weapon it *must* be used."

I gaped at Celestina and Killian, but neither of them looked surprised, so I guess this was not a one-time behavior of Josh's.

"There was a fresh delivery of blood today, if you would like to partake in some before we leave, Your Eminence." Celestina stood up and tossed her blood pouch in the trash.

"Oh." Josh set the chip bag down and shuffled off to the walk-in cooler. "Shall I fetch you one, Your Eminence?"

"It's fine," Killian called after his Second Knight. He raised an eyebrow at me as he watched me consume another strawberry, but he asked Celestina, "You made arrangements for a fresh blood delivery at the Curia Cloisters, I presume?"

Celestina checked her wrist watch. "Yes—it should arrive around the time we do. I wanted the freshest delivery to keep any of the other Families who usually use blood donors from complaining."

"Well done," Killian said.

Josh reappeared from the cooler, carrying three blood pouches.

Killian stared at him for several moments then took one.

Josh set the second down on the table and poked the straw taped to the pouch through it. "Are you sure you don't need another one, Your Eminence?"

"I said it was fine." Killian didn't open his blood pouch, but stared down at it for a moment before swiveling his gaze over to me. His eyebrow twitched, and he flicked me in the forehead.

"Ow," I said automatically, even though it didn't hurt.

Killian left before I raised my hand to rub at the spot.

"Stay safe, Hazel," Celestina called over her shoulder as she followed him out.

Josh merely nodded to me and left, tossing his emptied blood pouch in the trash on his way out—leaving behind the unopened second pouch.

"Good luck!" I called.

By the time I finished my snack of strawberries, Oreos, and chips, a few of the blood donors had drifted into the kitchen, searching for dinner. I chatted with them as the sun sank beyond the horizon, leaving the sky enveloped in velvet black.

It wasn't until we finished and were tidying up the kitchen that I remembered the extra blood pouch.

"Oh, I can put that away, Hazel," Amanda—the chatty blood donor I'd met the day I arrived at Drake Hall—offered.

"It's fine! I know where everything goes—I used to organize the blood after every delivery." I trotted over to the walk-in cooler and set the blood pouch on the frosted shelves. I made a face when I noticed that no one bothered to arrange the blood by expiration date, so there were some expired packs pushed to the side.

But I couldn't blame anyone—I knew personally the kitchen staff were busy. And it's not like we could expect the vampire that made the deliveries to do it. Wait.

I paused just outside the cooler and mentally reviewed my thoughts. "A vampire makes the blood deliveries," I said.

Only Amanda was left in the kitchen. "Hmm? Oh, yes. She's been the delivery person for months."

There was something about this—I felt as if I was on the edge of making a huge discovery if I could just puzzle it out correctly. "It's the same delivery person every time?" I asked.

"As far as I know." She tapped her lower lip. "I haven't seen anyone else. You've met her, haven't you? A female vampire—I *think* she's Unclaimed..."

I briefly closed my eyes as I tried to organize my wild thoughts. "I have to go." I grabbed my katana from the chair I'd balanced it on and tore out of the kitchen, pounding down the hallways.

I needed to find a vampire—there was something I had to confirm. Because if I was right, there *was* a vampire who was allowed through all the layers of security at Drake Hall without suspicion and *didn't* belong to the Drake Family: the vampire with the blood delivery company.

CHAPTER NINETEEN

Hazel

"Celestina? Josh?" I shouted, cursing under my breath when I remembered they had left well over an hour ago for their meeting.

I didn't know who else was here, and I *still* didn't have a cellphone, so it wasn't like I could phone Celestina up.

Desperate, I flung open the front door, nearly colliding with Rupert, who was coming up the front stairs, having parked his car in the turn around.

"Rupert! I need your help." I grabbed the front of his suit with my free hand, ignoring the possibility that he might maim me for it—this was too important to let him go, even if he was a jerk.

Rupert reared his head back and went to cover his nose for a moment—from the stench of my blood probably. "*What?*" he snapped, his hair more of a gold color than red in the yellow cast by the driveway lights. "Can't you do anything without Celestina or Josh around to protect you?"

"I'm serious!" I yanked hard on his jacket. "Tell me—do all of the local vampire Families use the same blood delivery company?"

Rupert tried to extricate his jacket from my grasp without actually touching me. "Of course. There's only *one* major company that services the Midwest. There are a few smaller local brands, but here in Magiford blood distribution is a contract awarded by Killian."

"Then it's possible." I let Rupert go and slapped my hands on my head as if I could forcibly keep my whirling thoughts under control. "Depending on her route, she could have access to *everyone*...including—the meeting!" Reacting entirely on instinct I jumped down the stairs, sprinting for Rupert's car.

"Call Celestina!" I shouted over my shoulder. "Tell her the murderer is there!"

Rupert strolled after me. I couldn't see his face in the darkness of night, but I was pretty sure he was scowling. "Where do you think you're going?"

I opened his car and slid in the driver's seat, tossing my katana into the passenger's seat. "To the meeting!"

"*What*?!"

I slammed the door shut and, thankfully, the keys were already in the ignition. I turned the car on and slammed from park to drive, already rolling forward as I hurriedly buckled my seatbelt.

"Stop—you stupid rat-blood!" Rupert howled.

I ignored him and drove the car down the driveway. When I glanced in the rearview mirror it looked like Rupert hadn't bothered to follow me—hopefully he at least thought to phone Celestina.

I reached the gate that divided off Drake lands and peered up and down the fence-line, but I didn't see any vampires on duty. I rolled a window down and shouted into the shadows of the night, "Hello?"

There was no response.

This made a string of expletives drop from my lips as I'd been planning on snagging one of them and driving to the meeting as they contacted the other Drake vampires.

I bit my lip and impatiently tapped my fingers on the steering wheel.

It was a very real possibility the murderer was going to the meeting. Celestina *said* she'd made arrangements for a fresh blood delivery. If the delivery vampire had a new target…

I set my jaw and floored it, making the sharp turn and speeding down the abandoned country roads, driving for the city like a bat out of hell.

I hadn't been this frightened since the night Mason threatened Felix—not when I was thrown off the roof, not even when the fae monster nearly killed me. My palms were clammy and itched as I tried to recall the exact way to the city.

"Why didn't you give me a cellphone!" I shouted at Killian—who obviously couldn't hear me. "You're dripping with cash! But nooo, can't give the wizard a *phone*—even though we'll happily give her a freaking *sword*!!" I glanced over at my chisa katana. "Sorry—I mean, I love you a lot, but I could really use some backup right now!"

The tires squealed when I took a turn too quickly, but I could see signs of civilization in the distance.

It took too long to reach the Curia Cloisters. I circled around to the back to the staff parking lot, my heartbeat doubling when the car's headlights lit up a familiarly colored blood delivery van.

I abandoned Rupert's car in the middle of a parking row and ran inside, clutching my chisa katana to my side.

"Excuse me, no weapons," a secretary shouted from the information desk.

I ignored her and sprinted through the building, my shoes squeaking as I flew across the tile floor.

I made it all the way to the assembly hall, where I was pretty sure the meeting had to be held again. This time, however, there were armed vampires outside the doors. (So much for no weapons!) One wore armor that wouldn't have looked out of place on a knight, the other wore a flowing robe—definitely *not* from the Drake Family.

"Quickly—you've got to get Celestina—or Josh—or Gavino!" My lungs ached, and I took such large gulps of air it hurt my throat. "They're from the Drake Family!"

The vampire in the robes narrowed his eyes. "Non-vampires are not allowed through these doors."

"That's fine," I wheezed. "Just go get one of them!"

The armored vampire shook his head.

"I'm Killian Drake's pet wizard!" I shouted—hoping they might hear me inside. "Go get any Drake vampire! Celestina—Josh!" I waited, having finally recovered my breath, but the doors didn't open.

The robed vampire peeled back his upper lip so his fangs showed. "Why do you have a sword?"

"That doesn't matter—just *open the doors*! This is taking too long—" I froze when I felt a floral sensation brushing my senses, filling my mouth with the familiar rose-water jello block taste. "She's getting started," I said blankly. "She's using fae magic!"

I stared at the doors in horror, when my memory kicked in, and I recalled the room had *three* floors—two for observation purposes. I turned on my heel and ran back the way I'd come, weaving around the walled-in room as I searched for the closest staircase.

I found it and went up it as fast as I could, taking two stairs at a time. The flowery feeling grew stronger the higher I went up, so I raced past the second floor and up to the third.

Sure enough, there weren't any vampire guards on the third floor to stop me, so I sprinted down the hallway, rounded the corner, and slammed into the double doors. I hoped I was being paranoid and I was way off base on this.

I *wanted* to be wrong.

But every muscle in me tensed when I saw the blond, female vampire crouched a car's length from the banister. A wood staff topped with a black crystal sat on the ground at her side, and a dagger with a metal dragon sculpted around the hilt was stabbed into the ground—the dragon's glowing eyes seemed to be the source of fae magic that I felt.

I was right. The delivery vamp was the murderer—and she was here for her next mark.

"*Killian!*" I screamed. "*Get down!*" I tore across the landing, weaving around chairs as the female vampire rolled to her feet to face me.

I was vaguely aware that a shrill scream pierced the air from the lower floor before there was lots of shouting. *Hopefully* Celestina and Josh would stash Killian and then come back me up.

The delivery vampire smirked, and as I jumped a table I could see the blue shimmering cloud that marked out the large area around her—a magical barrier.

But I didn't slow. I unsheathed my katana and pulled my little flicker of magic through my blood. I blew through the fae barrier —which closed up behind me. That took the smirk off her lips.

"Fae magic doesn't work on wizards, idiot!" I snarled.

"Insolent *rat-blood*." She made a grab for the staff, but I was close enough I was able to perform a serviceable overhead chop, which made her back away. I tried to kick the staff free of the barrier, but it got caught on a chair leg halfway there.

When I scrambled to kick it farther, she grabbed me by the hair and yanked me backwards.

I fell on my back, the delivery vampire kneeling next to me. My scalp burned, and she raised her free hand—her nails pointed and talon-like as more of her vampiric nature leaked through. I struck out with the palm of my hand, cracking her nose. I realized about then that she obviously was not up to the same caliber as the Drake vampires, and didn't train. I'd never been able to get a hit on *anyone* in Drake Hall unless they purposely let me, so this was encouraging news. It meant I stood a chance.

Swearing, the vampire leaned backwards, her eyes watering in pain as blood dripped from her nose.

I rolled away, but I wasn't quite fast enough. Even with her eyes pointed up at the ceiling, the vampire struck like a snake, her claws ripping through my workout clothes and slicing my side.

I ignored the pain as I grabbed the staff, intending to toss it through the barrier.

Bleeding everywhere, the vampire grabbed the end of the staff and yanked it from my grasp. I pivoted to face her, and was shocked to see a number of vampires—including *Killian*—standing outside the barrier.

The fae magic sparked angrily with the closeness of their presence, but while the other vampires hovered out of reach, Killian stood close enough that one of the sparks could easily brush him. Celestina stood just behind him, her lips moving fast in a hushed whisper as she gestured away from the barrier, but Killian ignored her.

When he realized I was staring at him, both of his eyebrows rose in obvious irritation. *What are you doing, you stupid wizard?*

He didn't have to speak—his irritation was settled into the way he had his arms folded across his chest.

But wait—the vampires were here. I could get out of the barrier and leave them to handle it, couldn't I?

"Mortem Basium!" the delivery vampire screamed. Black light lashed from the black crystal on her staff, careening straight for Killian.

I kicked the vampire in the back of the knee, making her reflexively fold backwards, then chopped down on her throat with the hilt of my katana. She fell into a heap, but jabbed the staff at me.

I brought my katana up into a guard stance that blocked it, but she hit with such force it made my arms quiver and my teeth rattle.

This is what a vampire was like when they were at full

strength? This was crazy! I had been so wrong—there was no way I'd win! But I didn't have to, backup was standing just outside the barrier.

"Give up," I snarled. "You can see you won't make it out of here alive if you attack again."

The delivery vampire laughed. "I already knew I wasn't going to survive this. But that's fine—as long as I can take that tyrant down with me!" She snapped her teeth at Killian, who had avoided the attack and was unscathed—though now Josh stood behind his other shoulder and was also trying to get him to leave.

Why wasn't he, anyway?

The delivery vampire was on her feet faster than my eyes could track and jabbed her open nails at me.

I ducked sideways, but she followed with her speed and sank her nails into my shoulder, piercing my skin. She twisted, shredding my muscles in her claws.

I shouted, and my back arched in pain.

She dropped me and raised her hand to her mouth. Her tongue hovered just over her claws before she gagged, the scent of my blood too powerful to overcome.

On the ground, I made a change to my strategy. I couldn't leave—she'd attack Celestina, Killian, and Josh again. But I could dispel the barrier and let everyone else *in*.

The vampire stepped over my prone body, murmuring in fae under her breath as the staff glowed black.

I made a show of moaning—it wasn't too hard; pain had made my injured shoulder *numb*, and I couldn't really move that arm, making my katana useless. I reluctantly released my weapon and curled my body as I tried to discreetly look for the dagger with the dragon on it. There—at the center of the circle.

I rolled twice and managed to grab the dagger. I even pulled, but it was shoved too deeply in for me to free with one hand.

The vampire clubbed me in the head with the bottom of her staff, and I collapsed, seeing stars.

I felt the surge of fae magic as the vampire triggered the spell.

Someone screamed, and the awful smell of burnt flesh filled the air.

I peeled myself off the floor and twisted around, relieved to see Killian, Celestina, and Josh were still standing. Celestina and Josh had drawn further back and were arguing with each other, but Killian had moved even *closer* to the barrier. He even rested his fingertips on it—which must have been blistering. Off behind him, though, an injured vampire moaned on the ground, and all the other vampires had fled halfway across the balcony.

The delivery vampire didn't seem to care. She was unearthing a few more enchanted items from her black bag, her back to me.

Killian's eyes lingered on me, then he tipped his head to the side, telling me to leave.

By now it was pretty apparent I couldn't do much of anything—and if Killian was telling me to leave, he must have a plan.

I nodded and tried to stand, but the pain in my head ached with such fierceness I could barely see straight, so I slumped back down onto my knees.

Killian made a quiet exhale of irritation. "You betray your own kind for what—the *fae*?" His voice was dark, and he stared at the female vamp, the tilt of his chin saying he was unimpressed.

"They pay well, but that's not why I took this job." Her hands shook as she pulled out a wood carving of a phoenix and set it on the ground. "You made me! You're a vampire—how could you limit the number of Unclaimed in the area?"

As I discreetly edged toward the side of the barrier, it dawned on me that her hands didn't shake from fear, but *rage*.

Killian impassively stared at her. "Unclaimed vampires are liabilities at best, and most often live short lives. As a species, we cannot allow such a thing any longer."

"You took away all my options—my choice!" she shrieked. "The rest of the Regional Committee didn't want to ratify the law because they considered it cruel, but *you* did!"

Killian scoffed. "You are using a law that has only recently passed to defend murdering innocents and vampires alike for months."

"Because I *knew* you'd pass it!" she snarled. "You're Killian Drake—you'd never let it go until you have *all* of us under your thumb and your control." She laughed, the sound staccato and unhinged. "And you don't even care! You'll do whatever you wish with no regard for who it harms or hinders!" She rested her hand on the phoenix. "Well, no more. You can't escape the building before I release this magic. You will pay for everything you have done."

I stopped edging sideways and stared at the phoenix, a bad feeling boiling in my gut.

She squatted on the ground, one hand resting on the phoenix carving, the other on the dragon dagger, and once again started to murmur in melodic Fae.

The phoenix statue glowed, and the wood actually started to singe while fire churned around the vampire's feet as power built.

This wasn't a single strike like she'd been launching with the staff, this was a *massive* spell. If the power was any indication, it would clear through the entire floor—perhaps the building. "Are you crazy?" I shouted. "There are innocent people here!"

"Collateral damage," the vampire said coldly. "Sacrifices are necessary for new beginnings. This rebirth will cleanse the vampire race so we can live as we deserve with no regard for laws of any sort."

She was totally off her rocker, but I couldn't let her kill everyone.

"Hazel," Killian started. "Don't—"

I ignored him and bolted for the crazy vampire. This time I wetted my hand in some of my blood that was flowing at an alarming rate from my mangled shoulder, then smacked my hand over her face, thrusting one of my fingers between her lips.

She wrenched herself backwards, retching and gagging. She

kicked me as she scurried backwards, kneeing me in the chest so I lost all my air. I wheezed for a few moments, then grabbed the phoenix sculpture.

It was *a lot* heavier than I had estimated. I could barely lift it with one hand. I tried to throw it, but I couldn't get it high enough to get any sort of lift on it. So I leaned back onto my butt and kicked it.

It didn't clear the circle, but it skidded a few feet away.

I tried to scramble after it, but the vampire darted in front of me. "You cockroach! Just *die*!" She grabbed me by the neck and lifted me off my feet, then threw me, slamming me into the ground.

Something in my injured arm crunched. The pain was so overwhelming I couldn't breathe. My stomach rolled, but all my muscles were already bunched in pain. My neck hurt, and for a few moments I wondered if she had crushed my windpipe. I tried to gasp for air, my hair matting in the dribble of my own blood. After what felt like an eternity, I was able to take in a shallow breath, and then another.

But when I tried to move, my body wouldn't listen.

I heard gunshots, but it sounded like they ricocheted off the bubbling surface of the barrier.

The delivery vampire laughed and said something, but her voice was muffled as my ears rang.

I blinked until my vision cleared, and what I saw made my chest hurt.

The other vampires had fled, but Killian, Celestina, and Josh remained.

Celestina and Josh must have realized Killian wasn't going to leave. Rather than seek safety for themselves they stayed, loyal until the end.

Josh had the tip of his broadsword stabbed into the barrier, his muscles straining as he pushed everything he had into his sword.

Celestina picked up a chair and threw it at the barrier. It splintered and fell in a shamble. Next, she picked up a table and hammered at the magical barrier. The red of her eyes was stark—she knew it was hopeless, but she wasn't going to go down without a fight.

Killian must have been the one to fire the gun. He held a handgun at his side and still had his other hand planted on the barrier, ignoring the painful sparks and flickers of magic. His eyes were obsidian black, his lips curled back in a snarl that showed more of his prominent fangs than usual.

They were going to die.

Even if the vampire set off the massive fae spell, I'd probably survive with my magic blood. But Celestina, Josh...and Killian...they'd die.

The female vamp stood just on the other side of the barrier from Killian, a mocking smile on her lips as she held the phoenix statue out, rambling off the fae spell.

Get up! I screamed internally at myself. *I have to do something! Anything!*

I tried to move my arm, and hot agony knifed through me—though I was too weak to do more than whimper. I tugged on the magic in the air and pulled it through my blood, but I couldn't concentrate long enough to get it to flicker at my fingertips. Everything hurt too much.

Flames ate up the phoenix statue, and I could tell by the ever-widening circle of fire around the vampire that the spell was almost complete. She would win, and kill Killian. She would kill the vampires I had slowly come to think of as my friends.

My eyelids drifted shut against my will.

Get up! Hit her—take her out. The thought came unbidden from the darkest bits of my mind: kill the crazy vampire to save them. Commit what House Medeis labeled as one of the greatest atrocities- for Killian Drake, a horrific vampire by nature.

But he had laughed and smiled with me. He'd protected me from my own kind—from *his own* Family! I didn't know what we were—friends seemed a weird definition, and one Killian would probably scoff at. But he had stood at my back, and every teasing poke, every challenge, every smirk had drawn me from my own bitterness and made me laugh despite my terrible situation.

Yeah. I'd kill someone for Killian Drake.

It went against everything I had been taught. Every rule I'd sworn to follow. Heck, it would probably make my parents *cry* if they were alive to hear of it, and it was almost certain that House Medeis would not welcome me back after this even if Mason was kicked out.

But I didn't care.

I'd spill blood and kill the vampire if it meant saving people important to me. *That* was doing what was *right*.

CHAPTER TWENTY

Hazel

I snapped my eyes open and again reached for my magic.

My body shook, and weirdly I began to glow a bright blue hue. Something in me crackled, then shattered, and I could *feel* it: magic. Not the faint flickers I had to fight to take in, but the vast, endless stretch of wild magic that cradled the world.

I pulled more and more of it through my blood, and it made me feel *alive*. I felt a part of me unwind that I'd never realized how crushed it made me feel. It was stronger than a shot of adrenaline, simultaneously beautiful and terrible.

With magic pulsing through me so much I probably glowed in the dark, I found I could stand. My face burned as I felt my wizard mark appear on the left side of my face, but this time the sensation lasted longer and stretched up my forehead to my hairline, and down my cheek, past my jaw, flowing over part of my neck. I inhaled, then picked my way toward the vampire, whose flames now stretched knee high.

"I'm giving you one last chance." My voice was stronger than I thought it could be, and I smiled as I felt magic thread through my hair and twine around my fingers. "One last offer of mercy: stand down."

The vampire didn't bother to look back at me—she was staring at Killian with a mad delight. "Never!" She laughed. "Not now—not ever!"

"Then die." I reached out and grabbed the back of her neck, unleashing the magic my blood harbored.

Blue bolts of electricity shot from me, surging through the encircled area with such bright intensity I couldn't see anything.

The vampire screamed—but it only lasted for a moment before magic consumed her body, turning her to ash.

But the magic wasn't done.

More electricity poured from me, until it felt like I had magic coming out of every pore. The phoenix statue split and crumbled, and the dragon dagger started to melt in the heat.

A huge bolt of my magic that cracked with a deafening boom punched through the top of the barrier, shattering the whole thing like glass. It soared up, smashing into the ceiling of the meeting room, cutting a gaping hole clear through the roof.

The entire building shook, and magic swirled around me.

Everything was too clear, too crisp. I could barely breathe because of the overwhelming sensations. Every part of me tingled and burned—but there was *so much magic* out there. A *world* of it! Why didn't we do more? Why didn't we *use* it the way it was meant to be used?

Overwhelmed, I felt my knees fold under me, even as lightning still crackled around me.

"She's going into shock!" Josh yelled from what sounded like a mile away.

"Your Eminence—*don't*! She's too dangerous right now!"

The world was bright blue with magic, and everything was so *hot*. I tried to sever my connection, but now that magic freely floated through my blood it wouldn't leave. I collapsed on the ground, my fingers twitching.

Something cold covered my eyes, offering a bit of relief.

"*Breathe*. You're not a passive wizard, Hazel. This isn't going to end you—magic would have to take you complaining and arguing every step."

I breathed, and clenched my jaw as I forcefully cut off the pull of magic. I could still feel it around me, but it no longer seeped through my blood like it wanted to.

The hum of electricity faded, and I relaxed. Something cool wrapped around me, and I was vaguely aware that I was being moved before my blood roared in my ears, and I passed out.

I woke myself up with my own snores.

Yeah, how's that for smooth? I was so loud I woke myself up with a snort that made my throat hurt.

I opened my eyes and promptly scrunched them shut. The shades were drawn, letting the orange-y gold light of sunset stab my poor eyes. I fluttered them open and closed, snort-sniffing in irritation when they teared up, making my vision blurry. Eventually, though, I was able to see again.

I was in my bedroom. My chisa katana was polished and arranged on its sword stand on my dresser, and even from here I could see my open closet stuffed with petite-sized suits. But for a moment I wasn't certain where I was...because sitting at my bedside was Killian Drake.

And this time he wasn't sitting back in his chair or looking like a model leaning against a wall.

No, he was artfully leaning forward, one forearm resting on my bed. His other hand—weirdly, strangely?—was intertwined with my own. He held my forearm up, propped up with his, and held my arm so close to his face I could feel his breath on the inside of my wrist. It was a weirdly intimate position—like something you would do for someone you really loved.

So...what was he doing? More importantly *why* was he doing it? I mean, this was *Killian Drake*. Even after all my time in Drake Hall I wasn't optimistic enough—or deluded enough—to think he loved *anyone*. Not even himself, probably.

Killian unashamedly met my gaze, his obsidian red eyes bored. "Hardly the fairy tale awakening," he said. "You look more like a troll."

It took two tries to speak. "Your bedside manners suck."

Killian's right eyebrow twitched up. "You think I care?"

"What happened?" I tried to pull my hand from his so I could rub my eyes, but he wouldn't give it up.

"You decided to make a go of securing the title Most Muleheaded, Stupid, Inept Idiot in the history of the world," Killian said wryly.

"I remember that." I shifted in bed a little, relieved to find I could move my body—with pain, yes, but at least I could feel everything again.

I froze abruptly as the details of the fight came back. "The seal broke."

"I imagine you are referring to the seal on your magic, in which case you are correct." Killian studied my wrist with puzzled interest. "Though from what I saw—and Celestina reported to me—there was no physical trigger. Do you know what did it?" He finally raised his gaze from my wrist, the red in his eyes more expressed in the flush of sunset bathing my room.

I leaned into the pillow propping me up and stared at the ceiling. My memory was slowly piecing itself together: the vampire, my injuries, and the overwhelming clarity the full force of magic brought to me. What had I been thinking right before the seal broke?

Hazily, it returned to me. I had decided I would spill blood and kill the murderous vampire if it meant saving people important to me.

"No," I said out loud. "No—it can't be."

Killian was back to inspecting my wrists. "Hm?"

"Seals can't be broken by *thoughts*, can they?" I asked.

"Can't they?" Killian returned the question. "Isn't true love and all of that junk nothing more than inner resolve?"

"But there's no way my parents would do this to me." My voice shook as tears threatened my eyes. "They wouldn't seal my magic and condemn me to a constant fight against bullies and make the only way out to decide to *kill* someone. That's against everything House Medeis stands for!"

Killian peered at me with interest. "That's what broke the seal? You decided to kill the vampire."

"To save you, Celestina, and Josh—yes." I flung my free arm over my eyes and held my breath, trying to ward off the sobs that threatened to shake my shoulders.

How could they do this to me? *Why* would they do this to me? They were my parents, but it seemed like they did their best to make my life a misery! And why wouldn't they want me to have stronger magic when they did?

In my pain, I twitched, automatically squeezing Killian's hand.

I was shocked when, after a moment, he returned the squeeze.

He exhaled deeply. "I can't believe *I* am the one suggesting this, but are you certain there isn't a part of this you're missing?"

I kept my arm over my eyes. "Like what?"

"Isn't everything done for the House?" Killian asked. "It seems strange that your parents would paralyze the Heir when all of your kind revere the House and model their lives around its existence. Technically, they've hurt House Medeis even more than they hurt you in all of this. So perhaps there is a reason behind it all—you just can't see it yet."

I slowly lowered my arm as I mulled over his words.

He was right. As much as I had come to hate and loathe the saying, "The House comes first." It had been drilled into *all* wizards since they could sit up as babies.

And obviously my magic—or lack of—had a *huge* effect on House Medeis.

Was it possible? But what reason could possibly justify all of this? It's not like Mason could have been plotting already when I was born—he would have been *ten*!

The condition for breaking my seal had shaken me, but at least now I didn't feel like crying. Maybe—when all of this was over—I'd ask Mr. and Mrs. Clark and the other senior wizards. They might know something. And in the meantime, I'd lose myself in training.

I awkwardly cleared my throat and shifted a little, making the bed creak and my muscles stiffen. "Did you find out anything more about her?"

Up went one of Killian's eyebrows. "The murderer? Yes. Her name was Solene—previously Solene Flores. She was turned in the early 1900s by the Flores Family before opting to become an Unclaimed four years ago."

"Why'd she leave?"

"It seems she bucked heads with the Flores Family Elder." Killian brushed my wrist with his thumb, his touch cool and strangely comforting. "I don't have certain confirmation of it, but it seems he disliked her and made her time with the Family...difficult."

I grimaced in sympathy. "That's why she freaked about the law limiting the number of Unclaimed."

Killian shrugged. "She could have been adopted into another Family. With our numbers dwindling, most Families welcome adopted vampires now."

"Yeah, but that's a pretty new thing, isn't it? I heard some of the Drake Family chatting, and it seems like being adopted usually puts a vampire in a lower position."

"If you are trying to talk me into feeling pity for her, it won't work," Killian darkly said. "She killed vampires and humans alike."

"Yeah," I agreed. "She clearly had a loose screw. I'm not at all trying to justify her actions, but it doesn't make you second-guess your new law?"

"No," Killian said. "Because every vampire life is precious. And Unclaimed don't survive long."

"Why is that?" I asked. "They can purchase blood—it's not like you guys are reliant on other vampires for provision."

"No," Killian agreed. "We rely on our Families for power and protection. Unclaimed don't survive long because they are walking targets. They have no allies among the vampires, which makes them easy prey for the rest of the supernaturals."

"I don't believe that," I protested. "As a community we have to get along—or we'll collapse."

Killian raised his other eyebrow. "And I suppose *your* experience has disproven this?"

I shut my mouth so hard my teeth clicked.

When the other Houses had refused to help me, I knew I was dead. *Everyone* knew what would happen, and the werewolves hadn't tried to stop it, and the fae nobles my parents had been allies with hadn't sought me out after I pledged servitude to Killian.

I was able to survive because of the Drake Family, not because of the goodwill of our community.

It was heartbreaking. Knowing that magic was dying should have united us...but while on the surface everything seemed okay since there weren't many conflicts and no wars, in reality the magical races had drawn lines of separation.

Except I'm a wizard living here in Drake Hall. Does that count for anything?

"Isn't there a way you could make things safer for the Unclaimed?" I asked, not quite ready to let go yet.

Killian tilted his head as he thought.

"I mean, you're the all-powerful, intelligent Killian Drake," I said, buttering him up for all I was worth. "Creating an alternative should be easy for you."

The flat set of his eyebrows and the line of his mouth said he knew what I was doing and wasn't falling for it, but he played with my fingers as he thought. "I could require contact or nearby living quarters with other Unclaimed. If they form their own sort of community—even if it's small—it would provide more protection than living alone as a sitting duck."

The light in his eyes was curious now—he was thinking about it.

Which surprised me. I didn't honestly think he'd be willing to change something he'd done. Maybe his concern for the preservation of the vampire race as a whole really *was* what drove him, rather than a general thirst for power.

"You don't regret your decision?"

"Huh?" I snapped my eyes to Killian's face.

He finally set my arm down on my mattress—though he still held my hand. "You don't regret your decision to kill the vampire?"

I furrowed my brow. "No. Why would I?"

Killian raised his eyebrows. "Because of your sanctimonious and precious House rules?"

"Oh. That." I briefly pursed my lips, then shook my head. "No. I did the right thing. It might go against House rules, but I feel it here." I thumped my chest with my free hand, breaking off in a wheeze when I realized it was my mangled shoulder. When I recovered my breath I added, "I'd rather fight and spill blood than let my friends die in front of me."

"Even if it means you can't lead your House?" Killian asked.

I considered his words. "Yeah. It was right," I repeated.

He stared at me with an intense scrutiny in his eyes I couldn't quite place. Did he think I was stupid? Did he believe I had fallen into whatever plan he had concocted? (If so, he had another thing coming to him; just because I'd stop someone from killing him didn't mean I was going to do his bidding.)

I figured he'd keep pestering me about it, but he abruptly replaced his stare with a smug smirk. "Then you consider me a *friend?* My wizard, you are more naïve than I thought." His voice was such a rich velvety purr it was obvious he was playing it up to cover whatever he was thinking.

"Let's just say I don't want to see you die," I said.

"An acceptable beginning." He leaned closer, his eyes at half-mast. "I can't say I've ever seduced a wizard, but it might be fun to give it a try."

I sucked my neck into my shoulders. "No," I said. "Don't do that."

Killian inched closer. "Do *what?*"

"Look here. You need to learn about personal boundaries and comfort zones."

"Quite right," he agreed, his faint British accent thickening into something much stronger. "Why don't *you* teach me?"

I scrunched my nose at him. "Come any closer and I'll purposely open my shoulder wound and stink you out of the room."

Unexpectedly, Killian froze, his head half-cocked. "Touché, little wizard." He leaned back in his chair just as the door thumped open.

"I thought I heard your voice!" Celestina had a big smile on her face—and a smoldering potion in each hand. "I'm so glad you're awake!" She set the potions on my nightstand and sat at the edge of my mattress, leaning in so she could give me a hug. "You were amazing."

"She was no such thing." Killian let his head loll on his neck in exasperation. "She nearly got herself killed with nothing to show for it. Idiotic, that's what she was." He reached around Celestina so he could flick me on the forehead. "Once she is healed there is going to be a *discussion* about the stupidity of flinging herself into danger."

I was pretty surprised Killian would have anything to say about that—particularly since he only gained from me attacking Solene. But I ignored his comment—and the flick to the forehead—and leaned into Celestina's hug. She was nice and cool, and I felt a little warm.

Celestina, however, didn't ignore her boss. "She nearly bested a vampire without magic, *and* she destroyed her seal all by herself," she said. "I think we should celebrate."

"You're going soft," Killian grumbled. "Throwing the wizard a treat just because she survived—ridiculous."

Celestina pulled back and gave me one of the smoldering fae potions. "Drink these—your shoulder is still in rough shape."

"Is Rupert complaining that I'm stinking the house up again?" I took the glass bottle from her and chugged the potion. This one had a thick, chalky texture, but it looked more appealing than the liquid-y bright pink one she passed off to me next. Right before I tipped it to my lips, my brain caught up with my mouth. "Oh—gosh. Did someone get his car back to him? He's going to hate my guts if the city towed it!"

"We brought it back," Celestina assured me. "And he wasn't at all put out about it."

I sniffed the potion—which oddly smelled of coconut. "Yeah, and if that isn't the biggest lie I've heard this year, I don't know what is." I threw my head back and tossed the potion down. It fizzed almost painfully in my mouth and throat, but my shoulder ached enough I didn't care.

Celestina watched with the care of a nurse. "You should eat. Think you can make it down to the kitchens, or should I call for someone to bring something up?"

"I can make it." I rolled my shoulders, making my body creak. "I think it'd be good for me."

Celestina backed up so I could slide out of bed. I stared down at my pajamas (Drake issued and silken, of course) then shrugged. Pretty much everyone in Drake Hall had either witnessed me screaming or dripping with sweat. I didn't think pajamas could hurt my reputation.

I limped for the door, my joints getting looser with each step I took, but paused in the doorway.

Killian remained seated while Celestina circled my bed, collecting the empty potion bottles and a few used blood pouches.

"Thanks for taking care of me," I said.

"Of course," Celestina said. "Go eat. I got some fae bath bombs online. When you finish eating we'll throw one in the tub for you."

I nodded and glanced at Killian, waiting to see if he'd look at me. (He wouldn't.)

I shrugged and padded from the room.

"Remember, Wizard. We will discuss your actions later," Killian called through the open door.

I grinned as I started down the hallway, feeling better than I had in ages. Killian probably just wanted to lecture me before forcing more training on me. But after my fight with Solene, I was more than happy to accept more free training.

Yeah, life still sucked. My parents were dead and Mason had taken over House Medeis…but I was starting to appreciate the Drake Family—even if I didn't approve of Killian's ways. And somehow…I felt *better*.

Maybe it was that my senses were now blasted open to the magic that soaked the air, but a part of me suspected it was more than that.

Over the past few months I'd come to realize how *off* some of House Medeis's rules were—like the no killing, even in self-defense one. But I'd made up my mind that I wasn't going to follow that law, and it weirdly made me feel freer.

I wasn't sure what I was going to do about Mason or House

Medeis, but I was also pretty sure I first needed to get used to my new powers. Given the other Houses' attitude, I was probably safest testing them out and training here in Drake Hall.

I stalled briefly in the hallway as I thought of Killian. I was pretty sure he was the one who had picked me up as I passed out—and what was with the hand thing? *Did* he have some sneaky plans he was going to use me in?

My stomach growled loudly. I took a deep breath then lurched into a walk.

Staying was going to be a gamble I'd have to take. But while I didn't trust Killian, I felt pretty certain that he wouldn't actively try to ruin my life. He found me amusing—maybe diverting and potentially useful. After what I'd gone through, that was enough for me.

CHAPTER TWENTY-ONE

Killian

I stood and let my arms drop to my sides as Hazel Medeis walked down the hallway, leaving me with a very troubling question.

I rubbed my head and glanced at my First Knight. "Celestina."

She straightened and swung around so she could face me. "Yes, Your Eminence?"

I paused, carefully choosing my words. I couldn't reveal too much. Not even to my second-in-command. "How bad does Hazel smell to you?"

"You mean her wizard blood?" Celestina adjusted her grip on the empty potion bottles. "She's smelled quite neutral to me for a few weeks."

I kept my expression still. "Neutral?"

"Yes. She doesn't smell bad, but she doesn't smell good like humans."

"You trust her, then."

Celestina tapped the bottles against her thigh. "To an extent.

I know she would never mean to hurt any of us, but she is a wizard."

"Yes." I stared at Hazel's bed, as if it could give me answers. "She's still a virtuous idiot—which, as she's proved, can make her dangerous."

"What do you mean, sir?"

"She doesn't regret killing the vampire," I said. "She didn't bat an eye or stop to think about it when I asked."

"The vampire was a mad murderer."

"Even so, she was trained to avoid physical conflict. With years of conditioning, I would have thought she'd be an emotional wreck. But she's not…because she believes strongly in what's right." I gazed at the door Hazel had disappeared through. "If she believes in what she's doing, I don't think there's a force on earth that could stop her, or make her double guess her decisions. *That* is why she is dangerous. That earnest, unflinching belief."

I was no fool. I lived in a world of gray. Yes, there was darkness and light, but between the political maneuvering and selfish ambition, most supernaturals were varying shades of gray. Even *I* wondered from time to time if I'd made the correct decisions about issues.

Hazel apparently had no such problem. Once she decided what was right, she did it. No matter what others thought.

"I don't think that's something you'll be able to change about her, Your Eminence," Celestina carefully said.

When I glanced at her, she had a bland, unconcerned expression on her face. But I had known her long enough to see the flicker of concern in her stance.

Celestina had become fond of the wizard. She didn't want to see me break her.

Unfortunately, it seemed like that was already beyond me.

"Naturally," I dryly said. "I have seen her in action long enough to be certain of that." I swatted a hand at her. "Go after her. Some members of our Family are rather exuberant about her actions. If they happen upon her in this state, they might accidentally hurt her."

Though my voice dripped with sarcasm, Celestina nodded, taking the charge seriously. "She has become a favorite. I will see to it, Your Eminence." She slipped out of the room with the softness of a leopard stalking its prey, leaving me alone with an untimely- and *galling*- discovery.

I rubbed my mouth, grimacing in distaste.

To Celestina—who doted on the stubborn wizard and clearly counted her a friend—she smelled *neutral*.

To me, Killian Drake, Elder of the Drake Family, Eminence of the Midwest—paranoid and hardened beyond feeling...Hazel Medeis smelled amazing.

I couldn't pin the scent down. She didn't smell like *food*—as other humans did. Rather, she smelled like sunlight used to feel before I was turned and found it less pleasant—warm, inviting, and *dangerously* pure. There was an undertone of wildness to her scent, too—something almost electric. I suspected that was her magic flowing in her veins.

But here was the problem. If she smelled that decadent, that welcoming...just how much trust had I placed in the smart-mouthed wizard? And how on earth had I let it happen?

To be continued in Magic Redeemed: Hall of Blood and Mercy Book 2

HOW TO ADOPT A WIZARD

A Hall of Blood and Mercy Short Story

"Ah." The sound Ling, my driver for the evening, made was so soft I would have missed it, if not for the infinitesimal rock of the brake being stepped on.

I looked up from my cellphone.

"I apologize, Your Eminence," Ling said.

I ignored the apology and peered out through the front windshield in time to see a short, blonde-haired young woman sprint to the sidewalk, cutting it so close that the breeze created by the Drake limo stirred her hair. She looked back—not at the limo but across the street—with wide blue eyes.

"Slow down," I ordered.

Ling slowed the SUV to a crawl as I took in the scene before me.

I didn't immediately place the woman—I was more distracted by the singed hole in her shirt that encircled her shoulder, which she held at an odd angle.

Someone shot magic at her. Idiots—they're fighting in public, in the middle of the day?

I followed her gaze across the street to the wizard that had most likely attacked her. He glared at the woman, though his shoulders visibly tightened with fear when he glanced at the emblem on the limo that marked it as my property—and the property of the Drake Family.

I didn't even need a moment to place Gideon Tellier as an easily recognizable man-child due to his distinctly flat face that looked as though someone had repeatedly smashed him with a shovel in an attempt to get any sort of intelligence wedged into his empty brain.

Most wizards are useless. They worry a lot, or live in dream worlds where they think everything is safe and secure. As if magic wasn't dying out at an unsustainable rate that would soon make our society crumble.

As I watched, Gideon's lips moved as he said something—something stupid, most likely—and turned on his heels and ran off.

I didn't know much about Gideon—except that his intelligence was pretty lacking and he covered it up with a lot of bluster about his magic. Which probably meant the woman was his victim.

I shifted my gaze back across the street, to the blonde who'd almost gotten herself hit by the empty limo I usually ordered at the front of my motorcade procession. (It was a lure to bait any of my enemies stupid enough to attack me, as most everyone mistakenly assumed I rode in it. An illusion I was happy to keep.)

It was the look in the woman's eyes that made me realize who she was, Hazel Medeis, the Heir of House Medeis.

I make it my business to recognize all the leaders of the magical community—it was how I recognized Flat Face. For the wizards, that meant knowing the leaders' child that would inherit the House after their parents croaked as humans are all-so-prone to doing.

Hazel Medeis stood out in my mind because she was such an

unusual case. She had less magic ability than her parents—which had become common as of late—but while her parents were notably strong in their magic, she was practically a dud.

That would have been enough to make me write her off, but in the pictures included in the reports my staff gave me, there was a very pronounced look in her eyes.

She didn't have the dreamy happiness or the studied politeness most wizards wore. Rather, she had the eyes of a hunted animal determined to survive and willing to fight for it.

It was an odd look given how complacent we supernaturals had become.

I leaned back in the bench seat and thoughtfully watched her as she jogged down the sidewalk. "She was running from the man, wasn't she?"

"I believe so, Your Eminence."

I narrowed my eyes. *She knew what she was doing when she crossed in front of the motorcade. It seems there's a reason she looks hunted. It's because she is.*

"Very interesting," I said.

"Your Eminence?"

"Nothing. Drive on."

I didn't care about wizards—or anyone besides the vampires, really. And so Hazel Medeis slipped from my mind with ease, until several weeks later.

"It is not my intention to offend. Rather, I am here to request refuge. A member of my House has staged a coup," Hazel Medeis said. She half-cowered, half-bristled with her back set against two doors on the far side of the room.

She had introduced herself after bungling her way into the large, vampire assembly meeting I had called to address the rampant murders of lower leveled vampires and those who worked for us.

I didn't need the introduction, though. The hunted look in her eyes had become even more pronounced since I last saw her. Now she resembled a cornered rabbit, and though I couldn't hear it across the room, I was fairly certain her heart was pounding in fear—of the vampires she faced, and the wizards who knocked on the door behind her.

"No self-respecting Family would take on a refugee of your diminutive and unimportant status. We don't bother ourselves with the politics of ants." Louis, Elder of the Lorraine Family, sneered.

"I am aware of this, which is why I would like to request a servant's position," she said as she tried to push the bargain.

Louis looked down his obnoxiously large nose at the wizard. "What use would a *rat-blood* be to us?" he scoffed.

While a few other vampire Elders piped up to question the wizard, I tapped my fingers on my desk.

A wizard, offering to serve the vampires?

It was a tempting proposal.

Although fragile and terrible at fighting, Wizards had their uses. And with the Night Court picking fights with me, it would be useful to have a wizard—even one as poorly skilled as Hazel Medeis—on hand.

Besides, even if she was on the run, she was the Adept of House Medeis. I could manipulate wizards through fear—a single look and most of them cowered—but I wasn't opposed to having a legal hold on them as well…

But was she *too* fearful? If she didn't have a spine she'd be useless. There wasn't really a way to know for sure. Granted, she apparently had the guts to face a roomful of vampires, but it was clear we were her last resort. And she seemed prone to running from her problems instead of fighting them.

"You really are useless. Off with you," another Elder told the wizard as I tuned back in

The man who was probably responsible for the coup Hazel Medeis had mentioned called through the door. "I beg your pardon, but I believe a dangerous renegade has impeded upon you. Please allow my men and me to peacefully retrieve her."

Hazel Medeis had given up on the vampires. I could see her studying the walls, looking for an alternative exit.

She may be a runner, but at least she's smart about it.

"You were told to leave, rat-blood," a female vampire—one of the House Richardson underlings who had come to represent her lazy elder—snarled.

I studied the frightened wizard for another moment or two.

Would she be worth the work and the effort? I didn't know. Weighing out my options, the chance that she *might* become something would override what little trouble I'd have to put myself through to get her.

I smiled.

This could be fun.

"The Drake Family will accept your pledge of servitude."

The wizard froze, then slowly raised her gaze to me.

I could see the fear in her eyes, and her shoulders hunched.

Good. At least she was smart enough to be afraid of me. And I wanted the name of Killian Drake to be dreaded by outsiders.

I raised an eyebrow as I studied her. "A pet wizard sounds amusing—even one so weak as you, Adept Medeis."

She appeared frozen for several long moments, then abruptly started to lower herself to one knee.

Ahhh, she's going to take it.

"Come closer, Adept Medeis," I said. "You should see the eyes of your new master as you swear fealty."

Now, it was only a matter of time to see if this gamble was going to pay off.

I LEFT Hazel Medeis to stew among my staff. I had enough to handle with the murderer running loose, and I didn't want to bother training her until I knew she'd be worth the effort.

She proved herself after roughly a week when she took down a fully grown mantasp—a large fae creature that was a disturbing mix of wasp and praying mantis.

She'd occupied it so two maids could flee. They'd found one of the vampires on guard duty, and it took them an exorbitant amount of time to tell the vampire what was going on between their tears and babbles.

I came because I could smell the disgusting scent of the wizard blood—Hazel had shed so much of it she stunk up the front yard—from where I was watching a few of my vampires train.

I—and the vampire the maids had notified—reached the fighting wizard at roughly the same time.

The mantasp was turning in a circle, thrashing around the underbrush of the forest as it tried to yank out what looked like its own claw that was stabbed in its abdomen.

The wizard was flat on her back, her eyes no longer focusing, and her shoulder bleeding heavily.

Tasha—the vampire that the maids had informed—roared fiercely and launched herself at the mantasp.

The ferocity was unnecessary. The mantasp had collapsed and was now twitching, although its stinger was coated with blood.

It seemed the wizard got herself stung in the process of fighting the monster. She'd need a few doses of fae healing draughts—mantasp stingers were poisonous.

Still...she'd taken the creature down. And with very little magic.

Not many wizards could do that.

As Tasha beheaded the monster, I prodded the wizard's forehead, but she didn't react.

"Tasha, call Celestina and tell her to prepare a fae healing draught."

"Yes, Your Eminence."

I grimaced as I looked down at the wizard. She reeked like a decayed carcass thanks to the magic in her blood that naturally repelled my kind. I wasn't that eager to touch her as she bled like a wounded animal, but this was the proof I was looking for.

Hazel Medeis wasn't mindless prey.

When backed into a corner she'd fight. And if the mantasp's own claw sticking out of its carapace was any indicator, she'd be *vicious* when incentivized enough.

I could work with that.

There was the matter of her tiny amount of magic, but I had my own theories about that. For now, this was enough.

I kept my expression smooth as I scooped the smelly wizard up.

"Your Eminence?" Tasha said in bewilderment, her phone almost dangling from her grasp.

"Make the call."

"Yes, Your Eminence!"

It was settled. I was going to make Hazel Medeis into my attack dog, and train her up the right way. She'd be a weapon.

It was my mistake to think that.

I never considered that she could be amusing and entertaining, and would manage to ingratiate herself among my Family. I never thought I'd come to *like* her, much less that she would ever stop reeking to me and would instead begin to smell as enticing as the sun itself.

The repercussions of my decision would rock the Drake Family, House Medeis, and magical society for years to come. All because I decided to adopt a pet wizard.

THE END

HAZEL'S ADVENTURE CONTINUES IN...

Magic Redeemed- Available on Amazon!

I thought my life would be easier after I unsealed my magic.

Spoiler: it's not.

Even though I have more magic than I know how to use, I can't be a one-person army and take my traitorous cousin down because he has multiple wizard Houses guarding his back. So I'm still stuck living at Drake Hall.

My best bet to free my family and reclaim my House is to find the Medeis signet ring, which will prove that I'm the real Adept. Unfortunately...no one knows where the ring is.

To complicate things, Killian's conflict with the fae Night Court is heating up. War will break out soon if something doesn't change, and Killian seems to think I might be the key to that change.

Plus, he's suddenly gotten really weird about smelling me, which wouldn't be such a big deal if he didn't make my heart leap every time he invaded my personal space.

Can I find the signet ring, or will Killian get me killed in his fight with the Night Court?

ABOUT THE AUTHOR

K. M. Shea is a fantasy-romance author who never quite grew out of adventure books or fairy tales, and still searches closets in hopes of stumbling into Narnia. She is addicted to sweet romances, witty characters, and happy endings. She also writes LitRPG and GameLit under the pen name, A. M. Sohma.

Hang out with the K. M. Shea Community at...
kmshea.com

Printed in Great Britain
by Amazon